THE DAISY FIELD

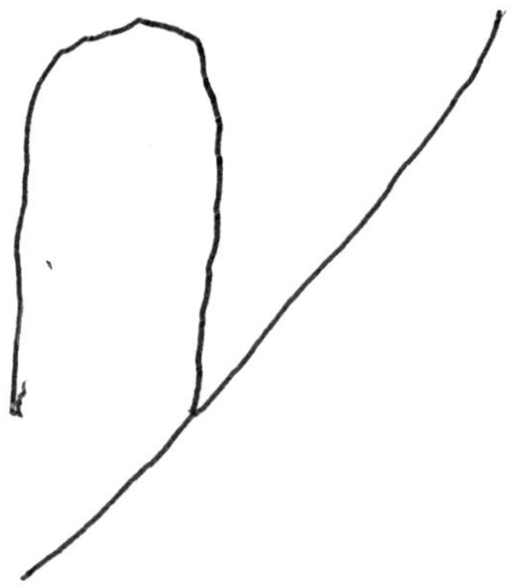

THE DAISY FIELD

AMY SUTTON

Two Harbors Press
212 3rd Avenue North, Suite 290
Minneapolis, MN 55401
612.455.2293
www.TwoHarborsPress.com

ISBN-13: 978-1-936401-51-2
LCCN: 2011904300

Distributed by Itasca Books

Cover Design and Typeset by James Arneson

Printed in the United States of America

TABLE OF CONTENTS

Acknowledgments

First and foremost, I thank my father, Zook. He has read each of the books I have written and, upon finishing *The Daisy Field,* he insisted I seek to publish. Because of his help and encouragement I have been able to pursue my dreams. I also thank my "regulars," those friends and family members who have kindly taken the time to read and comment on my books. In addition to Dad, my gratitude extends to Mom, Walter, Cheryl, DD, Amy, Kate, Garrett, Jenny, Linda, Pedro, Roger, Jeannie, Jeff, Ron, Bob, and Barbara. Your insight and feedback have been invaluable. Finally, a salute to Scott for his expert advice in how to successfully market my book and a hats-off to the staff at Two Harbors Press for their astute attention to detail and eagerness to assist.

On an emotional level, because this tale focuses on those who love and nurture, I thank my mother and the beloved live-in helper our family had while I was growing up. Though Mom and Daisy are now in heaven, I will never forget their generosity and willingness to support me in times of need.

Because Zook's Books is about giving back, twenty-five percent of the proceeds from the sale of this book will be donated to The Children's Place Association. When I lived in the Chicago area, back in the eighties, I was a member of the original board that helped to establish this residential care facility for HIV-infected children and their families. Upon opening its doors, The Children's Place Association was the first facility of its kind in the entire Midwest. Over the years the organization has expanded upon its mission, adding a plentitude of worthy programs and services. The agency remains a beacon of hope for those most vulnerable in society, locally as well as internationally. The service providers and their duly engaged supporters set a stellar example of keeping everyone's best interests in mind while diligently, and with compassion, addressing the needs of the children and the community at large.

Now enter into *The Daisy Field* and "Read with clarity, while gifting to charity."

Chapter One

Choosing what to plant

He was in the daisy field. Everything there seemed so real. He could laugh, talk, cry or sing. He could do most anything...in the daisy field." They were lyrics to a song she'd composed some seventy years ago, back when she was about twelve. As a youngster she composed lots of songs, her guitar being one of her best friends, always within reach. And now because arthritis had set in, she could no longer grasp the instrument. It rested in its brown case like a corpse in a coffin. Most of the songs she'd written and tunes she'd sung had faded from mind. But for some reason this one never had. The song was glued to a wall in her memory bank. As she happily hummed the melody, Lily powdered her nose and pinched her cheeks. She wanted to look pretty for the boy next door, the one she planned to give her guitar to, the one to whom she would teach the song; because, after all, as it'd turned out, it was so much about him.

His name was Presley. He lived in the neighboring apartment complex. An alleyway separated them. In the alley was a row of wooden boxes that a local hardware store had donated. And into those boxes Presley had shoveled a mound of rich-smelling soil that a local nursery had gifted. That same nursery also contributed the seeds that Presley had adroitly planted one by one. He was a slave to perfection even at a young age. He was also patient and persistent, the task of creating an urban garden having taken him the better part of two weeks. Every day after the school bus left him off on the corner, he ran to his prized project, watering when necessary, resituating the soil if a pesky bird had dropped in for a snitch of seed, and overall, taking tremendous pride in his endeavors to breathe a little life into the decrepit, destitute surroundings in which he lived.

Lily resided in a rest home. Presley lived in a low-cost housing complex. Both their doors opened onto Sedgwick, across the street from Chicago's Cabrini-Green. Lily had been there since 1968. Her husband, Richard, had died of a heart attack and shortly thereafter her grown daughter had insisted she be placed in some sort of senior assisted living quarters. Silver Trails was the least expensive one the daughter could find. Presley had moved in next door at the age of nine, in 1974. He'd been placed in foster care after his original adoptive mom divorced and remarried a man who refused to play father to a mulatto. So back he'd gone to the Department of Care and Family Services until a couple who, needing more in the way of welfare benefits, adopted him.

It was a while before Lily got up the nerve to talk to the boy next door. She'd done a lot of observing, though, gazing out her window into the alleyway where the youngster busied himself. Sometimes at night, when the parents were too lazy to shut the blinds and turn off the lights, she peered into their flat. She didn't consider herself a peeping Tom. Her concern was that no one paid much attention to the child. Most nights he ate dinner alone. And usually, from what she discerned, it was a bowl of cereal or some crackers with a hunk of cheese. There was no dining table, so the boy plopped on a beat-up sofa in front of the television set. The TV had a big screen; the console looked to be the nicest piece of furniture in the entire place.

Lily felt sorry for the youngster, felt like she needed to somehow lend a hand. Maybe she could serve as a surrogate, grandmother figure. Nurturing was ingrained in her. She'd always been a doting mother to her only child, Ivy, and her granddaughter, Heather. Even though she was forced into the lonely digs where she now resided, she'd managed to forgive her daughter for placing her there. Actually, there were a lot of things she'd forgiven along the way.

The day she finally talked to Presley was the day Ivy called to say she wouldn't be making her annual visit to the rest home. She said she'd heard about the violence surrounding Cabrini-Green and she didn't want to take any chances.

"Nothing's changed, dear. It's been this way since you put me here," Lily tried to explain.

"Sorry, Mom," is all Ivy could offer.

So, that afternoon when Presley was out watering his second year's bounty of tall Shasta daisies, Lily made her move. Placing a plump pillow atop the only chair in the room and pushing her seat as close to the window as possible, she hunkered in. Then taking a deep breath, Lily called down, "Those daisies are the happiest flowers I've ever seen."

Presley looked up, spraying the hose in the same direction. "Oops," he said, water drops splattering the window below Lily's.

"Aw, don't worry. That's old Sal's place. From what I hear he rarely opens his curtains during the day. He's kind of a night owl. He won't know the difference. "

"I didn't mean to," Presley said, redirecting the spray to his flower boxes. "You kind of startled me."

"I know; I'm sorry. I should've tried another approach. Unfortunately I'm pretty much stuck with calling out from my window."

"How come?" Presley asked, interested but not willing to divert his gaze.

"For one I'm not supposed to wander around too much on my own. Can't leave the house unassisted."

"How come?" Presley asked again.

"Because I'm in what's called senior assisted living."

"Oh," Presley said.

Knowing that wasn't enough, Lily continued, "I'm not handicapped, mind you. Not in a wheelchair or anything like that. I do have a walker, but that's something they insist I use. Quite frankly, I don't need any help. My legs can still support me."

"That's good."

Lily smiled. "Yes, as a matter of fact, at my age, it is." She readjusted her position in the chair, her body already succumbing to stiffness. "Looks like you have some strong muscles. Gee, all that dirt you shoveled last spring...that was quite a job."

Making sure to keep the hose pointed forward, Presley finally looked up and asked, "You saw me doing that?!"

"Yep. I was glued to my chair, right where I am now."

"Really? What kind of glue do they use on old people?"

Lily tittered. "No, I didn't mean I was actually glued to my chair...I was just intent on watching you...all the hard work you were doing." Thinking to herself that she hadn't been outdoors for nearly a year, she added, "Anyway this window here is the extent of my fresh air."

Presley didn't respond. His gaze was now locked on a swallow hopping about.

"Worried that little guy is going to take something that's not his?" Lily queried.

"Nah, I think he's okay. The only time I don't like the birds being around is when my flowers are seeds."

"Well, you've managed to protect your seeds for two years now. And the flowers that you've grown are a godsend."

"A godsend?"

"Yes, for me at least."

"What's a godsend?"

"Oh, it means...well, in my case...something I wasn't counting on, a gift."

"A gift from God?"

"Something like that."

"Well," Presley said in a serious tone, "these redwood boxes are a gift from Acme Hardware, and McCall Nurseries donated the dirt and seeds. They're the stores I went to last year to help start this project. They told me as long as I take good care of the flowers, I can come back every year for more dirt and seeds."

"Oh, I see. That's very nice of them."

Still pensive, Presley added, "But I guess you're right. God's still the one who gets the flowers to grow."

"Or maybe his sister, Mother Nature…"

Presley finally broke a smile. And oh, what an infectious smile he had. Lily beamed as she absorbed the boy's warmth and took in his features for the first time. He had coffee-colored skin, chiseled cheekbones, dark eyes and brows, curly cropped hair, little round ears and a wide smile that revealed a missing tooth. Immediately Lily worried. Was the missing tooth merely age-related?

"You're funny," Presley was saying as Lily tuned back in. "I like you. What's your name?"

"Lily. And what's yours?"

"Presley."

"Ah, such an unusual name."

"Yeah, my first mom liked Elvis a lot."

"Then why not call you Elvis?"

"I don't know."

"Well, you're the first Presley I've ever met and I think I like the name."

"How come?"

"Because I like you."

The smile was back and the chit chat went on for another twenty minutes. Suddenly the foster dad appeared at the back door. Big and burly, he stormed into the alleyway and hollered at Presley to "Get the hell in here! Forget the flowers. You've got chores to do!"

Lily shuddered at the man's deep, stern tone of voice. As she feebly waved goodbye, fretfulness consumed her.

Chapter Two

Deciding upon the appropriate place to plant

Presley was shoved through the open screen door into the family room. He cowered at the clenched fist raised above him.

"What don't you understand?" the father demanded. "You have the garbage to take out, this floor to sweep, and our laundry to fold before you so much as step outside to glance at those flowers of yours. I've warned you before. I'll rip them out stem by stem. Is that what you want?"

Presley shook his head vehemently. "No, please don't! I promise. From now on, I'll do my chores first. I only went out there because it was so hot today and the flowers really needed water…"

"Those flowers can wilt and die for all I care."

"But I have to take care of them. People are counting on me."

"What people? The only people you should give a damn about are your mother and me. Hey, look…bottom line, we could've taken in another child, but we chose you. You're one lucky kid, got that? Who knows where you'd be right now."

Presley nodded, his gaze cast downward.

"Now close the screen door and get to work!"

"Yes, sir."

The dad trudged heavy-footed to the fridge for a beer while Presley located the broom and started to sweep.

"And by the way," the father called over his shoulder, "you need to find a real job. Start pulling your own weight around here. Your mother and I can't afford squat on what we're making."

"A real job?" Presley whimpered. "But I'm only ten."

"There's a lot ten-year-olds can do."

"Well, I can't quit school."

"Think I'm stupid? I know you can't quit school. Unfortunately the law says you have to attend school. Not sure why. You're never going to amount to much. Maybe some 'mow, blow and go' guy. But not a three-piece-suit character who can earn a respectable living. No way."

Presley held his tongue. There were so many things he wanted to say, but he didn't dare.

"So, yeah, a job after school. Maybe a shoeshine boy on Michigan Avenue. There's a bunch of those high falutin' businessmen up that way who'd take pity on you. From what I hear those lawyers in three-piece suits tip pretty well."

"But when will I have time to do my homework and chores and tend to my flowers?"

His voice was a jack hammer. "FORGET THE FLOWERS!"

The conversation ended there. Presley swept in silence. When his foster mom walked in the door at six-thirty she chided Presley for letting the father slurp down too many beers. He was conked-out on the sofa and, though the television was blaring, his snoring was even louder.

"Why does he do this to me?" she moaned, setting down her heavy purse and stepping out of her platform shoes. "This is what I come home to practically every night!" The foster mom ranted some more as she unbuttoned the snug blazer that flared at her hips and yanked away the paisley scarf she'd chosen to complement her attire.

"That's a nice outfit you're wearing," Presley offered.

"There you go again, changing the subject."

Presley shrugged.

"What is that supposed to mean? You could care less? Well, I've got news for you; I work an eight-hour day. I deserve better than this."

Meekly Presley reported, "I did my chores. You don't have to fold laundry tonight."

"Well, that's a plus."

"Can I go out now and finish watering my daisies?"

"You and those blasted flowers. Fine. Go. And tell your father when he wakes up that I went over to Olive's place. She invited me over for some leftover barbecue."

When Presley returned to the alleyway he looked up toward the window where the old lady had been. Her window was shut and that made him feel a little sad. He turned on the hose and doused his flowers. He took a pair of shears and snipped off all the dead blooms. The man at the nursery had shown him how to properly deadhead his daisies so that more would grow. As he was picking up the spent foliage, Presley spotted the elderly woman peering down at him. He stood and waved.

Opening her window, Lily said, "Well, there you are again."

"Yes, I had to do my chores before I could come back out."

"Have you eaten dinner yet?"

"No, not yet."

"A boy your age? Aren't you hungry by this hour?"

"Kind of. But I'll grab something when I go in."

"And what's on the menu for tonight?" Lily asked, trying to hide her concern.

"Oh, whatever's in the fridge. I'm not very picky."

"Doesn't your mother cook for you?"

"Not usually. She's too tired after work. And like tonight, she went to her friend's for leftovers."

"What about your father?"

Presley looked through the screen door and relayed, "Well, he's taking a nap."

Lily wasn't sure what to say, so she changed the subject. "Do you have homework at your age?"

"Not too much. I have one page of arithmetic and one of spelling to do tonight."

"What's your favorite subject?"

"I'm actually pretty good at spelling. I won a spelling bee last year in third grade."

"Bravo!" Lily exalted, raising her hands to the level of the window so Presley could see her applaud. "What word did you spell correctly?"

"Raucous."

"Really? That's a hard one. The word's spelled differently than it sounds."

"Yep. I almost spelled it with an 'o' instead of 'au.'"

"Do you know what the word means?"

"Something like 'rough.' I saw the word on the front page of the *Chicago Tribune* once before. There's a newspaper stand on the corner where I catch the bus. The headline read in big print, 'Raucous Gang Goes Rioting.' And there were these pictures of men shooting their guns somewhere in Cabrini-Green."

"Yes, I'm afraid the violence has become common. Things *are* raucous around here. My own daughter won't come to visit me anymore because she's afraid of getting shot."

"That's too bad. I doubt it'd happen, but you never know. There was a high school kid from Edwin Cooley who was killed by a stray bullet. Our teacher at Schiller had him as a student and Mrs. Clover said he was a really good kid. She warned us to be very careful."

"And you should be. But for me...well, I hardly ever get out of here anyway."

"I think that's bad."

"What? The random gunfire?"

"No, that they don't let you out of that place."

"Well, I don't live in a prison; but sometimes it feels like one."

"Are others allowed to leave?"

"Oh sure, if they have loved ones that come to visit. In the past when my daughter's dropped in, she's taken me to the Drake Hotel for afternoon tea. Afterwards she'd bring me back here, kiss me goodbye, and I'd wait entire year to be treated to the excursion again."

"Where does she live?"

"In Wheaton."

"She lives that close and she doesn't come see you more than once a year?"

Lily responded with a sad shrug.

Presley sensed her dismay and added, "That's wrong. You know what? If I had a real mother, I'd be so nice to her. Especially if she was like you."

"I'm sure you would, Presley. You're a very thoughtful young man." Changing the subject so she didn't appear mawkish, Lily asked, "Say, Presley…I brought back a hard crust roll and a brownie from my dinner tonight. Do you want them?"

Presley brightened. "I'd sure like to have the brownie. But I better not take the roll. I can't really bite off anything hard 'cause I lost a tooth."

Grateful to learn without prying, Lily nonchalantly asked, "How'd you lose it?"

"My father yanked the thing out 'cause he was tired of my whining."

"Ouch, that must've hurt."

"Nah, not too bad. Besides, he was right. I was being a baby."

"Did the Tooth Fairy come to visit?"

"Who?"

"You've never heard of the Tooth Fairy?"

Presley shook his head. And just as Lily was about to regale him with stories about the favored fairy, she saw the father stumbling toward the screen door. "I think you'd better scoot now," she said, pointing behind Presley to alert him.

"What're you doing out there?" the father grumbled as he stepped into the alleyway.

Timidly setting down his shears, Presley replied, "I did my chores and when mom came home she said I could finish taking care of my flowers."

"Where's your mother now?"

"She went over to Olive's for leftovers."

"Well, that's just swell. Leaving me alone again to get my own supper." Glaring at Presley he seethed, "Guess what...you're gonna get me something to eat tonight."

"There's hardly anything in the fridge."

Lumbering back to the sofa the father barked, "No excuses! Hustle your butt!"

Lily opened her window and gestured to Presley that she had his brownie. Mouthing the word "Enjoy," she speedily wrapped the gooey dessert in a tissue and tossed the treat down.

Presley caught the flying bundle and stuck it in between his flowers for a late-night snack. "Thank you," he mouthed back.

The next three days brought torrential rains. Presley's parents told him not to go out into the alleyway after school. The child was aggravated because now he had a purpose above and beyond his precious flowers. He wanted to see Lily.

"Quit with your fidgeting," his mother ordered on the third eve of confinement. "Your flowers are fine. These thunderstorms are bringing plenty of water to your plants. Finish your homework and come help me with dinner."

Presley kerplunked on the sofa. He picked up a spelling book and tried to focus on words meant for students at the middle school level.

"Practicing for future spelling bees?" his mother asked.

"I guess," Presley answered, lackluster.

"Well, that's good. You keep winning those and maybe you'll get into college some day. And if you do, maybe you'll land a decent job."

"That's not what Father thinks."

"Oh, never mind your father. He's the world's biggest pessimist."

"He said I'll never become more than a gardener. And that even though I have to go to school, I need to get a real job now."

"At your age?"

"Yep. He told me again before leaving for work that I should go to Michigan Avenue and start scouting out shoeshine places. He thinks I'll make good tips doing that."

"Well, now. He didn't talk to me about this. There's no way you're going to take a job like that! You're only part-Black. No need to act like someone's slave child just to earn a pocketful of change."

He knew his mother meant well, but suddenly he felt darker than dark. Eyes affixed to the word "obsequious" in his book he pondered the meaning while memorizing the spelling.

On the fourth day the electric skies finally subsided and the plump clouds parted. Presley charged home after school, eager to enter the alleyway. This time before even reaching for his shears, he peered up to the second-story window. Like a favorite portrait that hangs in a chosen spot, there was Lily, her kind eyes searching for him.

Opening the window she exclaimed, "My goodness, I thought those storms would never go away." She wanted to add, "I've missed you," but she decided to hold back.

"Yeah, I really missed coming out here."

Allowing herself, "And I missed your *being* out here."

"Guess what?" Presley asked excitedly.

"What? Give me some good news."

"Tomorrow's the last day of school."

Using the heel of her hand to clunk her brow for emphasis, Lily exclaimed, "Is it really that time of year already?"

"Yes! No school or homework until after Labor Day."

"So, will I see all the more of you?"

Presley shed his scintillation. "Actually, you might see less of me."

"Really? Why?"

"Because my father said I have to find a job."

"What kind of job? Watering other people's plants?"

"That's what I'd be good at and I wouldn't mind that kind of work. But nobody has plants. I think mine are the only ones around here. Everything else is ugly cement."

"True. This neighborhood is falling to pieces. I hear Cabrini-Green used to be a decent place to live. But now, gosh, the buildings and houses are in shambles. There's litter and filth everywhere. I guess people just don't care."

"Either that or they're working too hard to notice."

"Do both your foster parents have a job, Presley?"

"Yes. My father works at a gas station, 'bout a mile away. He walks because we can't afford a car and none of the buses go in that direction. When it gets dark early in the wintertime, my mom kind of worries about him because the area's not very safe."

"How about your mother?"

"She takes the bus."

"No, I mean where does she work?"

"Oh, she has a job at Marshall Field's."

"That's a nice department store. And its smack dab in the heart of the shopping district."

"Yes, and we don't have to worry so much about her getting home because she catches the bus on Michigan Avenue and her drop-off is right across the street."

Lily lowered her head. She was statuesque, contemplating.

"Are you okay?" Presley finally asked.

"Yes, of course. I was just thinking…can you come to the front desk of our building after school tomorrow?"

Presley tilted his head. "Sure, I guess so." He waited to hear why, but Lily was gone.

Chapter Three

Gathering the proper gardening tools

When Presley hopped off the bus the next day, he made a beeline for Silver Trails. He dashed up the stone walkway and halted at the front door. He couldn't see a doorbell to ring. He was unable to reach the heavy, brass door knocker. There were no panes of glass to peer through. Not knowing what else to do, Presley used his knuckles to knock on the door. No one answered. He made a fist and used the side of his hand to bang on the door. Still no one answered. Finally, he pulled a decorative pot over and stood on its edge so that he could reach the brass knocker. Suddenly the door was thrust open and there before Presley stood a short, stocky woman in a starched, white uniform.

"And just what do you think you're doing?!" she bellowed.

Presley shuddered. He was speechless.

"Step down from that planter right now! You're trespassing on private property, boy."

"I'm...I'm sorry. I didn't know how to get in. I was trying to..."

"We don't let strangers in."

"But I'm not really a stranger. I live next door. Lily told me to come by."

"Lily Wilson?"

"I'm sorry, ma'am. I don't know her last name. I just know her by Lily."

"There's only one Lily here, but I doubt you know her." The woman looked Presley up and down and added, "She rarely says a word to anyone."

"Well, I talk to her a lot."

The starched official raised a brow. "Really? And how is that?"

"When I'm in the alleyway, she talks to me through her window."

"Is that so? And why, when she doesn't talk to anybody else, is she going to talk to *you*?"

Presley shrugged. "I don't know. Maybe 'cause she's lonely."

"What's this all about?" an official asked approaching the front door.

"This boy claims Lily Wilson told him to drop by."

The man was tall and had a thick mustache that matched the brown vest he was wearing. Lowering his gaze he asked in a kind manner, "Are you Presley?"

Relieved by the friendlier tone, Presley replied, "Yes, yes that's me!"

"It's alright, Myrtle. Lily did mention the boy to me."

The stout woman huffed and went back to her business, mumbling mean things under her breath.

"Come in, Presley. Sorry for the confusion. We don't usually have youngsters coming to our door."

"That's okay. I only came over because Lily asked me to." He hesitated and added, "And I don't even know why."

The dapper gentleman led Presley to his office. "Well, my understanding is that you're looking for a job." He gestured for Presley to have a seat and then he lowered into his throne-like chair behind an ornately carved desk. "Is Lily correct?"

Presley was taken aback, but managed to reply, "Uh, yes. Yes, she is. I told her how my father wants me to find work."

"Do you know what a busboy is?"

"I think so. Isn't that somebody who helps out at meal time?"

"Yes. Not so much serving the food. That would be a waiter or a waitress. What we need is someone who can set the tables and pour water. Make sure there's rolls and butter at each table. Help set up for buffets. Have you ever had any experience doing that sort of thing?" the cordial administrator asked.

"Well, sir. I've never worked in a restaurant, if that's what you mean. But I do help out at home. And I'm sure I could do those things here."

"How old are you, son?"

Presley straightened. "Ten, sir."

The man twirled one end of his mustache. "My, you seem much older. Are you sure you want to work for us? Mind you, I need someone who is responsible."

"Oh, I am, sir! I'm used to doing all kinds of chores." Somewhat embarrassed Presley added, "And I need the money. I mean, my family does."

"Well, we won't be able to pay you very much..."

"That's okay. Anything will do, sir."

"And what about your schedule?"

"My schedule, sir?"

"Yes. When are you free?"

"Oh, well, except for taking care of my flowers and my chores at home, I'm free any time."

"And school is out now, correct?"

"Yes, sir. Until Labor Day."

Standing again, the official said, "Well then, let's bring you on board for breakfast, lunch, *and* dinner this summer. If things go well, maybe when school starts up again we can keep you onboard for at least the dinner hour."

Presley jumped out of his chair. "Yes, sir! Thank you!"

Approaching with a hand ready to shake, the tall man in brown said, "My name is Mr. Taylor. I'm in charge here at Silver Trails. I have two other senior homes that I oversee, so I'm not always here; but generally you'll see me a couple of times a week. I'll let Lily know that we spoke and I'll get things set up with the restaurant staff so that you can begin tomorrow. Is that too soon?"

"Oh, no, sir. That's fine," Presley said excitedly.

"All right, then. Can you be here at six in the morning?"

"Yes, sir."

"Normally we'll have you show up at seven. But on your first day here I'll have, Rosie, our head cook, come in early to show you the ropes. Sound like a plan?"

"Yes, sir."

"Call me, Mr. Taylor. Everybody else does."

Unable to contain himself, Presley saluted. "Yes, Mr. Taylor!"

"No need to salute. This isn't the military," the man said with a cunning smile that reminded Presley of the Scare Crow in *The Wizard of Oz*. "By the way, have you ever worked with the elderly?"

"The elderly?"

Chuckling, the man said, "You know...older people?"

Presley shook his head, hoping that it wasn't a prerequisite for the job. "I had a grandpa with my first set of foster parents. But I was pretty young. I don't really remember him."

"Ah well, sounds like you're getting along famously with Lily. She sought me out and spoke very highly of you. And that's saying a lot because my understanding is Lily hasn't really talked to anybody for all the years she's been here at Silver Trails."

Presley didn't know what to say, so he simply grinned.

"She also told me that you grow and take care of some beautiful flowers."

"Yes, in the alleyway."

"I'll have to duck my head around the corner when I leave this evening. I'd like to see them."

"Do you have flowers here to take care of?"

"No, but maybe we should."

Presley nodded. "They are a godsend, you know."

The tall man patted Presley on the shoulder as he led him out. "I think you're going to be a big help to us, Presley."

"I sure hope so, Mr. Taylor."

"I know so!" Lily shouted from the front hall. She threw her arms up in a "V" for victory.

Those in the entryway looked on in awe. Never had they heard Lily make a peep, let alone a whooping exaltation.

"Don't let go of your walker," Myrtle chided.

"Aw, who needs the dang thing?!" Lily huffed, shuffling over to Presley for a hug.

After leaving Silver Trails, Presley planned to hustle home so that he could sweep and fold laundry. He was going to hurriedly water his daisies and then come back inside to prepare some dinner for his parents. He couldn't wait to tell them the good news! Unfortunately, when he walked in the door he saw his father tanked out on the couch again. There was a cardboard box on the rug with two beers inside. The other four were empty, strewn about on the floor. Presley noticed the couch was slightly wet. He was pretty sure the damp splotches weren't due to spilt beer. Apparently, his father had been crying. As he stood gawking, wondering what could've prompted the tears, Presley saw his dad's eyes opened to narrow slits of red.

"What are you looking at?" the father grunted. He closed his lids again.

"Just seeing if you were awake?"

"I was asleep until *you* came in."

"Sorry, I didn't know you'd be home this early."

"Done your chores yet?"

"No, I just got here," Presley answered, anticipating the usual reprimand.

"Where've you been? You weren't out back when I walked in. Not hanging out with any bad actors, are you?"

"No. When the bus leaves me off, I come straight home. Except today..."

The father sat up awkwardly. "What is this, some sort of guessing game? Tell me where the hell you've been!"

"Next door," Presley replied timidly.

"Last time I looked we have two next doors," the father said, popping open his fifth beer with the back of his fake gold ring. "Be specific, kid."

"I was at Silver Trails."

"That home for zombies? Why'd you go there?"

Trying to sound upbeat, Presley explained, "Well, there's an old lady there who likes me a lot and…"

"And she's a dimwit who thinks you're her long lost grandson. Is that right?" the father broke in.

"No, that's not it at all," Presley said, feeling crushed.

"Oh, come on, Presley…fess up. You don't know anyone from that dingy, old codger's place. This is just another one of your daydreams; and it's all make-believe from the land of la la daisies, no?"

"No! What I'm telling you is true. Starting tomorrow, I have a job at Silver Trails."

The gulp of beer the father had downed came back up with a wet cough. "Give me a break," he choked, "you're telling me you landed a job next door at the old folk's home?" He caught his breath and continued, "And you got the job today, after traipsing over there with no skills to offer, just a mere mention of the fact that you happen to know some old bag who lives there?"

"I do know a lady who lives there and she's not an old bag. She's nice. And she's the one who told them about *me*!"

The father raised his beer and made a toast. "To my kid…a better liar than the best of 'em."

Slinking off to the closet to get the broom and commence his chores, Presley said under his breath, "I'm not lying. It's the truth."

The father took another fat swallow of beer and said in an altered tone, "I sure hope you're not lying because we're going to need every cent we can get. I lost my job today."

Chapter Four

Designing the flower beds

The next morning a gleaming dawn gave Presley the extra nudge he needed to rise and shine. It had been a trying night. His father was assuredly downcast and, as he sobered up, matters only got worse. Presley didn't know how to quell his father's angst so he swept and cleaned while he listened and absorbed. Then instead of tending to his needy flowers where solitude would've welcomed him, Presley went to their pint-size kitchen and threw together a dinner of sausage and beans while his father ranted and raved some more. By the time Presley's mother walked in the door the dad was wallowing in self pity and belligerently blaming his dismissal on the boss, the patrons, the owner of the gas station, the city of Chicago, and the entire in-the-toilet economic system.

So much for my good news, Presley thought to himself that night as he served up supper for his parents. He resigned to tell his mother later. But he didn't intend to broach the subject again with his father because, after all, maybe his dad was jealous of the fact that his foster kid had so easily and readily snagged a job. No sense in tormenting him any further.

Thus, wearing his only dressy outfit, gray slacks and a collared shirt, Presley tiptoed out of the flat before the sun managed to rise. No need to tell anyone he was leaving. He was certain his father intended to sleep in. His mother was in retail and didn't rise until eight o'clock. Most days he was on the bus headed for school at that hour. Rarely did they cross paths in the morning, so she never knew if Presley was home or not.

When the young boy made his way up the stone path to Silver Trails he immediately assessed the front door situation. *Shoot,* he thought to himself, *I should've asked how I'm supposed to enter.* Just then the door magically opened.

"Hi, I'm Rosie. You must be Presley, our new busboy. Mr. Taylor told me to be here early to show you around."

Presley smiled up to the heavyset woman with skin the color of coal and eyes that twinkled brightly. Her hair was graying, a plump portion of it molded into a mesh hairnet. Like the orderly woman who'd answered the door the day before, Rosie also wore a starched white uniform. But she looked relaxed in her dress like it was hugging, not annoying her.

"Well now, come on in," Rosie sang. She reached for Presley's small hand and drew him inward. "Let me lead you to the kitchen." Humming happily, with Presley at her side, she waddled along and noted, "We go down this here hallway to the left, straight down to the end and then make a right." She stopped and gestured. "Now, be careful with this door. It opens in either direction so the kitchen help can come and go easily. If you look over there to the left, that's the dining room. So, as you can see, we use this door a lot. What you don't want to do is push into the door too hard or too fast because a waiter with a full tray may be on the other side." Rosie put her hands on her wide hips and laughed heartily. "We've had run-ins occur on too many occasions. And what a mess to clean up!"

Presley nodded, wide-eyed, absorbing every word. Rosie gently pushed the door open and into the kitchen they gallantly stepped where two cooks stood wedged up against the enormous stove, waving with their spatulas.

"Thomas and Anthony, this is Presley. He's our new busboy," Rosie announced.

"Nice to meet you," they said in unison.

"Same here," Presley replied as he thought to himself, *I like these two guys already. They remind me of Yogi Bear and his sidekick, Boo Boo. One's a big hunk with kind of a dopey look and the other's short, squatty and chipper.*

"Now," Rosie went on, "just so you know, at breakfast time, Thomas is in charge of our egg orders. The residents can choose between sunnyside up or over-easy. There's also an omelet of the day three days a week and scrambled eggs on the alternating days. Those egg dishes stay out in warming bins on the buffet table."

Presley's gaze took an elevator up to eyeball Thomas. He was more than just a big hunk; he was a towering figure of a man—so tall that Presley had to wonder why he was flipping eggs and not playing basketball for the Bulls.

Sensing he was being sized up, Thomas told Presley, "I've been the egg chef here for the better part of five years. There's a real art to it," he said proudly. "So, if you hear any complaints from those seniors out there, set 'em straight for me. Okay, bud?"

"Yes, sir, I will."

Rosie continued, "And Anthony..."

"Have the boy can call me Tony," the short cook interjected. "Everybody else does."

"...he is in charge of things like French toast and pancakes. We have those available four days a week and waffles on the alternating days."

"I'm also the muffin man," Tony said, gesticulating with floury hands. He rattled off, "I make blueberry, cranberry, banana, and bran. The seniors love the blueberry best, but what they need is the bran. 'Eat your fiber,' I keep reminding them."

"Do you bake the desserts here, too?" Presley asked, remembering the rich chocolate brownie Lily had tossed him.

"No, Poppy does. After the breakfast hour I switch over and make my specialties like lasagna, pizza, and stew."

"So, Poppy's another cook that comes in?"

"Now don't start confusing the boy," Rosie ordered. "He hasn't even met the entire morning shift yet." Realizing that Presley really did want to know about their baker, Rosie tacked on, "Yes, Poppy is yet another cook at Silver Trails. But you probably won't meet her because she goes to college during the day and after her studies she comes by to bake about nine o'clock at night." Taking a deep breath Rosie concluded, "Gees, this is a ton of information to throw at you your first day here."

"That's okay," Presley said. "It's a lot to know, but I'm sure in a day or two I'll have it down pat." He paused and asked, "Does anyone stay and cook all three meals a day?"

"I'm the only cook that's here all day," Tony answered, gloating.

Rosie raised a thick brow, making Tony cower a smidgeon.

"Oh, except for Rosie. But she's head cook so she does a lot more than play chef. She's a master at making marinades, jarring jellies…her fudge is so rich you could hibernate on a single brick of it. She's an expert when it comes to grilling, barbecuing, sautéing, and baking. And if that's not enough…" Tony wiggled his hips for emphasis, "…she can polish all our pots and pans until they glow like a big brass band!"

"Aw, go on," Rosie said humbly. "I only polish those darn pots when they get so black you taste smoke. Brass band…now where'd that come from?"

Rather than wait his turn, Thomas jumped in, "I'm here for breakfast and lunch. Then I leave and come back for a few hours in the evening. I coach basketball after school lets out."

All a' sparkle, Presley enthused, "I knew you were a basketball player!"

"Ya mean my height gave me away again?" Thomas chuckled, slapping his knee with a humungous hand.

"You must be really good. Bet you can hold onto the ball with just one hand, huh?"

"And I can twirl it on my index finger just like the Globetrotters do."

"Really?!" Presley asked, eyes glinting with wonder.

"All right, gentleman," Rosie interjected. "That's enough about sports. We're here to cook and serve." Steering Presley over to a wall of cabinets, she continued, "Here is where you'll find the water glasses. The silverware's in these drawers and if you need clean table cloths, they're folded on the shelves down below. Each table should be set for six people and there are a total of twenty tables. Some tables will only have five seniors seated at them, but set those for six anyway. You never know when a family member or a new resident might join us." Rosie caught her breath and underlined, "It's assigned seating, meaning it's the same group at each table for every meal. Don't let any resident try to tell you differently."

Presley hesitated, somewhat confounded.

"If you're questioning the system we have...you're right...it's a pain in the...*behind*. There are spats and quarrels constantly brewing over seating arrangements." Rosie acted out a scenario: "Amaryllis doesn't want to sit with Dahlia because Dahlia habitually smacks her lips. And Dahlia doesn't want to dine with Amaryllis because she's a glamour puss who still has enough hair to sculpt into a beautifully coiffed, Texas beehive thick enough that you can't see through it. Besides, Dahlia has a crush on Frankie five tables away. But then good old Frankie doesn't even know Dahlia exists because he's living in his own little world, galaxies away from the maddening crowd. See what I mean?"

At first Presley nodded, then slowly shook his head.

"Talk about *me* confusing the boy," Tony called over. "What she means, Presley, is the system is not foolproof. But if we let the seniors sit wherever they want to, this place would be a zoo, not a dining facility."

"Where does Lily sit?" Presley asked innocently.

"At table sixteen," Rosie said, "Come, I'll show you."

When he entered the dining room, Presley immediately felt like he belonged. In the center of each table was a vase of daisies. They were smaller than his Shasta daisies, but they still made him feel right at home. "The flowers are pretty," he said.

"We use daisies a lot. They last longer than most flowers."

"Yes, I know," Presley replied cheerfully. "I grow daisies. They're my favorite flower."

"Is that right?"

"Yep. I live next door and…"

"Those are your flowers in the alleyway?!"

"Yes, ma'am."

"Well, I'll be… Those are the prettiest I've ever seen. And they just keep blooming! You must take awfully good care of them."

Presley nodded, but before he could say anything more a blaring alarm went off.

Chapter Five

When using planter boxes, determine their layout

Presley stood petrified. Rosie threw up her hands and ran toward the kitchen. Seconds later she reappeared, waving her arms in a panic. "Don't just stand there!" she screamed. "Fire!"

Chaos ensued as residents were rudely awakened by the alarm. Cries for help echoed throughout the house. Rosie pointed to a back doorway. "That's your exit. Now git!" she exclaimed, breathlessly.

"But what about Lily?"

"Don't worry about nobody but yourself. We've been trained. We know what to do."

At that point Thomas and Tony burst out of the kitchen, fire extinguishers in hand.

"It's not in the kitchen," Thomas shouted over the cacophony.

"It's not a grease fire and no smoke coming from the ovens," Tony added.

Rosie gave Presley a shove in the direction of the back door. She barreled forward. "It must be on one of the upper floors! Check to make sure everyone's getting out. Remember, unless you see smoke or flames comin' from underneath, open every door that's shut. We don't want anyone left behind!"

Presley felt helpless. He desperately wanted to lend a hand, especially if Lily needed him. But he didn't know which room she was in. From the alleyway he could figure it out, but now that he was *in* the rest home... "I'll go outside!" Presley yelped, ignited. Charging toward the back door he tripped over a bundle in the hallway. The light was so dim he couldn't see what the big lump was. But as he rose to get up he heard it moan.

"Ooooh," groaned a deep voice.

Presley squinted and through the darkness saw a blanket with movement underneath. "You okay?" he asked, leaning over to pull back the coverlet.

A chuckle escaped and then pained laughter. "Okay? Hell no, I'm not okay! These floorboards feel like rocks 'gainst my ribs."

"Here, let me help you up," Presley volunteered. "We've got to get out of here. The building's on fire!"

"There's no fire," the corpse-like figure grumbled.

"What? I can't hear you, sir," Presley urged, trying to gather the gaunt man up. "Come on, we have to get out of here!"

"I said there's *no* fire!!! I pulled the alarm."

Presley stood agog.

"Go see for yourself. Over there against the wall."

Heading in the direction the man was pointing, Presley quickly made his way down the hall. Sure enough, there on the wall was an alarm box that was open with the lever yanked. He scampered back to where the downed culprit lay and shouted, "Don't worry, I'll be right back!"

Presley charged through the house, weaving in and out of walkers and wheelchairs and the frantic seniors trying to vacate the premises. Finally he saw Rosie coming out of one of the rooms, carrying a frail woman piggyback. Presley called over to her, "It's a false alarm!"

Rosie motioned to get out.

"But it's a false alarm!" Presley shouted even louder.

Just then a firefighter slammed through the front door. "Everybody out!" he bellowed.

His crew followed, infiltrating and ordering everyone to, "Move quickly. Stay calm. Use the stairs. Don't worry. Keep moving."

It was useless, Presley realized. He couldn't douse the feverish panic even though there were no flames to extinguish. All the residents and what staff was inside the building ended up outside on Sedgwick that morning. Luckily it wasn't winter. It was a cool, crisp morning that promised to turn sultry and hot. While waiting on the sidewalk, Presley scanned the crowd and the commotion. Never before had there been this much activity on his block. In a way, because he knew there was no fire to worry about, the chaos was comical. After all, the street looked like one big pajama party was being hosted there. Some wore jammies, some donned robes; one or two who slept in the nude wore nothing until cover-ups were availed, and then there were a few morning doves who were fully dressed and ready for their day. Presley listened in on a couple of the conversations surrounding him and smiled all the more.

"I've never been so scared in my life!" exclaimed one elderly woman.

"Well, at least you're in a wheelchair on the first floor and they could wheel you out," replied the other. "I live up on the third floor. We couldn't use the elevator and I nearly died getting down those stairs!"

To his other side he zoomed in on, "I bet it was Pyro Paul. He insists on having a girly perfume candle burning whenever he takes a bath...which is at least twice a day. I've always said there's something wrong with that guy."

"He can't do that!" his buddy said.

"What? Take a bath?"

"No, have a burning candle in his room!"

Then there was the couple who held each other and wouldn't let go. "Oh, Dickie, I never ever, *ever* want to lose you!" the woman gushed.

"Oh, Violet, never let go of me," the man replied.

They were syrup and glue combined. Presley had to wonder if they were *able* to let go. Maybe they were actually stuck in their snug-hug. And just as he was ready to ask them if they needed assistance, he noticed his mother pressing through the crowd.

"Presley, what's going on?! What the heck are you doing out here?!" The mother's voice carried over the crowd and suddenly countless eyes fell upon them.

Stammering Presley said, "I...I...I work here now, Mom...for Silver Trails."

The majority of expressions revealed doubt, his mother's included.

"You what?!"

"I have a job as a busboy."

"And just when did *that* happen?!"

Squirming, Presley felt like a juicy June bug being eyed by a murder of crows. "I...I just started today."

"We don't know him," one senior said icily.

"He's a stranger," said another.

The buzz became contagious until one elder suggested, "Maybe he's the one who started the fire." The comments catapulted into a barrage of unruly criticism and blame. At a point, Presley's own mother had to shield him from the verbal onslaught.

Finally, peering out over a patchwork of bald and silver-tinted heads, tall Thomas spotted the epicenter of the feverish outrage. He hailed Tony and Rosie, and the three of them bulldozed through the stifling crowd.

"Step back!" Thomas ordered.

As the seniors slowly made room, Rosie pressed, "Just what's going on here?"

Tony stood next to Presley, pillar-like.

"That boy claims he works for Silver Trails," hailed the original instigator.

"Never seen him before in my life," screeched a woman pointing a dagger finger. "His own mother didn't know anything about him working here."

"He's probably a real troublemaker like the rest of the hooligans around these parts!"

Thomas lifted one of his big hands as a stop sign and barked, "That's enough!"

Tony chimed in, "He *did* begin work for us today. You don't know him because you haven't even had breakfast yet. He's our new busboy." He threw up his hands and jeered, "And what a lovely way to welcome him into our home."

"Excuse me, y'all," Rosie said, raising her voice like she was ready to belt out the Hallelujah Chorus. "I think there's been a serious injustice made here this morning. I must say I've worked for Silver Trails for the better part of fifteen years…'bout the time it opened. And never have I seen this kind of mob mentality. Never have I seen anyone treated so poorly. Granted, we've never had a fire to deal with and I'm praying that's why you're all out of sorts. But please, come to your senses. This boy, Presley, had nothing to do with the fire. And when I say nothing, I mean nothing. I'm his eyewitness. When the alarm went off he was with me, talking about flowers. Okay? You think the boy next door who grows lots of beautiful daisies is going to set our house on fire?"

Just then four firemen came out of the building. The captain addressed the crowd, "It was a false alarm, folks! Somebody pulled the lever in the box by the back door. It's safe to go inside now."

The residents stood motionless. They turned their attention to Rosie. "See that? False alarm…" Rosie said with a humph. "Know what y'all? I think you owe this boy an apology."

Squeamishly, like reprimanded children, the elders called out in unison, "Sorry."

Humbled, Presley just waved.

"All right, then. Let's get back inside. Those who need assistance, wait for one of the staff. We'll get to you as soon as we can."

Presley asked eagerly, "Can I help?"

Rosie nodded, saying, "You're one of the staff, right? Sure you can help."

Looking to his mother, Presley smiled broadly. "Sorry I didn't tell you last night, but Father was so upset over losing his job and…"

His mother gave him a perfunctory hug. "That's okay. I'm sorry for doubting you." She sized up the crowd of seniors and said, "Better get back to work. Looks like a lot of those elders are going to need your help."

And they did need Presley's assistance. Suddenly everyone was clamoring for him to come to their aid. It was hard to believe that only minutes earlier they were ready to tie him up like a lynch mob, and now they were feebly calling out and waving to get his attention. It was Lily that Presley first approached.

"I tried to find you…" Presley began.

"I know. I saw you from a distance, but I couldn't call out. Don't have the cheerleader voice I used to." Lily reached for Presley's hands and held them in hers. "I am so sorry for what happened. I don't know what got into everyone. They're usually not like that."

"They probably got scared and took things out on me. It's okay."

"No, it's not. And I feel awful because I couldn't do anything to stop their rudeness."

"Well, I think they know I'm okay now."

"Sonny, can you help wheel me inside?" one senior called forth.

"I'll be there in a second. I have to help Lily first."

"No, no," Lily said. "You go on ahead. Remember, I don't need assistance." She gently squeezed Presley's hands before releasing them. "I'll see you for a late breakfast."

And breakfast was late that day, very late. Oddly, everybody had funneled out of the building and into the street in a matter of minutes, but it took over an hour to get them all back inside. On top of that, when Tony went back into the kitchen he found the tins of muffins he'd baked, four-plus dozen, had vanished. He was livid! He grabbed various ingredients and commenced with baking another batch. "Even the rats in this neighborhood couldn't have come in and stolen my muffins in that short of a time!" Thomas was waylaid, too. He had to redo most of the egg dishes he'd already prepared because the doors had been left open and the flies swarmed inward, sampling his tasty feast. Rosie put herself in charge of combating the flies. She took to swatting and slapping the black bugs like she was the victim of some neurological twitching disorder.

With all the zaniness surrounding him, Presley suddenly remembered the man by the back door! He charged out of the room.

"Where you going like a bat out of hell?" Rosie called after him. There was no answer so she decided to follow the boy.

"He's gone," Presley said, looking at the floorboards.

"Who's gone?"

Kneeling down, Presley said, "There was an old man under a blanket. He was lying right here."

"You sure you weren't hallucinating?"

"No, I talked to him. I tried to help him up so he could escape the fire. He just laughed and said he was the one who pulled the alarm."

"This old man under the blanket?"

"Yes, honest."

"Did you get a good look at him?"

"No, it was too dark. Besides he sort of hid his face from me."

"Well, just so you know, we don't have residents camping out in dimly lit hallways. Some of our rooms cost less than others, but to have a resident parked here on the floorboards would be criminal."

"Maybe he was a criminal," Presley offered. "Maybe he broke into the house."

Shaking her head, Rosie said, "I don't know. Maybe you have a vivid imagination."

"You have to admit, it's kind of weird…the alarm that went off was over there," Presley said, pointing down the hall. "The fireman said so."

"Yeess," Rosie said, considering the notion. "But still, if there was a man sleeping in this hallway, a man who set off the alarm, how'd he get in through double-locked doors? Why did he pull the alarm and where is he now?"

Presley could only shrug.

"Piece of advice. Keep it to yourself. We've had enough excitement for one day and I don't want the seniors thinking you had anything to do with that alarm going off."

"You told them I was with you."

"Trust me, they can forget what you tell them the instant words leave your mouth." Rosie made a 'shhh' sign. "Let's keep this little secret between you and me."

So Presley didn't utter another word about the cackling corpse in the hallway. He went right to work, setting the tables in the dining room, pouring the water, arranging the napkins, putting butter on each table and the bowls of individual jams, getting the buffet table ready, and finally putting on the white starched jacket they gave him to wear while busing tables. He was swimming in the jacket, so Rosie promised to alter it for him after supper was cleared and the kitchen was cleaned. As head cook she assuredly had innumerable duties to surmount! After just one day on the job, Presley stood in awe of her. Rosie was a forthright yet gentle matriarch, a leader he aimed to follow.

The latter part of June sped by like a wasp drawn to bacon. Presley flew out of bed at dawn and dropped to his pillow by nine every night. Between shifts at Silver Trails, he still made time for his precious daisies. They were thriving and as appealing as ever. In fact, unsuspecting pedestrians who walked down Sedgwick would glimpse down the alley at the fresh floral mass of white and jerk their heads back to admire and linger a little longer. The stark beauty of the plantings was such a contrast to the drab grayness and barrenness across the street in Cabrini-Green that even total strangers appreciated Presley's gift.

While he was in the alleyway, Presley still yakked with Lily through her window. They had all the more in common, all the more to talk about now that he worked where she lived. One time they were discussing what was going to be served at dinner. It was Italian night and Tony was cooking polenta. Lily hadn't tasted it before and she wanted to know what it consisted of. Before Presley could answer, a tapping came from the window below Lily's.

"Cornmeal," the resident said. The voice was muffled, but then the elder opened his window and shouted out, "Cornmeal!"

Lily leaned over the sill and looked down. "Rather than listening in, why don't you join us in our conversation, Sal?"

The man quipped, "Not interested!"

"Well, you certainly knew what we were talking about."

"That's because I'm Italian."

Presley chuckled. *Another testy elder,* he thought.

"Well, of course you're Italian," Lily said smartly. "Sal is short for Salvatore, is it not?"

"Damn right. And my last name solidifies my heritage."

Presley decided to jump in. "And what's your last name, sir?"

"Donatelli."

"Ah, such a lyrical ring to it," Lily noted.

"Italian names are like that," Sal said. Sticking one wrinkly hand out the window and moving it like he was conducting a symphony, he added, "Yeah, our names are musical. Hell, anything's better than those garbled Polish names I keep coming across. Hard on the ear, hard to pronounce, and why most end in 'ski' I'll never know. Had a buddy in the war, last name of Kraniscroakski. Who'd want to go through life with an idiotic name like that? We called him 'Toad' for short. He didn't mind. Better than us butchering his real name."

"What war were you in, sir?" Presley shot forth, pretty sure the man would like talking about his war experiences.

"Two," Sal replied curtly.

"Wow, two wars?"

"No, kid. World War Two." Sal paused and added, "Fought overseas against Hitler."

The empty quiet that followed had a bite to it, so Lily took her cue, "So, Sal, where've you been?"

"What do you mean where've I been?"

"Well, I don't think in the five or six years I've lived upstairs from you, I've ever heard your voice."

There was another awkward silence, so Presley took the lead. "I think it's because Mr. Donatelli chooses to take his meals in his room. I've been told to get his empty tray once in a while."

"Oh, I see..."Lily said. "You have a handicap that prevents you from dining with the rest of us?"

"No, I do not," Sal replied indignantly. "I'm not handicapped. I just don't like sharing meals with people I don't know or care about."

Getting his gist, not wanting to badger, Lily changed gears. "Are you going to come for the entertainment tonight?" she called down.

Sal was swatting at a thirsty mosquito, ignoring the question.

"I saw the flyers posted in the house," Presley called over. "It said the guy's a magician."

"He's been here before," Lily relayed. "Heard he has a very good act. Does some unbelievable tricks."

"That's what they are, all right…tricks. Never any magic involved," Sal grunted.

"Such a cynic you are," Lily chided. "Well, I rarely attend Happy Hour, but I think I'll go this evening."

Redirecting her attention to Presley, she asked, "Will you be there?"

"Yes, they asked me to come in ahead of dinner, to pass the peanuts and popcorn during the magic show."

Sal groaned, "Oh, joy. Peanuts and popcorn. All the more reason not to go. He gave a quick wave of his hand and shut the window.

"Don't take it personally," Lily said. "He's just an old fuddy duddy."

The magician that eve turned out to be a big hit. His name was Black Jack. He wore black leather and had a trained crow that perched on his shoulder. He asked that the lights in the living room be turned off. Everything about him was dark and mysterious. At a point during the show Presley was passing munchies to the seniors when Black Jack nabbed him and brought him forward to be part of a magic trick. It was a disappearing act. Presley was a little nervous at first, but then Black Jack whispered in his ear, giving him instructions.

The black cloak was thrown over Presley, the magician shouted some alien command, "*Iye con val dor mante!*" and the cloak was yanked off. The audience clapped wildly. Presley was nowhere in sight. That's when Lily got to her feet and made her way forward. She demanded Black Jack return Presley to the room. Her concern was genuine, but it made the magician laugh and the crow caw.

"Stop this nonsense," she demanded. "Bring him back!"

A scream came from the side of the room. In the dim light a figure could be seen waving frantically. "Turn on the lights…please! I think my Dickie's had a heart attack!"

Seconds later Presley pushed through the door nearest the ailing man. He flicked on the lights and lunged down next to the lifeless elder. In order to work at Silver Trails he'd been sent to a class in CPR, but this was the real thing, and he was awestruck.

"Somebody go to the front desk. Tell them to call an ambulance!" Presley ordered. Then he leaned over the barrel-chested man and put his ear to the elder's nose, trying to ascertain if he was breathing. Next he took his trembling index and middle fingers and put them on the man's carotid artery, begging to find a pulse. Sensing none, he tried to tilt the man's head back a little to start resuscitating him. But the man's head was heavy and awkward to move. Plus Presley realized that the man's mouth was much bigger and wider than his. "I don't think this is going to work," Presley announced as he got up and ran into the kitchen. Instantly he returned with a dazed Thomas by his side. It was tough for towering Thomas to get down into a kneeling position, but he did.

Just as he was ready to give breath, the magician appeared. He nudged Thomas aside, saying, "Let me take over. This is my specialty."

And it was magical because Black Jack expertly administered CPR and in a matter of minutes, right as the ambulance arrived, the man called Dickie opened his eyes. A team of medics hustled in with a stretcher. And *presto*, vitals were taken, the victim was lifted and strapped in place, and off they sped to the hospital. His wife, Violet, looked like a repeat heart attack waiting in the wings, so they took her along, too.

When Black Jack returned to the front of the room the seniors stood and applauded.

He bowed humbly and said, "Thank you, my friends, but I have to be honest with you. That wasn't magic. I'm a registered nurse who plays magician on my days off."

People murmured their admiration and clapped some more. The mood was once again upbeat and Black Jack was able to finish the rest of his tricks. Afterwards, as he was stuffing duffel bags full of props, he hailed Presley.

"Want you to know you did the right thing, young man. There's no way you could've given that gentleman mouth to mouth. You were smart to get an adult to help. If he pulls through this, he'll have you to thank."

Presley stood a little taller, beaming. Then he asked Black Jack, "Does your crow bite?"

"No, you want to hold him?"

Nodding with enthusiasm, Presley put out his hands.

"One arm will do. Jasper will walk up it and find your shoulder. That's where he likes to rest."

Presley giggled. "It kind of tickles." In no time the big black bird was perched on his shoulder, staring at him, beak to nose. "I thought crows were kinda mean. But he's nice. I like him."

"He seems to like you, too."

"How long have you had him?"

"A few years. Used to have a squirrel, too, but he died recently. Jasper and Scamp, they were best friends. 'Near about killed Jasper when we lost Scamp."

Unbelievably, the crow made a guttural knocking noise.

"I think he knows what you're talking about," Presley said.

"Yeah, they're no dummies." Black Jack put his arm out and Jasper hopped back on board.

"Can I help you out with your equipment, sir?" Presley offered.

"No, thanks. I can get it. Besides, there's a woman flagging you down. Over there by the kitchen."

"Oh, that's Rosie. Guess I'm supposed to clear these chairs and start setting up for dinner." Presley waved back, acknowledging. He turned back to the magician and said, "If you ever want me to watch your bird for a while, I can. I live next door and I grow daisies in the alley. Lots of birds stop by. Jasper might like it."

"Maybe I'll take you up on that one day. Thanks for the offer."

Presley nodded and took to his tasks. The magician smiled and said to his feathered friend, "Now that's a nice kid."

That night after dinner Presley returned home to find his mother sobbing.

"What's the matter?" he begged to know. But all she would do is cover her face and cry some more. Later that evening his father came in more inebriated than he'd ever seen him before. He literally stumbled through the door and fell face-down on his belly.

Presley sat alone on the sofa, watching *Mod Squad*. His mother had already slunk off to bed, sullen and forlorn.

"Get me a beer!" the father demanded with his face smashed into the floor.

Presley could hardly understand the command because it was so garbled. "Excuse me?" he said.

On his knees Presley's father dragged himself to the base of the sofa. "You heard me…get me a beer…damn it!"

Presley totally understood the second time around, but he was torn. He knew his father was already drunk. Another beer? That might make him pass out or give him a really bad hangover. He'd seen enough of those, so he decided to get his father some water instead. He got up and went to the kitchen, returning with a glass of water. At the sight of the glass and not a bottle, the father got to his feet and with whatever strength and coordination remained, clobbered Presley over the head with both arms. Down the boy went, glass shattering around him. The father fell backwards and, with the impact of his fall, passed out. Presley felt dizzy from the blow. He got up slowly and saw that he had a bad cut. A shard of broken glass was digging into his calf and blood was oozing forth. Pulling the glass out, Presley hobbled over to his father's side and, as he had done earlier that evening, he put his ear to his father's nose to see if he was breathing. To find a pulse, he took two trembling fingers and placed them on his dad's neck. There was an arterial beat, all right. In fact, blood was pumping wildly. Satisfied his father was alive, Presley laid on the sofa and sobbed.

Chapter Six

Consider the soil's Ph factor (sweet vs. acidic)

"Yes, I'm the one who called for help," Sal said. "You're lucky I'm a stargazer. I happened to be looking out my window when your father nailed you over the head."

"Sorry you had to see that, sir."

"Young man, your father beat you! What he did is inexcusable. I wasn't going to turn and look the other way. I had to report it. Care and Family Services should know."

"Yes, sir."

"He beat your mother, too, I understand."

"Yes, sir. I didn't know that at the time. When I got home she was crying. She tried to hide her black eye from me." Presley took a feeble breath and said, "My father's had a hard time lately. He lost his job over a month ago and he hasn't been able to find any other work."

"That may be, son. But there's absolutely no excuse for him to take his anger out on you and your mother. Got that?" Sal paused, in profound thought. "I'm going to tell you a little secret. I was physically abused as a child. My Italian father made his own wine. Drank way too much of it. Got mean when he drank and he laid into me a few times."

Presley nodded and then was still. Suddenly, as if they sensed his anguish, Sal's two tiny dogs hopped up and nestled in the boy's lap.

A gradual grin replaced the frown.

"Oh, they're so cute," Presley said, petting them. "What are their names?"

"The brown one is Chimp and the white one is Squirt."

"I can see why you call this one Chimp," Presley said. "He looks like a monkey."

Zooming in on the white, scraggly dog, he asked, "Is this one Squirt because he's so little?"

"No," Sal replied, pointing toward his bed. "Squirt likes to pee on my bed post."

Presley couldn't contain himself. He laughed for the first time in days.

"All right, so here's the deal…I didn't call you to my room to rattle on about your father's loathsome behavior. I summoned you to see if I can hire you to walk my dogs."

"Me?"

"I don't see anyone else in this room…" Sal said sarcastically.

Presley gasped and yelped out his response, "Okay…sure!"

"Good, then, here's what I'd like you to do for me, Elvis..."

"Excuse me, sir, but my name is Presley."

"Okay, Elvis…" Sal repeated. He paused and said succinctly, "Whoever named you Presley meant to call you Elvis."

Confounded, Presley uttered, "Sir?"

"We all know Elvis is the pop star's first name. You don't use a last name as a first name. Who named you Presley anyway?"

"The first mom who adopted me."

"And when did you move in with her?"

"About two months after I was born. That's what she told me anyway."

"So, you don't know your blood parents?"

"My blood parents, sir?"

"Your real parents."

"No, sir. But I overheard my first mother say I was born up north, near Lake Forest."

Sal sat forward, scratching his balding scalp. He knew the area to be a wealthy suburb of Chicago, but he didn't let on or pry any further. "Lake Forest, eh?"

"I think so, sir," Presley murmured as the two dogs launched off his lap and scurried toward the door.

"They must know you're here to take them out," Sal said, dangling their leashes as the dogs danced on their hind legs.

"How long should I walk them, sir?"

"Until they do their business. Usually half an hour is ample, but I'll pay you for an hour because there are two of them."

"Wow, thank you, sir." Presley knelt down and was covered in wet kisses while he put on the dogs' leashes. "Is there anything else I need to know?"

"Chimp will yip at other dogs while Squirt will nip at other dogs, so just keep them in tow. Tight leash all the way."

"Are they used to a certain route?"

"They're used to the one block behind the house here, so this is going to be a treat for them. But please, don't venture across the street into Cabrini-Green. I don't want you or my dogs being the target of a stray bullet."

"Don't worry, sir. I never go over that way."

"Smart boy. Well, then, we'll see you back here in about half an hour, Elvis."

Stepping out into the hallway the youngster said, "Presley, my name is Presley."

Once the dogs and the boy were gone, Sal went to his window, opened it, leaned out and used a broom handle to tap on Lily's above. He tapped twice before she heard him.

Looking downward, Lily said, "Hello," like she was answering a phone call.

"It's me, Sal."

"I figured as much. You're the only one who lives right below me."

"Yes, well, I wanted to ask you something."

"And you can't come up to my room to ask me?"

Sal was tongue-tied. "I don't know how to get there," was his bogus response.

"Oh, for heaven's sake..." Lily said. "If you'd come out of that dang room of yours once in a while...Never mind...Here's what you do. Walk out of your room, make a right, take the elevator that's three doors down, go up one floor, come out and make a left, go three doors and knock. That'll be my room. It's not that difficult."

"You sure it's okay?"

"Yes, Sal, we're allowed to have visitors."

"All right, I'll be up in a flash."

"Don't hurt yourself," Lily called back as she heard the window below slam shut. She hustled to the vanity and slicked back her waves of white. She went to her bed and pulled up the comforter so her room looked tidier. By the time she finished, there was a pounding on her door. "Yes?" she called out like she was expecting one of many suitors.

"It's me, Sal."

"Oh, of course," Lily said, opening the door with a flourish. "Please, do come in." Lily led Sal to her vanity chair, which was too small and dainty for his stocky frame. As he clumsily managed to lower his wide base atop it, Lily said, "I'm sorry, I wish I could offer you something to eat or drink."

"No, no. That's quite all right. I just came up to discuss Elvis with you."

Lily hesitated. "Elvis Presley?"

"No, the boy, Elvis."

"Oh, you mean Presley."

Sal said stubbornly, "Well, I call him Elvis." Uncomfortably, he shifted in his seat and continued, "Did you know that Elvis's father beats him?"

Lily's body contracted, her spirit being stabbed.

"I called Care and Family Services about it. I could hardly believe what I saw. The blasted father hauled off and knocked Elvis over the head. He evidently gave the mother a black eye, too."

"Oh dear, I didn't know about the incident. Presley never said a word."

"Well, he wouldn't. He's either too shy or too scared."

"Or both. Oh, that poor boy. What are we going to do?"

"We?"

"Yes, obviously you wouldn't be here if you weren't concerned for his welfare."

"Well, I did my part. I notified DCFS."

"That won't guarantee it doesn't happen again." Lily relayed.

"I also hired him as a dog walker. He's out with my two dogs as we speak."

Lily raised an arched brow that was overly penciled in.

"Here's the way I see it. Keep him all the more busy outside of the home and you'll keep him away from that SOB father of his. Eventually, the jerk will find another job, but until he does, he's over there drowning his sorrow in suds. Beer after beer can only equal trouble."

"Yes, I know." Lily took a seat on the edge of her bed. "Maybe you're right. As much as possible, remove Presley from the problem. Besides, the family could use the extra money." Thinking, she asked, "But what can I do? I don't have any dogs to walk."

"Hmm..." Sal rubbed his bristly, unshaven chin. "You're the one who got to know him first. And you did it by talking to him about his flowers. The kid loves growing those flowers. What if we got permission from Mr. Taylor to have the boy build flower boxes and plant daisies here at Silver Trails? If there's a question about the money, you and I can be in charge of asking the residents if they care to chip in."

Lily surprised Sal by jumping to her feet. "Great idea!" she exclaimed.

"Thank you," Sal said proudly. "I think so, too." Awkwardly rising from the cramped chair, and listing a little too much to the right, he nearly tripped over a big brown case lying on the floor. "Whoa..." he declared.

"Oh, my. I'm sorry. That's my guitar. It's in the way no matter where I put it."

Regaining his balance, Sal said, "I used to play guitar...back in the day. Mind if I take a peek?"

"No, be my guest. I don't think Blossom has seen the light of day since I've been here."

"You even named her," Sal said, leaning down stiffly to open the case.

"Yes, she and I have gone everywhere together. Ever since I was a teen."

"Ah," Sal inhaled as he partook of the beautiful instrument. "A Gibson, acoustic. Absolutely the best. I had a twelve-string years ago." He strummed the six strings and cringed.

"Worse than fingernails on a chalk board," Lily noted. "My fault. Blossom hasn't been tuned in eons."

So, for another fifteen minutes Sal and Lily shared vintage memories of their guitar strumming days. Sal was able to retune the guitar while Lily looked on through youthful eyes. She erased Sal's balding head, his paunchy gut, the sun craters on his somewhat bulbous nose, and saw him as a handsome, strapping young man who could woo starlets with his musical expertise. Suddenly, Sal deposited the guitar back in its case.

"Oh, my gosh. I've been here too long. Elvis will be back with my dogs any minute." He shuffled quickly to the door. "We'll continue this conversation tomorrow when he's out with the dogs again. Same time, okay?"

"Okay by me," Lily said cheerily.

Even before the two elders met the next day, Lily approached Mr. Taylor and secured his okay to start a flower garden on the back patio of Silver Trails.

"Glad you're spearheading the project," Mr. Taylor said. "I meant to discuss it further with Presley, but I got so busy with other things, I plum forgot. I think the seniors here will enjoy a place of respite. Nobody ever seems to mingle out on the patio."

"Now they'll have a reason to," Lily relayed. "In fact, if there's enough money you may want to buy a few chairs or benches. The residents might like a place to sit and enjoy the flowers."

"If the budget will allow, as soon as Presley has the flower boxes planted, I'll look into that, too."

"Oh, thank you!" Lily exalted.

As Lily left his office, Mr. Taylor couldn't help but think to himself that this eager and able youngster named Presley had already brought so much joy to the seniors at Silver Trails. He mused: *Lily sure is a changed person. Hardly ever spoke. Never really smiled. Now she's friendly and engaged and she supports whatever cause the boy undertakes. Down the line, might have to see if Presley's willing to lend his zip and zeal to our sister facilities, Silver Journey and Silver Venture.* Mulling it over further, the administrator acknowledged, *both those homes could use a boost. Between the two homes there've been four deaths and two traumatic injuries since June. Silver Trails has endured one heart attack, but Dick Cunningham survived and though he's on oxygen and confined to a wheelchair, he and his wife are not moving out. We need more happy endings like that!*

When Lily told Sal the next day that she'd arranged for Presley to have a flower garden at Silver Trails, he was so ecstatic he hugged her. She was taken aback and the two fell sideways onto the bed. Scrambling to get to their feet, with the dogs bouncing all over the room, Presley moseyed in.

"Oh!" he exclaimed. "I'm sorry. The door was open and I…I…"

"Never you mind," Lily said, giggling. "Come right in."

Sal was mortified. He kept losing his balance as he tried to stand up. "Damn, I can't get my feet to do what I want 'em to anymore!"

Presley moved in to assist. "There you go, sir. You steady now?"

Shaking his head, Sal replied, "Yes, yes, I've got it. But God knows there'll be a day I won't have it. I'm turning into a scaly lizard without legs…a slug."

Brushing away the frustration like she had a fairy's wand, Lily foretold, "Sal has some good news for you, Presley. Tell him, Sal."

"You tell him. You're the one who arranged things."

"But it was your idea."

"No, initially I believe it was yours…"

"But you're the one who got things rolling…"

Presley took a mini step forward between the two elders.

"Oh, all right. I'll tell him," Lily declared. "Sal and I agree you should plant a garden here at Silver Trails. I directed the notion to Mr. Taylor and he said it was a great idea."

His mind traveling at warp speed, Presley coughed forth, "Wow, I wonder if I have the time to take care of more daisies."

"You've got a couple of weeks before school begins, right?"

"Yes, but I'm busing three meals a day, doing my chores, taking care of my planter boxes, studying for next Fall's spelling bee, and now I'm walking three dogs." He gasped and updated Sal, "After Mrs. Cunningham saw me walking Chimp and Squirt she asked if I'd be Boomer's dog walker, too."

"Oh, she did tell me that at dinner," Lily said. Then explaining to Sal she continued, "Violet Cunningham sits nearby at mealtime. Her husband, Dickie, is the one who had a heart attack not long ago. Ever since then he's been unable to exercise their dog."

Readdressing Presley, she said, "That's very kind of you to agree to all these odd jobs. I'm sure it means a lot to the residents."

Sal regarded Presley who looked overwhelmed. "Maybe his plate's too full."

But Presley exclaimed, "No, no it's fine. I can make time." He was thinking of how his father had no work and how much the extra cash would mean to their struggling family. "I won't be able to start the flowers from seed, though. It's too late in the season."

"I'm sure that'll be fine with Mr. Taylor. Start by putting together your redwood planters and he can call a nursery to deliver the soil and flowers. He said there may even be funds enough for some patio chairs. After all, we're going to want to sit and partake of your garden's splendor."

Sal handed Presley the leashes. "You've got the dog days of summer going on. Better get moving, Elvis."

"His name is Presley," Lily insisted.

"Not to me it isn't," Sal said with a twisted smile. "Oh, and I've got one more request I'm going to make of you, Elvis. From now on I want you to bring me my meals, instead of Myrtle. That woman is nastier than a sow in heat. Whenever she drops off my tray, she dumps her bad mood in my lap, too. I'm tired of it."

"As long as it's okay with Rosie, sir. I'd be glad to bring you your meals."

Lily shot Sal half a grin. "Maybe one day you'll manage to get yourself down to the dining room so no one has to *bring* you your meals."

Presley snickered at the bantering as he skipped out of the room with Squirt and Chimp. When he opened the big front door onto Sedgwick Street, a spray of bullets met him.

Chapter Seven

Check drainage, avoid root rot

"Raucous youth and another drive-by shooting," screamed the newspaper headlines. Lily saved the article for Presley because she knew he'd appreciate seeing the word "raucous" again in print, especially as it applied to the gang that had attacked him. There'd been several drive-by shootings around Cabrini-Green that summer, but this was the first on Sedgwick. The previous month two boys had been killed by gunfire. Trite though it seemed, word was they were in the wrong place at the wrong time. Presley was fortunate. He was merely grazed by a bullet. Sal's dogs were traumatized, but neither were harmed.

Myrtle was first on the scene that afternoon. She fell to her knees and wailed, "No, not our busboy!"

Presley couldn't believe her reaction. *She doesn't even like me*, he thought. "I'm okay," he told the starched assistant. As a dribble of blood revealed itself, he added, "Don't worry. It doesn't really hurt."

"Call an ambulance!" Myrtle hollered.

With the battle-ax's strident alert reverberating through the hallways, seniors peeked out their doors and over the balcony. Sal grabbed Lily's hand and urged, "Come on! Elvis has been hurt!" The two moved faster than was safe for them, huffing and puffing until they were by Presley's side.

"I'm sorry about your dogs," Presley said with a worried expression. "I hope they're not too scared to go out with me again."

Sal leaned over and took the two leashes from the boy. "Don't worry about my pups. You're the one who's been hit."

"Yeah, and I wasn't even in a bad part of The Green."

Lily put her hand on Presley's head. "You have a guardian angel watching over you, know that? This could have been a lot worse." She eyed his wound. "A graze I'd say, but you still need a doctor to look at that."

"Here comes the ambulance," alerted Myrtle.

"Do I have to go in it?" Presley asked reluctantly. As the vehicle pulled up he watched as a familiar-looking man jumped out of the back. "It's Black Jack!" he declared. As the medic approached, Presley asked excitedly, "Where's your crow, Jasper?"

"Can't bring him with me when I'm on duty. Only when I'm doing my magic."

"Are you going to wave a wand and fix this boy's arm?" Lily asked hopefully.

Descending to assess the damage, Black Jack replied, "The magic's already been done. This boy is safe. And as far as tending to his arm, it's a cinch. Don't even need to take him in. I'll clean it up and bandage it right here. Have him on his way in no time."

"And what about that motley bunch who shot at him?" Sal asked sternly.

"I'm not a police officer, sir, but I will report the incident."

"We all will," Lily affirmed. "Things are getting too rough around here."

"Raucous," Presley said under his breath.

Instead of working the dinner shift that evening, Presley was told to go home and rest. When he appeared at the door, his father immediately started in on him. "What're you doing home so early? Did you get fired?"

"No, I got shot."

"By a disgruntled senior?" The father thought himself funny and laughed.

"No, by a gang member."

"You walkin' those dogs down near Locust? You know that's

Death Corner, right? That's a fact, boy; been 'bout fifty murders on Sedgwick and Locust."

"No, I was in front of Silver Trails. The drive-by happened right next door."

"Best watch your back from now on. In case you hadn't noticed we're living in a cesspool."

That was the end of the discussion. Presley's father popped a beer and plopped on the sofa. When his mother learned of the shooting she was much more sympathetic. But the bottom line was nobody had a remedy. There was no omnipotent panacea to cure the social ills that were afflicting them. The disease was widespread, precarious, and vile.

When Presley took to walking the dogs again, he was extremely careful. He would slowly open the front door and peer outside to the street to see if any cars were speeding by. His father had warned him, and Presley heeded his advice. Now he knew to watch his back and use his keen vision to scout out any unusual activity surrounding him. He was also on the lookout for shady characters, especially the carload of punks that'd blasted him.

On one of his many walks he told Boomer, the Cunningham's Corgi, "I wish I had a sixth sense like you dogs do. Then I could *feel* when something's wrong. Things have gotten so dangerous around here, you hardly ever see kids out playing anymore. It's sad."

The short-legged, honey-and-white dog with the pointy ears barked twice as if to say, "You're right!" and went back to sniffing weeds and tugging.

Just days before school commenced, Presley, who had toiled relentlessly on the back patio of Silver Trails, finally finished erecting his redwood planters. He created something very unique and different from those he had built in the alleyway. He made them circular rather than rectangular, thus accentuating the design and layout of the patio. The residents were so enamored with his work that, even before the soil and plants arrived, they came outside to ogle and chat.

"Artistic young man," one said.

"Well-skilled to be calculating such clean geometric patterns," another commented.

"Hard to believe he's just ten," remarked a third.

"And he's our busboy, to boot," praised another.

The seniors were so pleased that they decided to hold a party on the patio. They agreed to have the gathering on the night the garden project would be finished. Presley got wind of their idea and prayed that everything would go accordingly. He begged Sal and Mrs. Cunningham for a day off from walking their dogs. He pleaded with Rosie to cover him during the lunch hour when the truck would be arriving from the nursery. Realizing it was a lot to ask, but very much needing extra hands, he sought Lily's aid in planting the flats of flowers. All were more than willing to oblige, especially Lily who showed up with her own trowel and knee pads. They went to work at noon and didn't stop until five.

Taking a deep breath as she rose stiffly to her feet, Lily declared, "Well, I'll be! If that isn't the most beautiful garden I've ever seen. And bravo! Look what an improvement to our patio. It's glorious! Mr. Taylor's going to need to order a bundle of chairs because everyone's going to be flocking out here to partake of this utopia!"

"Utopia?" Presley asked, brushing the dirt off his knees.

"Yes, my dear boy. Utopia. It means wonderment. Something to marvel at."

"Do you spell it u-t-o-p-i-a?"

"Very good. Yes."

"I'll have to remember that; the word may come up in one of my spelling bees."

At that point, Rosie sauntered out with a pitcher of lemonade. "You two need some refreshment? It's getting kind of steamy out here." She turned and, upon seeing the new garden area, nearly dropped the tray she was carrying. "Lordie be!" she exclaimed. "Never have I seen anything so pretty! Surely I'm in the midst of a dream."

The complimentary chatter continued to pour forth into the evening as the residents convened on the back patio. Neither the

Chablis nor the lemonade poured as freely or as plentifully as the praises directed toward Presley.

Standing to the side with Sal, Lily said, "A couple of months ago they were ready to eat him alive. And now look…they can't get enough of him."

"He's a hard worker. People like that."

"No, people like *him*," Lily underlined. Cozying up a smidgeon, she added, "He's somewhat of a catalyst."

"And just what do you mean by that?" Sal asked taking a gulp of his lemonade.

"Well, look at you."

"Me? Why look at me?" Sal said deadpan.

"I don't mean literally. I mean look how Presley has made a change in you."

"How so?"

"Oh, please. How can you be so blind? Surely you can see how you've changed since Presley came into your life."

Sal rolled his eyes like a little kid ready to be reprimanded. "Don't hold back. I'm sure you're going to tell me one way or another."

"You're darn right," Lily said, elbowing Sal. "First of all, you're here!"

"That's a given," Sal said, swirling what was left of his beverage. "Your point being?"

"This is the first Happy Hour, the first social event, the *very first* time you've ever come down to mingle with the rest of us."

Shifting his weight side to side, Sal finally said, "You're fairly new to all of this, too. From what I understand you've been sort of a recluse the past few years."

"Actually, pretty much the whole time I've been here. Up until this summer…when I finally befriended that young man over there."

Sal allowed for a squeamish smile. "Okay, I'll admit it. He's managed to bring some of us out of our shells."

"Yes, indeed. Crabs that we are." Lily replied. "By the way, why is it that we get so testy in our old age?"

"Probably because we're being tested all the time."

"Oh, ha ha ha."

"No, I mean it. Life gets more trying. We lose loved ones and lots of us are lonelier than hell. We have aches and pains, arthritis and what not. We're stubborn and become creatures of habit, get set in our ways...that sort of thing."

"And that makes us cantankerous?"

Sal raised a thick white brow. "I think so."

"I don't mean to pry, but how long ago did you lose your wife?"

"I've been alone for damn near twelve years now. Sweet Pea, that's what I nicknamed the love of my life." Sal looked off in the distance, continuing in a somber tone, "Yeah, my beautiful Sweet Pea died of cancer in her early sixties. She did her utmost to fight, but that disease is pure dread, nothing quite as miserable. After three years, my beloved couldn't hold on any longer. Sadly, she was waiting for me to give her permission to move on. Once I did that..." Sal gulped back a groan and repeated, "Once I did that, Sweet Pea died the next morning."

"Oh, I'm so sorry. My Richard died of a heart attack. It was a shock, but it was fast. And in a way I'm grateful I didn't have to endure years of him being seriously ill."

"How long we're you married?" Sal asked, getting personal for once.

"Fifty-six years." Lily gazed off like she was watching a slide show of her life.

"Did you live around these parts?"

"We spent the first five years in a little bungalow not too far from the Brookfield Zoo. Then we moved to Lake Forest."

"What a leap forward. Or should I say upward? Some beautiful homes in that area." Sal took the final swig of his sour drink and added, "Ya know, Elvis was born there. At least that's what he tells me."

"Lake Forest?! No, he must be thinking of someplace else." Regarding Sal's expression, Lily said, "I don't mean to be unkind, but let's face it, there aren't a lot of blacks who reside in that town."

"He looks to be a mix."

"Even still…" Feeling uncomfortable with the subject matter, Lily made a quick change. "So, Sal, where did you and your wife live?"

"In Cabrini-Green."

Gasping, then trying to hide her surprise, Lily asked, "Across the way here?"

"Yep, smack dab in what is now a rat-infested, gangster-laden, poverty hellhole." He could sense Lily needed more. "We were one of the first to move into the Frances Cabrini Row houses. Sweet Pea and I planted roots there in '42. The residents back then were predominantly of Italian ancestry. We had the Bellinis to our left, the Puccinis to our right, the Marconis above us, and the Stuzerellis below. There were a couple of Irish families and one Polish family as I recall, but for the most part we were hard-core Italians with olive oil pumping through our veins."

"And garlic on your breath?"

"Now don't go getting mean."

Lily laughed. "I'm not. I love Italians. They're all about family. Do you have children, Sal?"

"Michael and Camellia. But both live out of state; far away from here. How about you?"

"A daughter, Ivy. She doesn't live far, but I rarely see her. She's afraid to come to this area now."

"Can't say I blame her. If you read the headlines, everyday there's something rude, crude, or lewd going on in this here neck of the woods."

"Did you move out of the Row houses because of the violence?"

"It's what they called 'white flight.' I'd say by '62 most of the people in the complex were black. We moved out in '65 when crime got so bad we feared for our lives. It's tragic because in the beginning the housing was affordable and safe. And the location was desirable because the majority of us had jobs in the nearby factories."

"It was after the war, right? Isn't that when they closed down those factories? I remember hearing thousands were laid off."

"Yes, that was the crux of the problem. But, too, the city was strapped for cash so they stopped providing police patrols, routine building maintenance and transit services. I'll never forget when they started paving over a number of lawns because they couldn't afford to maintain them any longer. And God forbid if your complex fell victim to a fire. Instead of rebuilding the units, the Housing Authority simply boarded you up."

"Hard to fathom. You'd think Cabrini-Green would be prime property sitting between two of the wealthiest neighborhoods in Chicago."

"Yep, but having Lincoln Park and the Gold Coast as neighboring communities didn't do us any favors."

Lily tilted her head, wanting more.

"Think about it. Because of the wealth nearby, Cabrini-Green became a popular site for illicit drug sales. And *presto*, where there are drugs, there is suddenly competition to sell those drugs and in no time you've got a bunch of gangs on the loose. About the time we left, there were specific gangs controlling certain buildings. Believe it or not, we as residents were being pressured into siding with the gang associated with our complex. Our allying with them was the only way to protect ourselves from their violence."

Putting a hand to his slightly slumped, dowagers back, Lily said sincerely, "And here I was living just miles away…wearing my blinders, unaware of the problem and its severity. Dare I say clueless?"

"Unless you lived in the squalor…unless you feared for your family's safety on a daily basis…how would you know? Look, don't beat yourself up over the issue. We survived."

Lily smiled up at Sal. "Gee, Silver Trails must seem like a picnic ground for you."

"A few fond memories allowed for my return here. But don't kid yourself," he said in an austere tone. "What happened to Elvis the other day in front of our house; that was no joy ride. If those unruly kids wanted to kill our little friend they would have. We reside on the edge of peril, Lily. Don't take it lightly."

"Oh, trust me, I don't..." Before Lily could finish her comment, she heard angelic singing in the background. She twirled around to see who was performing and there was Presley!

Chapter Eight

Apply soil that is friable and fertile

"I didn't know the kid could sing," Sal said, leaning in toward Lily.

"Neither did I! You'd think I'd have heard him at least once while he was out in the alleyway, watering those daisies of his."

"Is there anything he's *not* good at?"

"Promoting himself," Lily replied. "See that? He's not the entertainer that was hired for our gathering. There's a musician over there with a keyboard."

"Guess Elvis asked the guy if he could sing."

"Are you ever going to quit calling him Elvis?" Lily chided.

"Why should I? Turns out he is a star."

"Well, it's not an Elvis voice he's showcasing."

"That's because he's ten. Trust me; that high-pitched falsetto will drop to bass one day."

An astonished Sal and Lily made their way across the patio to where Presley was performing for the crowd. When he finished singing "Love Me Tender" the seniors applauded like they were at the Philharmonic. Pop music was not necessarily their favorite, but they were mesmerized by the pure and resplendent voice they'd just heard.

"Bravo!" hollered one.

"Encore!" yelled another. "Do something we know, something by Sinatra or Deano."

Presley was mortified. He brought the microphone closer and said, "I don't really know too many other songs. I sing stuff by Elvis because my first mom loved him so much." He coyly added, "That's why she called me Presley."

Violet called forth, "How about the song, 'Teddy Bear'?"Several of the seniors looked at her askance, so she added, "Not that I listen to this kind of music. But my granddaughter does and she simply loves that tune."

In his wheelchair, Dickie rolled forward, concurring, "Violet's right. Our granddaughter, Sage, can't get enough of Elvis. And that's her favorite. Do you know the song, Presley?"

"Yes, sir, I do, but...." Presley eyed the musician. "But I don't know if I should keep going. I only asked to sing one song."

"Sing for us!" came the unquenchable chant.

The musician waved Presley on. "It's fine. Go ahead. They want to hear you, so give 'em your all."

And Presley did. He even jived a little, allowing for the trademark undulation of his pelvis and hips. He was a miniature of the star for which he was named. When the seniors begged for more, Presley declined, promising that he'd entertain them another time. At that point, the keyboard player took over. And with the ballads he crooned, the mood changed from stoked to stodgy, sending everyone back to their idle chit chat and tame libations.

About half an hour later, after the flock of seniors had finished smothering Presley with their acclaim, Lily and Sal moseyed up to the boy.

"What a hit you were!" Sal said, shaking Presley's hand with zeal.

"Where did you learn to sing like that?" Lily begged to know. "Why haven't I heard you before? How come you don't sing while you water your flowers? It'd be like singing in the shower."

"Yeah, and when I do that I get in trouble. My mother doesn't mind too much. But my father said when I sing in the shower it's annoying."

Sal gave Presley a supportive slap on the back. "Well, he must be tone deaf. Because you're very good, young man. And I don't say that to just anyone."

Lily interjected, "It's true. Sal used to play guitar and sing. He knows a pro when he hears one."

Sal added, "And Lily, too. She still has her guitar."

"Really? You have a guitar?" Presley asked excitedly.

"Yes, I do. And you know what? I want you to have it."

Presley nearly toppled over. "Me? You want me to have your guitar?"

"Yes. Do you think you can play it?"

"I've never even *held* one."

"Well, this one may be a little big for you now, but you'll grow. And I'll give you lessons so you can learn to play Blossom."

"Your guitar has a name?" Presley asked, eyes wide.

"That's how special it is," Sal noted. "When you've played a guitar as long as we have, your instrument becomes your best friend. I wish I'd kept my twelve-string. My son took off with it when he went away to school. Never saw Long Neck again."

"You didn't tell me you named your guitar, too," Lily said.

"Have to keep *some* things secret from you," Sal replied with a wink.

Presley was practically dancing in place. "So when…when can you teach me?"

"When do you want to start?" Lily asked. "Remember, your plate's pretty full as it is. And school starts in a few days."

"That's okay. I'll fit lessons in somehow. Pretty soon I won't need to spend so much time on the flowers here and in the alleyway. They'll die back when winter comes."

"Magnifico," Sal said. "Take up guitar in the off season. By next summer we'll have you hired on as our busboy, dog walker, gardener, *and* entertainer. Yet another job for you, my man."

"I'll start making diagrams of chords right away, so you'll have a picture of where the fingers go on the various strings and frets."

"Frets?" Presley asked.

"Don't confuse him before he even gets going," Sal suggested.

Lily halted her left hand from making instinctive chord formations mid-air.

"It's okay. I'll learn in time. I'm pretty good at picking things up."

"You sure are!" Lily praised. "I've never seen anything like it!"

That instant, Rosie appeared. "Speaking of picking things up, young man, I covered for you at lunch today, but I sure could use your help right now." Pointing to the hors d'oeuvre table she requested, "Bring the empty plates and glasses in, please. And then let's get going on setting the tables for supper, okay?"

"Did you hear him sing?" Lily asked, happy wrinkles forming.

"All the way in the kitchen, even with the fans on," Rosie replied.

"Isn't he the best?"

"Hey, I've been singing his praises ever since he got here." She cocked her head and kindly commanded, "Now let's git to work, young man."

His final compliments for the day came as he stepped into the kitchen, carrying a tray of teetering glasses and plates.

Tony exclaimed, "So we have a star in our midst! How long have you been singing, kid? Since you popped into this world? Did they give you a mike instead of a rattle?"

Thomas inquired, "Did you sing Elvis before they named you Presley?"

"Let the boy get to his chores," Rosie ordered. "There'll be plenty of time to ask questions later."

Presley stood on his tippy toes. He set the tray down into the big deep sink and, as he raised his gaze, on the other side of the window he saw a skinny-framed man scoot by. "Did you see that?" he gasped.

"Was it a scraggly, hunched-over hobo in a blanket?" Tony queried.

"Yes, yes it was!"

"Got it, Chief!" Thomas declared, mimicking the bumbling Maxwell Smart. "That dweeb is a regular around here. He's an oddball; means no harm, though. Whenever we have Happy Hour he drops by, hoping to snitch any leftovers we might be tossing out."

Pointing wildly, Presley said, "But...but that's the guy who pulled the fire alarm. He was sleeping in the hallway when I tripped over him. He even told me he was the one who pulled the alarm."

Rosie bustled forward and stared out the window. "Did you just see him, Thomas? Is it Willie Waggers?"

"Yeh, it's him. He's hiding over there behind the fence."

"Then *he's* the one who stole all my muffins that day," Tony said, making fists with his Crisco-covered hands. "Figured a measly rat didn't do it! Had to be a rodent with a huge appetite."

Rosie stormed to the back door and hollered, "Willie Waggers! Get your butt over here! Now!"

Sheepishly the man slunk over to where Rosie stood stonefaced. He crumpled to his knees and brought the blanket up over his head.

"Take that filthy thing off. You need to get yourself a new blanket or you're going to be ravaged by bedbugs."

Quivering, the man replied, "But I don't have a bed to sleep in, so how could my blanket get bedbugs?"

"Oh, never mind!" Stabbing her finger like she was a bully bursting a kid's bubbles, Rosie laid down the law. "You and I have some talkin' to do! We have an eyewitness here that says you're the one who set off our fire alarm few months ago. Is that true?"

Under his coverlet Willie was trembling.

"Willie, you answer me. Right now!"

Slowly the man nodded and put his hands over his head in shame.

"Okay. So, are you also the thief who stole all our muffins that day?"

Like he was confessing to murder, Willie wailed, "Yes. Yes, I did it. I was so hungry and they smelled so good. I got a whiff of 'em before dawn. I just had to have 'em."

"And how'd you weasel your way in here?" Rosie insisted.

"When Tony came out to empty the garbage, I snuck in and hid."

"So, why'd you pull the alarm, Willie?"

"I had to create some sort of disturbance. I had to get everyone out so I could sneak in and take those delicious muffins." He inhaled the air like he was savoring the scent all over again. "They were to die for."

"And did you ever think, ya old coot, that you could've killed one of our seniors by setting off that alarm? People have heart attacks over stuff like that all the time."

Heaving deeply, partly for show, Willie begged for forgiveness. "I'm so sorry. I'll never, ever do it again. I promise. I'll be good. Please don't banish me."

Rosie shook her head, finally taking pity. "All right, Willie. Wait here. I'm going to get you a clean blanket. Go chuck that one in the garbage can. I'll gather up some scraps from Happy Hour and then I want you to be on your way. Got that?"

Groveling at Rosie's feet, Willie babbled on, "Oh, thank you. Thank you. I'm forever in your debt. God bless you." His outburst of gratitude poured forth until Rosie came back with her offerings. Willie grabbed the blanket and food, hugging them like he might never let go. "I'll be on my way now. Thank you. Thank you. Thank you," he said, his craggily voice trailing off as he disappeared.

When Rosie returned to the kitchen, she was mumbling, "He's a jaybird is all. Dives in out of nowhere, snatching up this crumb and that..."

"Well, at least he's thankful," Presley noted.

"He ought to be." Rosie planted her hands on her hips. She was one big exclamation point. "Hard to believe that run-down soul was once a civil engineer. Such a waste!"

Thomas took a scouring pad to a greasy pot. He scrubbed mightily. "Lots of smart people have been losing their jobs, Rosie. It's not necessarily their fault."

"Never said it was, Thomas. What I'm saying is if you're smart you'll be resilient."

Thomas looked confused as he plunged his huge hands into a mound of soap bubbles.

"I know what resilient means," Presley said proudly. "I looked the word up when I found it on a list of spelling bee challenges."

"Tell Thomas, Presley."

"Well, when you get knocked down...you bounce back up again. It's like those blow-up clowns that are punching bags. You sock 'em. They tip over. But then they come right back up for more."

Rosie raised a brow. "Now that's about the best analogy I've ever heard."

Thomas sent a congratulatory nod in Presley's direction. "Got it," he confirmed.

"Best if we can all remain resilient," Tony said. "Times are tough enough as it is. We don't need to lose our jobs."

Presley exhaled, thinking to himself that he had too many jobs. And with school starting, he had no idea where he was going to find time for everything. He'd agreed to Rosie's request that he come in for just one hour in the mornings to help set tables. He'd have to start at five-thirty, but he wanted to oblige and he knew the extra cash would come in handy. He'd still serve as busboy at the dinner hour. He'd still walk dogs on alternating afternoons. And his most time-consuming job, overseeing two gardens, was gratefully nearing an end. For the first time Presley eagerly awaited the waning of the growing season. Through September the boy took very good care of what flourished in the alleyway and what was planted in the garden at Silver Trails. But when October was escorted in by an early freeze, he was thrilled to be moving on. It only took one Saturday and half of a Sunday for Presley to deadhead all the daisies. This time he cut the stems way down, just above the dirt. They'd have to sleep like that until near about May, but it was a given...they'd be back in full glory, ready to greet and please come June.

In the meantime, Presley took to the guitar. His appetite to learn something new was insatiable and simply groovy! The first two weeks of October, after walking Sal's dogs or doing homework or tending to his dining room duties, he begged Lily for a peek at Blossom. Lily would open the case and watch the boy's eyes zoom in and radiate. She offered to let him hold her instrument, but he always declined, saying that he'd wait until he had time for the proper instruction.

"She's beautiful, though," he'd praise. "Can't wait until I know how to play her."

At one point Lily suggested, "You know, Presley, since this is going to be your guitar, you can give the instrument a new name."

"No way!" the boy protested. "She will always be Blossom. You said she's been a close friend to you. I could never, ever change her name because your best friend is my best friend."

"Okay then, have it your way." Lily knelt down and gave her guitar a gentle pat. "I think you'll be in loving hands, Blossom."

"Yes, I will take very good care of her…just like I do my daisies."

"I'm sure you will," Lily said, glowing.

His first lesson was set for Friday, October thirteenth. Presley promised to walk Chimp and Squirt first since he'd walked Boomer the day before. He showed up at Sal's shortly after the school bus let him off. With the two dogs in tow, Presley raced up a floor to tell Lily that he'd be back in half an hour. When she heard his knock, Lily quickly pinched her cheeks and powdered her nose. She opened the door and stood there gleaming, every bit as anxious as Presley. Finally, they were getting underway with guitar lessons. "Okay," Lily chirped. "Hurry on back from your walk. Blossom and I can't wait."

But Presley didn't return.

Chapter Nine

Be proactive about pest control

An hour passed. It was nearly five o'clock. Lily heard a knock at the door and quickly hobbled over to answer it. But it was Sal, not Presley. Sal was fraught with concern; his furrowing brow creased in places she'd never noticed before.

"Have you seen him?" he asked, stone serious.

"No, I thought you were Presley at the door." Lily clasped her hands and brought them to her chest as if she was praying. "What could've happened to him, Sal? He came up here with Squirt and Chimp to say he'd be back in half an hour. It's been over an hour. And it's starting to get dark."

Sal paced the hallway, his cloddy feet shuffling, threatening his stability.

"What are we going to do?" Lily pleaded.

Raising a hand like a traffic cop, Sal halted in his tracks. Determinedly he announced, "I've got to go look for him."

"But, Sal, you have no idea where he is."

"Do you have a better plan?"

"Yes, call the police."

"And you really think they're going to send out a patrol for a boy who's been missing a little more than an hour?"

"But Presley's so reliable. He's always on time. Something terrible must've happened."

"Lily, they don't care. Policemen avoid Cabrini-Green like it's the plague. They're not going to risk their lives for a kid who's lost his way home."

"He isn't lost. He knows his way home!"

"But, don't you see? That'd be their rationale—that he's dawdling or that he took a new route home or that he's merely lost."

Hesitating, Lily pointed at Sal. "You'd better go find him. Now!"

Just as Sal set off on a determined path, he ran into Rosie at the bottom of the staircase.

"You seen Presley?" she asked, perturbed. I've got seniors lined up for supper and the tables aren't even set yet." Absorbing Sal's angst, Rosie brought it down a few notches. "Everything okay with the boy? Father isn't beating him anymore, is he?"

"No, but something's happened. I'm going out to search for him right now."

Rosie grabbed Sal's arm. "You think it's that gang of kids after him again?"

"Hell if I know. But I'm going to find out!"

As Sal barged through the front door, Rosie called after him, "I'm going to send Thomas out with you."

But Sal was gone, intent on the rescue.

❀

It was six o'clock. The sun was sinking into a furious sky, shards of orange and red stabbing at the clouds. Presley was huddled together with the two dogs. They were all locked in a cage, petrified with their confinement. Trying to assuage the dogs fear, Presley made shushing noises. When that didn't work and the canines started shaking, the boy hummed an Elvis tune. He turned it into a lullaby and it calmed Squirt and Chimp until their arch enemy stormed back into the secluded garage.

❀

His name was Grenade, a wiry dark-skinned teen who was explosive in every way. He didn't need brawn because he was the leader of the pack, and he managed to surround himself with plenty of muscle power. The gang that nabbed Presley totaled twelve. They were a contemptible lot of subservient, testosterone-packed robots who didn't give a damn. They just as soon die as disappoint. And Grenade didn't allow for disappointment.

"*Que pasa*, lil jive turkey?" the teen seethed, leaning down to peer into the cage. "I see you got your spazmo doggies by your side, heh?"

Squirt growled and Chimp barked.

"Such a doofus duo. Might just have to feed you both to my pit bull."

Presley yelped, "Don't you dare hurt them..."

"Oh, go sit on it, Potsi!" Grenade hollered. "You're such a piece of work! What could you do to me anyway? Tie me up in one of your leashes? Paw me to death? Whine like a bogus mama's boy until I can't take it anymore?" He slammed the cage with the heel of his hand. "You're such a grody geek! Little dog walker out to make everyone happy."

Trying to sound tough, Presley said, "You're wrong, I walk dogs for the money."

Grenade grinned like a wily coyote, "Oh, is that right, pansy man?" He slithered down onto his haunches. "Gnarly. So the skinny is that you're stoked by mullah, too?"

"Why don't you just let us go? We haven't done anything to you."

The cage was slammed into again. This time Presley trembled along with the dogs.

"Fool that you are, chill out or I'll ream your ass! My turf, my rules! Got that, ya little rah rah raunchoid?!" Grenade's volcanic outburst alerted his gang. They stormed in, begging to know how they could best serve.

"Need us to take care of business, Grenade, drown 'em in Lake Michigan?" a husky kid with a helmet-like afro called out.

"What're you, trippin', bro?" shouted another. "What a drag. That's how we dumped the last dork. Nah, let's chuck 'em off the roof of some ritzy hotel. Way more sweet."

"Get real, dude! Diablo's gang did that six months ago. Talk about copycat."

Grenade launched to his feet. "Shut the hell up...all of you! You don't know Jack! I'm the boss and whatever I say is going down!"

The gang looked on in restrained silence. Finally the kid with the fat afro said, "Yo, man. Don't freak out. It's cool; we're hangin' with ya."

Another deadhead groveled, "Everything's copasetic. Peace, love, and granola, man. You're the bomb."

Feeling in charge again, Grenade rose to his feet and dusted off his flared jeans. Pointedly he remarked, "Okay, so we're slammin' now, right?" Those in the huddle nodded or gave a thumbs-up. "Bitchin. Here's the gig then. This dog walker gets around. I've seen him truckin' along the borders of our turf. But until today, he's never stepped foot in The Green."

"I've been told not to," Presley mumbled.

"Zip it, Ace! We already know you're a goodie-two-shoes who takes care of stupid flowers and old farts." Then Grenade turned to his pack and underlined, "All the more reason no one will suspect him."

"Of what?" one gang member timidly asked.

Grenade exploded again, "You freakin' airhead! Of moving drugs for us!"

Presley squirmed; the dogs squealed.

This time Grenade hauled off and kicked the cage. "Crap! Get those dogs to veg out or they're history! I swear I'll wring their necks!"

"If you do that," Presley said, trying to sound brave, "whatever plan you have will fall through."

Leaning forward with dagger eyes, Grenade hissed, "And why is that, my little dog walker?"

"Because if you kill these dogs then there's no reason for me to be walking through Cabrini-Green."

"He's got a point," breathed one of the younger gang members.

Grenade slugged the kid who dared to interject. "You're pissing me off! Let me repeat myself; I know what I'm doing!" The irate leader sunk a hand into the pocket of his leather jacket. He pulled out a burlap pouch. "See this, dog walker? Listen up. You want me to let you out of that cage so you can split? Want to boogie on out of here? Be free again to piss on your pretty flowers and play with the out-to-lunch potatoes at the wrinkle farm?" Presley could only stare, glassy-eyed and foggy. Grenade pressed on tauntingly, "Good night, John boy." Presley didn't move. "Ya maxed out? Later, Scater?" With emphasis Grenade jiggled the sack in front of the cage. "What gives, lil bro? Gonna make me wake your mama?"

"What's in the bag?" Presley finally asked, shaking off the trauma.

"It's for-sho, the real thing. And I ain't shuckin' ya when I say it's worth its weight in gold! So, if you open my stash or rip me off or screw up delivering the goods..." Grenade pointed to Chimp. "... that brown shaggy shit will be torn apart limb by limb."

Presley shuddered, but had to ask, "And what about Squirt? He's coming with me?"

"No duh! You're the dog walker. Gotta have a dog at your side, right?"

"But it's dark now."

Grenade mocked Presley, cowering and whining, "But it's dark now."

The gang realized it was okay to chime in, so they laughed and berated Presley, their voices loud and lunatic like a pack of hyenas.

Slicing through their banter, Grenade said in a steely tone, "Cabrini-Green will put hair on your chest, little dog walker. Book on down the street and get a taste of the wild side. It hasn't poisoned any of us yet. We're bangin'! You can, too. You say you make bread walking dogs? Well, if you sign, seal, and deliver for me, you'll be rolling in the stuff." Grenade pulled a key out of his pant pocket and unlocked the cage. Presley rose stiffly. Squirt broke bondage, running through his legs. Grenade slammed the cage shut before Chimp could escape. In so doing, Chimp's nose got bonked and the dog yelped. "That's nothing, you little wuss!" Grenade pointed at the dog, threatening, "If your trusty dog walker isn't back in fifteen minutes, you'll be on tomorrow's menu at the Asian restaurant 'round the corner, *capiche*?"

"Please don't hurt him," Presley begged. He put on Squirt's leash and faced Grenade full on. "I'll do what you say."

"Damn right, you will," Grenade assured, handing over the pouch. "Do you know Scott Street very well?"

"It's north of here."

"Yes. There's an Italian deli with a hair salon on one side and a Laundromat on the other. Know where I'm talking about?"

"The deli's called Mangiatti's?"

"Right on. Take this into the store and put the pouch in the owner's hands. Nobody else touches it, get my drift?"

"What if the owner's not there?"

"He will be. He's expecting this drop-off." Grenade set the bag in Presley's palm. "Now peel outta here and we'll catch you on the flip side. Not you or your lame dogs will be hurt if you just do as you're told. Dig it?"

Slouched over, Presley wandered off into the shadows with the phrase "Dig it" repeating in his mind. He couldn't help but think it might actually be a real grave he'd have to dig or be lowered into.

Sal was distraught. He'd canvassed three of the streets that bordered Cabrini-Green: Sedgwick, Chicago Avenue, and Halsted. He'd walked more than a mile and his entire being ached. He felt blinded by the eerie, thick darkness that descended upon him, but he pressed on. It had been ages since he'd crossed over into the bowels of Cabrini-Green, but he knew the trek was imperative, that he had to scour the area now. Alleyways filled with piles of rotting garbage, abandoned apartments surrounded by steel mesh, and littered remnants of buildings in collapse made his search all the more perilous. At one point Sal fell head first over a toilet someone had tossed off their balcony. Though it was too dark to see, he recoiled from the stench. Stumbling to get to his feet, Sal saw a tall looming figure in front of him. Raising his hands in surrender, he said in a timorous voice, "Please, please don't hurt me."

The towering shadow inched closer. Long, dark, menacing arms stretched forward, hands sifting through the black void of night.

"Please," Sal pleaded, "I'm just an old man looking for a young boy." Powerful arms dropped on his shoulders and Sal wailed, "Noooo…"

"Whoa! Don't go havin' a heart attack, sir. It's just me… Thomas. Rosie sent me out after you. Said you needed help looking for Presley. That he disappeared with your two pooches."

Sal exhaled his fright and inhaled relief. "Yes, the boy was supposed to be back by four-thirty, but no one's seen hide nor hair of him."

"Pretty tough to see anything in this darkness," Thomas offered. "How 'bout if we head back?"

"But I told Lily I'd find the boy."

"And you will. He's probably back at the home as we speak."

At first Sal scoffed at the notion of returning empty-handed, but he finally succumbed to Thomas's advice. Besides he told himself, *you can't manage another block of this hellish search. Your body is ready to break down like the demolition surrounding you and your will is in the toilet you just tripped over.*

Sal crumpled his shoulders in defeat. Awkwardly he clumped along behind Thomas as they took a shortcut back to Silver Trails. The silence surrounding them was like a psycho thriller, so Sal decided to break it. Casually he asked Thomas, "So, did you play basketball in college?"

"Never went to college. My mom worked two jobs, but her take-home was only enough to cover family expenses for my brother and me. I was offered a partial scholarship to USC, but I had to turn them down because I had no way of paying the rest of the tuition."

"Gosh, what an opportunity. Had I known you back then, maybe I could've helped you out some."

Thomas' laughter erased the eeriness around them. "Sir, I don't know anyone with that kind of money! But thank you just the same. 'Sides, that was five years ago. I've gotten kind of rusty when it comes to playing basketball."

"Bet those kids you coach don't think so."

Thomas nodded. "Yeah, you always look like a star to those who're just starting out."

❀

It took Presley exactly sixteen minutes to accomplish his mission. He raced back to find Grenade yanking Chimp out of his cramped cage. Standing by was a squirrelly gang member with a machete in hand.

"Stop!" Presley shouted. "I'm here!"

"You're a minute late," Grenade shot back. "Your doggie needs to suffer some."

"But it's not my fault. The owner was busy. And you told me not to hand the stuff over to anyone but him." Lunging forward, Presley put himself between the sharp weapon and the wiggly, terrified dog. "Don't do it! Please!"

Grenade gestured to his chum to withdraw the machete. He grabbed Chimp by the collar and let the mutt hang, gasping and choking. Finally he dropped the terrified critter into Presley's arms. "Next time you're late, the dog dies."

"Next time?" Presley muttered.

"Yes, next time! What don't you get? You're my new delivery boy. We're bros, doggie walker." Grenade extended a hand and then jerkily rescinded it. "Oh, and next time if things go down righteous, I'll pay you something for the gig."

"But…I have enough jobs as it is," Presley said, knowing his excuse was feeble.

"Why you thankless, little jerk! You're lucky I'm splitting any of my greenbacks! If you don't deal for me I can just as easily slit your throat!"

Though timorous, Presley tried another approach. "Well, this is going to be my last dog walking job. Because I'm really late and there's no way the man who owns these dogs is ever going to trust me again."

"We've seen you with other dogs," Grenade said, sneering.

"Only one other dog and I don't walk him every day."

Grenade readied for another explosion. "I could give a piss if you walk a freaking frog! Return to this very spot by the time the sun goes down tomorrow or we'll ream you out!"

"But I can't come at dusk. That's when I set tables."

Grenade thrust his hands forward, gesturing he was ready to strangle Presley. "Be here or you won't be around to set another table…ever again!"

With Chimp in his arms and Squirt close at heel, Presley scurried off. The gang's heinous laughter and bantering echoed throughout the empty lot, branding and banishing the boy all in the same madcap upheaval. Presley ran until he could run no more. Exhausted he crossed Sedgwick and stumbled up the stone path to Silver Trails. And there were Sal and Thomas coming from the other direction.

"Presley…" Thomas called forth. "Is that you?"

Stopping suddenly with Squirt colliding into the backs of his legs, Presley squinted to see through the darkness. Realizing who was approaching, he speedily focused on a plausible excuse for his disappearance. Lying was not easy for him. He really had to think this one through.

"Where have you been?" Sal asked, more frustrated than angry.

"We've been lookin' all over for you," Thomas added. "What happened?"

Letting the lie spill forth, Presley stammered, "I…I…I lost one of the dogs. Chimp tugged on his leash when I was busy watching Squirt take a pee. I accidentally let go of the leash and he was gone! He ran off into Cabrini-Green. He must've been chasing a cat or something because all of a sudden I couldn't find him."

"That's not like Chimp," Sal said.

"Oh, but he did run off…honest. I looked in the bushes and under piles of garbage and up and down the alleys…"

"You know not to go over there," Thomas interjected in a fatherly tone that aged him a decade.

"But I had to. I had to find Chimp. I couldn't return without him."

Sal tilted his head. "You should've come back and we would've gone with you to look for him."

Presley sighed and said, "I guess. Sorry. I was so upset I didn't think of that."

Sal patted the boy on the back. "Well, the bottom line is you're safe. And you have both my dogs and they're safe. Thank you, Elvis."

Thomas shook his head, "His name's Presley. Try thank you, *Presley*."

"Now let's get everybody inside," Sal instructed. "I know a few others who are going to be very relieved you're back."

Presley was only relieved that his fibbing had proved to be believable. But what was he going to do the subsequent eve? How was he going to explain to Lily that he had to forego another guitar lesson? How was he going to bow out of setting tables again? How was he going to walk Boomer, come back late and explain to Violet and Dickie where he'd been? The old "I lost the dog" routine wouldn't play out a second time. With stress sinking in and his mind all awhirl, Presley slunk through the doors of Silver Trails, wishing he'd never come there in the first place.

Chapter Ten

Sowing the seeds

When the phone rang Lily set down her book *Ragtime*. She spied her bedside clock and wondered who could be calling at eight-thirty. Presley was the big upset earlier in the evening, but everything had worked out. He'd made it back in one piece; Sal's dogs, too. What now?

"Hello?" Lily said in a quiver.

"Grandma?"

Lily hesitated. She had to think. Was it a prank call or could it really be Heather? "Hello," she said again.

"Grandma, is that you?"

"Heather, is that you?"

"Yes, it's me. Hi, Grandma! You sound like you're a million miles away. Are you talking into the receiver?"

"Where are you, dear?" Lily sat up in bed, trying to focus.

"I'm in Hollywood."

"Still?"

"Well, yes, Grandma. I live here, remember?"

"Oh, well, I thought maybe you'd moved home."

"No, I'm calling from California."

"That far, eh?"

Heather laughed and said, "Yes, Grandma."

"And what time is it there, dear?"

Heather hesitated and then poured forth, "Oh, I'm sorry. Did I wake you up? I keep forgetting there's a time difference."

"Not a problem. It's always good to hear your voice." Lily then thought. "My, how long has it been since we've talked?" she asked.

"I know…I'm sorry for that, too. I really should've called sooner."

"It's been nearly a decade, I think. I'm glad to know you're all right. I've asked your mother about you whenever she manages to drop by and see me, but she always shrugs me off."

"Yes, well. We didn't part on the best terms."

"You haven't spoken to your mother in all these years, Heather?"

There was a long pause. "No…but I've talked to Dad."

Lily didn't know how to proceed.

"Anyway," Heather continued, "I'm calling to catch up, see how you're doing."

"How'd you know where to find me?"

"Last time I called Dad I got your number."

"Oh, I see. How is your father?"

"The same. Busy, stressed out. You know how it is with Mom. She keeps spending big-time so Dad has to keep earning mega bucks. Doubt he'll ever get to retire."

"Hmm…that daughter of mine," Lily said with a hint of disgust. "I told your Grandpa Richard that he wasn't doing her any favors by catering to her every whim."

"He really spoiled her, didn't he, Grandma?"

"He sure as heck did. If your mother wanted the prettiest baby doll in the window, he'd buy it for her. If she wanted the most elegant gown to wear to the prom, he'd be there with an open wallet and his hand ready to dole out whatever cash was needed to buy his 'honey girl's' smile."

"Is that because she was an only child?"

"Probably. We wanted more children, but one is all God would give us. And your mother, Ivy, was it." Wanting to change the subject Lily asked, "So, how do you like Hollywood, Heather dear?"

"It's not all it's cranked up to be, but I'm still happy I came out this way."

"Well, you couldn't have gone any farther from home unless you moved across the Pacific to Hawaii."

"You're right. But as you recall, I had to leave Lake Forest. I had to get as far away as I could."

"Yes, but only because of your mother. Not because of me or your father. We would've stood by you."

"I know, Grandma. I only wish things had been different. If only I'd been a little older…If only I'd listened to you and Dad, maybe I would still have my baby."

Lily felt a resurgence of remorse setting in; her skin tingled like a ghost had mysteriously tagged her. It had been over ten years; something she longed to forget. Not for a minute had she blamed her granddaughter. She blamed her daughter! Her selfish daughter who only cared what the Lake Forest socialites might think when they found out Heather had given birth to a child out of wedlock, an "illegitimate."

Ted, Heather's father, wasn't happy about matters. But once reality settled in, he was upfront about his daughter's condition and, above and beyond that, he was willing to listen and help. Ivy, on the other hand, when she first learned, ignored the fact that Heather was pregnant. She went about her life like nothing had happened. At tea parties and duplicate bridge gatherings, she never breathed a word about family or home life. She corralled the conversation, steering it toward other women's children—those who were high achievers, those who would soon be off to topnotch colleges, those who were guaranteed a golden future. At charity events she made sure she held the most lauded volunteer position attainable. That way others would see her as focused on the esteemed philanthropic cause at hand. They'd never have to know that Ivy's own daughter was a charity case.

The screaming matches began when Heather started to show. Ivy forbade her daughter from leaving the house. "You can't go to school with that bloated belly of yours! You should've had an abortion months ago!"

Then reasonable Ted would enter in, "Now, Ivy, calm down.

We've been through this before. Heather can attend the vocational school for a while. She only has two more months until her delivery date."

Meanwhile, not wanting to hear another word, Heather would waddle off to her room and close the door, ashamed and defeated.

A few weeks before Heather's delivery date, Lily offered to take the baby. Her husband, Richard, was totally against the idea, underlining the fact that they were too old to be parents and that they'd already raised a child of their own. He sided with his daughter, Ivy, agreeing with her that Heather should give the baby up for adoption.

But then he *always* sided with Ivy. Gave her everything she ever wanted, even the emotional support she couldn't seem to garner from her own husband. So, the issue of keeping or putting Heather's baby up for adoption evolved into a family war—Ivy and Richard against Heather, Ted, and Lily. And though it was two against three, the former two were more vociferous and determined and they ended up the victors. Thus, on a sub-zero, snow-laden day in January, Heather was whisked off to the hospital to give birth to a son that neither she, nor anyone in her family laid eyes on.

After the birth, matters got worse. Ivy came home from a bridge party one day, ranting and raving that her friends had in fact learned of Heather's predicament. "I'm branded for life!" she screamed in hysterics.

Ted did his best to console her, but Ivy denied him access. Before clamming up all together she drew her line in the sand, "Because of this scandal we must move out of Lake Forest. I can no longer live here!"

From that moment on, Ivy wouldn't converse with anyone but her daddy, Richard. So, Ted, trying to keep the family together, scanned the real estate market in outer-lying areas. He needed to be within commute distance of Chicago, yet far enough from Lake Forest so that the hissy cat calls from Ivy's so-called friends would no longer be an issue. After enduring a month of Ivy's silent treatment and downright meanness, Ted found a mansion on a large, secluded lot in Wheaton. It was twenty-five miles west of downtown Chicago. He could take the train into the city and Ivy could hide in the prim and proper township where Billy Graham had laid down tracks. They had no trouble selling their Lake Forest property and within the month they were on their way. Everyone was satisfied but Heather.

"I can't go, Dad! My friends…they're all here in Lake Forest."

"Heather, I don't know what you want me to do. Your mother says she can no longer live here."

"Yes, I know. And that's because of me. And I'm sorry. I really am. But it's enough that I had to give up my baby. And now she wants me to give up all my friends. I'm a senior in high school, for God's sake! I can't move and start all over again at a new high school. Dad, I don't know a soul in Wheaton!"

"I understand, Heather. Honest I do. But I'm the one who has to live with your mother over the long haul. And quite frankly, I can't take another day of her anger. She lashes out and screams at me, even when I'm not the culprit. I'm a victim of her ire and I've been needled by her prickly venom long enough."

Heather's chin dropped to her chest. Looking down at her still swollen breasts and plump belly, she felt the antithesis, deflated and conquered. Even her beloved father had been wooed over to the other side. He had a point, she knew. Living with her mother was challenging enough. You didn't need her rage overcoming your sense of well being. After all, her contentiousness could cause undue stress, heart palpitations, ulcers, and quite possibly cancer. It might be more forgiving and expedient to ingest cyanide.

Heather had reached her limit! She knew the time was right to part ways. Even though she still cared about her father, it was not going to work living under the same roof with her dogmatic mother. She'd already been forced into lying to her dad about leaving her friends behind. Sure, she had a few girl friends that she liked well enough, but they weren't her reason for wanting to stay in Lake Forest. The real reason had to do with the fact that Heather was head over heels in love with the man who'd impregnated her, Malcolm Hawthorne.

Malcolm was a teacher at Lake Forest High. He was young for being a high school instructor, only twenty-three. He'd gone to Northwestern on scholarship and in five years had received an undergraduate degree in history along with his teaching credential. As soon as he graduated, he applied at Lake Forest High and was accepted. His family was so proud. He was pleased, too, but he knew not to gloat over his accomplishments. Malcolm was pretty sure his hiring had been speedily confirmed because he was a black man. He had a feeling the district had been coerced into hiring him because the faculty and student population therein was practically all-white, Caucasian marshmallow through and through.

The instant she took a seat in Mr. Hawthorne's class, Heather knew she would someday be more than just a student to the tall, dashingly handsome gentleman. He was visibly strong, intelligent, and mature; qualities none of the boys her age had or remotely cared about. In her attempts to vie for the teacher's attention, Heather studied extra hard so that she could correctly answer questions he posed in class. Too, she made a habit of approaching Mr. Hawthorne after class to reveal her voracious appetite for history. She wanted her professor to sense he'd planted the seed and that her desire to learn more was because of him.

"What's your favorite book on the Civil War, sir? I'm going to the library after school and I want to get a book that you'd recommend."

The crush Heather had on Mr. Hawthorne did not subside after first semester. Her ploys to nab him were steadfast, continuing on into second semester when the subject matter turned to the World Wars. At a point, Heather asked her history teacher to go to the movies with her because there was an epic documentary being heralded about the Nazi invasion on Europe. Malcolm kindly turned Heather down, deferring to his busy agenda and all of his assignments. What he wanted to tell her was that he could never accept her invitation because he could get in a heap of trouble for going out with a student, even if it wasn't really a date.

Deep down, however, he wanted to say yes. He'd grown to like the sassy blonde who was forever in his face. Not only was she cute, but she had a ton of spunk and wherewithal. Most of the teenage girls in his classes cared solely about how hot they looked in their miniskirts and halter tops. They tried to copy the styles of the models in *Glamour* and *Mademoiselle*, fussing over their hair, which they either parted center and let hang straight and long or they frosted and used hot curlers to achieve the Farrah Fawcett layered look. Heather was different. She let her natural blond hair rest shoulder-length; she barely wore any makeup, and what little she did was skillfully applied. Too, she didn't gab about such things—what was cool in cosmetics, what threads were the grooviest, which football player was a stone fox and what cheerleader he'd most likely shag. High school girls' interests were predictable and their hallway conversations were boring to the ear. Malcolm felt that even if Heather was faking her love for history, at least she was delving into her studies and the knowledge she'd gained was impressive. Her class with Malcolm ended right before lunch, so many times she stayed on and they'd get into a lengthy discussion on a certain ruler or conqueror or president, this battle or that war. The array of subjects they touched upon seemed as vast as the listing of books in their library.

When sophomore year ended, Heather felt like her life was being put to sleep. What was she going to do if she couldn't see her beloved Mr. Hawthorne Monday through Friday? Summer break became an infectious disease and Heather was riddled by it. The ailment produced fits of episodic crying, loss of appetite, mood swings, and overall, stultifying boredom. A month into summer, Heather managed to get a job at the local movie theater. It suited her needs because the theater was dark and cavernous and nobody could tell whether or not she'd been weeping.

Her father was gone most of that summer. His company positioned him in San Francisco at one of their training facilities. He stayed at a nearby Embassy Suites and worked from sunup to sundown, passing along his keen aptitude with regard to preparing financial summaries. Heather's mother remained in Lake Forest, but she split her time between the country club, her favorite boutiques, and various charitable organizations. As a rule she pretty much ignored her daughter. After all, Ivy's calendar took precedence.

One night Heather offered to work late. A new movie called *Flipper* had been released and the crowds that lined up to see it were taking theaters by surprise. The film about a friendly dolphin was tugging at the heartstrings of families and people of all ages. Ticket sales soared. Because of the sold-out performances, more help was needed. Heather figured it was the perfect night to work overtime. She flat-out didn't feel like going home to the loneliness that awaited her, but more than anything she was sick and tired of the TV dinners she was expected to eat.

That evening Heather was stationed by the front door, assigned as the sole ticket taker. As the masses shoved their way in, Heather caught a glimpse of her history professor toward the back of the line. She gasped and looked downward, wondering if her eyes were still red from crying the night before, wondering if Mr. Hawthorne would recognize her in the ugly taupe uniform she was required to wear, wondering if he'd remember her at all. Accepting tickets and returning the torn-off stubs, Heather finally came across a dark hand that reached forward. It was polished ebony, like a favorite stone she'd once collected.

"Is that you, Heather?" Malcolm asked in disbelief.

Gradually Heather looked up. Taming her inner fireworks, she nonchalantly said, "Oh, hi, Mr. Hawthorne. Come to see *Flipper*?"

Putting his arm around the shoulder of the child at his side, Malcolm responded, "Yes. I'm taking care of my niece this weekend. She begged to come see the show and I figured what the heck, a decent 'G'-rated film is doable once in a while."

"Better than historical documentaries and war flicks, right?"

"Hurry up!" a father with three cling-on kids ordered.

"Oh, sorry," Heather said, taking their tickets. Then to Malcolm she explained, "Well, I'd better get back to work. The natives are getting restless."

Malcolm grabbed his niece's hand and stood off to the side. "Are you allowed to watch the movie once you've taken all the tickets?"

Heather thought to herself, *Is he asking me to join them?* She hoped so and in turn replied, "Yeah, I'm free to go once I finish here."

"Why don't you sit with us then? I can save you a seat."

"Are you sure that's okay?"

"Hey, it's summer and we're not on school grounds. Even if someone sees us, doubt they're going to give our being together a second thought. Besides, this here is my heart throb." Malcolm squeezed his little niece. "You don't mind if Heather watches *Flipper* with us, do you Holly?"

The cherub-faced sweetie-pie cooed, "No, Uncle M. Your friend can come. I like her."

If Malcolm could've blushed through his dark skin he would've. He held his niece's hand and, as they trotted off, he called back, "Look for us on the left-hand side. Oh, and Holly likes to sit up close, so we'll most likely be toward the front."

The evening was a hit! The movie was truly a feel-good, happy high note. And to be asked out afterwards for a sundae at the diner down the street, well, that just couldn't have been topped. Even the luscious chocolate and caramel syrups being served couldn't compare with how delicious Heather felt inside. In a single night she'd been cured of her pathetic summer doldrums. And even though there were still two weeks until school started, the sadness Heather had endured since the middle of June was erased. Even her mother took note, commenting, "My, where'd you dump that frown you've been wearing all summer?" Heather didn't bother to respond.

September 4th was the commencement of Heather's junior year. She waited in the auditorium until her name was called out and having been handed her class list she then strolled toward the Home Ec room, her so-called homeroom where each day would begin. Once she took a seat, she scanned the six other subjects and teachers printed on her class sheet. She knew she wouldn't have History again. But she also knew Mr. Hawthorne had been asked to take on one Political Science course and she was praying she'd been assigned to his class. At first she didn't see his name on her list. That's when her stomach began to churn. Biology with Dr. Metcalfe, P.E. with

Mrs. Wisteria, French with Mr. Bowne, Algebra with Mr. Calvin, English with Miss Poplar, and Poli Sci with... with... The print had been smudged. Frantically Heather leaned over to zoom in on a classmate's form.

"Do you happen to have Poli Sci last period?" she begged to know.

The student shook his head, so Heather got up and made a beeline for a group of girls in the back of the room. "Do any of you have Poli Sci last period?" One of the girls nodded, so Heather hustled over and nervously asked, "Who's teaching it?"

The ditzy redhead picked up her class list and read aloud, "Mr. Hawthorne." She then looked up and added, "Oh, he's that sweet hunk of chocolate. I won't mind him teaching me a thing or two." The other girls snickered in agreement.

Heather mouthed "Thank you" and returned to her seat. *Phew*, she thought, *it's him!* And I have him last period which means if Mr. Hawthorne's free after school, he and I can hash over political phenomena on a national, maybe even a global level.

Feeling like a genius, Heather sighed. But suddenly she sat erect and rigid like she'd been stung. Heather freaked. *You'd better get a move-on,* she demanded of herself. You'll never be able to shoot the bull with Mr. Hawthorne unless you know your stuff. History was a cinch to digest and regurgitate because the events and characters were past-tense and you're lucky enough to have a photographic memory. Heather warned herself, *but Poli Sci's going to be very different.* You've heard from others who struggled in that class; that it's mind-boggling how much there is to know. Even the class description's a lot to absorb.

Squinting to take in the small print, Heather read to herself, "We will cover national, state, and local governmental institutions and their processes, political parties and their platforms, public behavior and issues which shape contemporary society, and we will survey the operation of institutions which compose our system for administering criminal justice." *Face it, you don't know squat about that subject matter!* Heather had to refrain from getting up and dashing off to the library. But when the lunch bell rang that's exactly where she headed.

In October, Malcolm suggested Heather join the debate team.

"You'd be great at it, Heather! You know the school library from top to bottom. You've browsed every inch of book shelves. And it's all about delving into the right data to support your platform and argue your case. I can't think of anybody who'd be better at that than you," Malcolm encouraged.

Heather was tickled that her teacher thought she was a star pupil, but she had her doubts. "Mr. Hawthorne, thanks for the suggestion, but I'm not that confident in front of a crowd."

"How do you think one gains that type of confidence? This is a learning experience and just like anything else, you have to start somewhere. To tell you the truth, most kids don't have anywhere near the poise you do. You're much more mature and credible. Trust me, you'll excel at this. I just know it!"

Heather was quiet in thought, weighing her options.

Malcolm interjected, "You know, the debate coach, Miss Clematis, no longer has her afternoons free, so I've agreed to take charge of Debate Club."

Without so much as making eye contact, Heather exclaimed, "Then count me in!"

Malcolm smiled broadly. He was pleased to know he wouldn't have to give up his afternoons with Heather. He'd come to enjoy the host of sparring matches they'd gotten into over politics and anything that warranted a war of tongues. Already he envisioned Heather as a prosecuting attorney, taking the courtroom by storm. She was savvy, driven, and more than capable. He wanted to say she was his, but he couldn't go to that extreme; at least not yet.

When the changing of the guard occurred and Malcolm took over the debate club, the team lost one of its prime players, Lilac Turner. She was brilliant and it was because of her that the team had gone to Regionals the previous year. But Lilac was Miss Clematis's pet and it was a given that if the teacher quit, so would the star student. The remaining eight members were dismayed, acting like total defeatists. "Why bother sticking it out?" one asked. "We'll never win anything without Lilac."

That's when Malcolm strode in and having overheard the wimpy comments, proclaimed, "You will win again because I have a secret weapon." Malcolm stepped outside the room and pulled Heather in next to him. "If you've never met, this is Heather Simone. Trust me when I tell you she is every bit as smart as Lilac. But above and beyond that she has the will *and* the skill, the capabilities of a champion. Mark my words, gang; she is going to lead our team to victory."

The four girl/four boy team applauded. Heather stood dumbfounded, reveling in the praiseworthy introduction made on her behalf. But seconds later she felt like throwing up. A fleeting thought slapped her silly. *What if I can't lead my team to victory? What if I fall short of expectations and disappoint everyone, including Mr. Hawthorne?* A twisted smile crossed her face as she found herself seeking a seat in the back row.

Within the month Heather moved forward to the front row. Shining forth, she was turning out to be the brightest, most dazzling and opalescent star the club had to offer. She was exemplary and set the standards high. With Heather leading, the team took on school after school, never failing to awe and inspire. Not every tournament was a trophy-case winner, but the team was assuredly holding its own, gaining respect and being lauded by parents and administrators as a worthwhile extracurricular school activity. This was important because it meant that in future semesters the funding would be allocated and distributed without hesitation. In essence, if Mr. Hawthorne chose to oversee the group again, he'd be sitting pretty, no questions asked. And this is what Heather wanted for her favorite teacher. That's why she worked as hard as she did.

The debate team took a breather after Thanksgiving through to New Year's. Studying for finals took precedence. Immediately thereafter the winter holidays were on tap. Everybody but Heather was excited about the two-week break starting on December 21st. Finals would be over and the yuletide could begin. But for Heather, not seeing Mr. Hawthorne was torture. She could care less about Christmas. Mulling over the holiday for the umpteenth time, she noted, *I'll get some old ladies perfume and a bunch of midi and maxi-length dresses that I'll never wear, ones my mother will explain have designer labels. Dad will fret over what Mom paid for my gifts, forcing a smile while trying to down the saccharinely sweet eggnog Mom insists on making every year. The rest of the day will be about cooking a prime rib while taking down all the decorations—another one of Mom's weird traditions.* Heather sighed and thought to herself, *I wish I'd never stopped believing in Santa Claus because all I really want for Christmas is Mr. Hawthorne. Yes, my teacher wrapped up in a big red bow, positioned under the tree as a huggable stuffed animal, awaiting my every whim.* The notion brought a smile, and for the time being the happy vision sufficed.

Fortunately, the holidays came and went. Though she missed her teacher it was nothing in comparison to what she'd endured over the previous lengthy summer. When the debate club kicked in again there was talk of a road trip. The Regionals were to be held in Indianapolis. The team had qualified! They accepted the invitation and were told to reserve the final Thursday through Sunday in March. Next the fundraising began. Heather took the lead and offered to head up three car washes and two bake sales. She was Queen Bee on a mission. Whatever she buzzed as an order, her helper bees sped off in all directions to accomplish.

By the end of February the club had more than enough money for its sojourn. Mr. Hawthorne could not have been happier. And he let Heather know it with winks and nods and thumbs-up gestures that were meant for only her. Classmates saw Mr. Hawthorne's praise for Heather as congenial, a teacher's pet type of thing. But both Malcolm and Heather knew there was more to the relationship than that.

Finally, the day of departure arrived. A small school bus used to transport the handicapped was borrowed for the team's trip to Indianapolis. Mr. Hawthorne and the nine club members climbed aboard and off they sped with their hired driver sitting amongst a pile of road maps. After what seemed much longer than it should've taken, the bus pulled up in front of a tired-looking motel. Grabbing their overnight bags, everyone disembarked. In the entry way of the motel they stepped over empty coffee cups, stir sticks, cigarette butts, strewn ashes, and discarded newspapers.

Heather mumbled in disgust, "Maybe we should've held one more car wash so we could've stayed at a place with a little more class."

Malcolm chuckled and replied, "Not to worry. We'll only be here to sleep."

After checking in, Heather found that she was the only member who'd been given her own room. The four boys split off into two rooms. And the other four girls did the same.

The rooms were spread out. Two of the boys were on the third floor and two were on the first. Two of the girls were on the second floor and two were down the hall from the boys on the first floor. Heather's room was on the third floor, around the corner and down the hall. Away from all of her teammates. She didn't like being separated, but then after getting settled and coming out of her room she noticed that Mr. Hawthorne was only four doors away. That made her feel safe and more at ease.

Peering down the dimly lit hallway Heather waved and called forth, "At least I know *somebody*'s nearby."

Malcolm strode toward Heather. When he got closer he said in a hushed tone, "Yeah, you can be my protector. This place is dark and spooky." He playfully put his arm around Heather's shoulder and added, "You'll take care of me, won't you?"

Heather laughed and said, "I'm here at your beck and call, Mr. Hawthorne."

Halting in the hallway, Malcolm said, "When are you going to stop calling me Mr. Hawthorne? It makes me feel ancient."

"Well, I can't exactly call you Malcolm when all the other students address you as Mr. Hawthorne."

"That's true. Shame on me for not being the adult." Standing still for a moment and then leaning in toward Heather, Malcolm asked, "Okay, but is it too much to ask that when you're alone with me...you call me by my first name?"

"Are you sure you want me to?"

"If it's not too weird."

Heather tilted her head, trying to discern what was going on. "No, it's not that. It's just that I don't want to get you in trouble..."

"Trouble? Why should I get in trouble if someone overhears you calling me by my first name?"

"Remember when we were first getting to know each other and I asked if you'd like to go see a certain documentary with me?"

Malcolm nodded. Removing his arm from Heather's shoulder, he tried to focus.

"And you turned me down?" Heather added.

"Yes, but then this summer I asked you to join my niece and me at the movies. And I even took you out afterwards for an ice cream sundae."

"I know. I got mixed signals from that. Your invitation was confusing."

Putting his hand to her chin, Malcolm made Heather look him in the eyes. "What we have going on between us is confusing. It's *very* confusing. And I don't know what to say except that I have strong feelings for you. I know it's wrong because you're a student and I'm a teacher. But you're a very mature young woman and I'm...I'm..."

"...a foolish man."

Malcolm was relieved he'd been cut off. He straightened and said, "Yes, another terribly astute comment on your part, Ms. Simone. Thank you for bringing that to my attention." He cleared his throat and stated, "You're absolutely right. For the time being let's keep it at Mr. Hawthorne."

But that didn't happen. On their final night in the motel things changed and Heather had no reason to be formal with her teacher again.

Chapter Eleven

Phosphorous promotes seed production

Part of it was they'd won Regionals! Thirteen teams competed and the club from Lake Forest came in first. The achievement was one to celebrate! Part of it was that in the finals Heather had gone head to head with the captain of another team. She'd brilliantly debated the given topic and convincingly won the judges' highest marks, a total turn-on for Malcolm. And part of it was because Mr. Hawthorne decided to splurge and take his debaters out for dinner. He was jazzed, juiced, and genuinely grateful to Heather for taking their team to such heights. And while sitting next to his star pupil at the table, being extremely careful so that no one would notice, he placed his hand atop her thigh. Mysterious tingles shot through Heather. Malcolm felt the quickening pulse beneath her skin, which in turn set him off. They both took a cleansing breath, hoping to contain themselves.

Finally, after mud pie was devoured, the team members excused themselves from the table. Malcolm stayed a bit longer, pretending to eye the bill when in fact he was doing his utmost *not* to lock a lustful gaze onto Heather. Once the teens had vacated the premises, the teacher looked up and caught a glimpse of his scintillating star traipsing off to the elevators. *Not to worry*, he told himself. *You'll meet up with her soon enough.*

While heading down the hallway back to his room, as he passed Heather's, he felt a rush of warmth overcome him. Her passion exuded through the door and was inescapable. His desire pleaded of him to partake. He had to stop and knock. There was no turning back or passing by!

Coyly, Heather queried, "Who's there?"

"Malcolm."

"Not my teacher? Not my debate coach?"

"No. Not Mr. Hawthorne. You know who I am."

With that, Heather unlocked the door and opened it part way. Malcolm stepped in and as soon as the door closed his hands were on Heather's face, drawing her in for a long, luscious kiss. He'd never tasted anything so sweet. So he kissed her even more deeply. When she came up for air, Heather gasped, "I've never felt like this before. What are you doing to me?" The intensity continued to rise as Heather let go of a gentle groan.

Malcolm then whispered, "I'm loving you."

The kisses, caresses, and lovemaking that followed were more than either expected or could have hoped for. Malcolm was Heather's first; she was a virgin for him. She'd been with other boys, but had never fully given herself to any of them. Heather was Malcolm's first in the sense that he'd slept with other women, but emotionally he had never fully given of himself. This dynamic gifting and sharing of each other's bodies and spirits was not only erotic, but sensually staggering. The two could not sate their desires and it wasn't until the first peek of dawn broke through the blinds that Malcolm and Heather let go of each other.

"Oh, my God!" Heather declared. "Oh, my God, you've got to get out of here!"

Malcolm rolled over and joked, "Certainly if I were a god, you wouldn't be shooing me away like this."

Returning to her seductive self, Heather stroked Malcolm's chest, gushing, "Don't get me wrong. You are indeed a god. But though you may be heaven-sent, you need to roll your butt out of bed or you're going to end up in *Hell*."

Sliding his body over Heather to feel her curvaceous tenderness one more time, Malcolm reached for the clothes that had been wildly ripped off of him just hours before. While dressing he felt compelled to ask, "So, where do we go from here?"

"You mean besides going to Hell?"

Malcolm zipped up his pants and knelt next to Heather on the bed. "It's going to be okay, you know. Nobody's going to find out. This is our little secret."

"And is that what we want it to be, a secret?"

"It has to be for now, Heather. You're not even eighteen yet. Theoretically, what we did last night...I could be arrested for. Some might call it rape."

"Not if I was a willing party."

"I'd like to see you argue that one in court. Trust me, should anyone find out about our little night of bliss, losing my job would be the least of our worries."

"Are you saying that because you're black and I'm white...?"

"That's just frosting on the cake, babe."

"So, back to your question then," Heather said, pulling up the sheet to hide her nakedness. "Where do we go from here?"

Malcolm stood to put on his cheesecloth shirt. He slowly buttoned it. Heather watched intently. How sexy and dexterous his fingers were. Upon finishing, Malcolm looked up and said point blank, "I'm in love with you, Heather."

Relaxing her grip on the sheet that now covered her, Heather sighed and readily responded, "I love you, too."

Malcolm's whole being smiled. He then reached for the leather watch he didn't recall removing. As he put it back on he continued, "Unfortunately, even though we agree that we're in love, your age is going to be a factor."

"But I'm seventeen."

"You might as well be twelve."

Somewhat indignant, Heather spouted, "You said I'm the most mature young woman you've ever met."

"And you are. But until you're eighteen..."

"That's next year. Are you saying you won't wait for me?"

"I'm not saying anything. Quite frankly, I'd like to be with you from this moment on, but I can't...we can't."

"So, that brings us back to square one..."

"Where do we go from here?" Malcolm repeated, discouraged.

Dawn forced an end to the conversation. Malcolm snuck out of Heather's room and back to his own. His first task was to shower because even though he liked the lingering sweetness of lovemaking on his body, beneath the skin he felt like a juvenile delinquent. It seemed necessary to wash away any trace of his indiscretion. As he lathered and scrubbed he reminisced about his amorous night with Heather. *That was no discrepancy*; he told himself, *that was pure euphoria. Maybe I should've contained myself, waited another year or two, but the moment felt so right, like we were meant to be together.* Toweling off, confident in his resolve, Malcolm said aloud, "Heather's mine and I'm not letting her go."

The driver of the school bus pulled up right on time. The four girls and four boys bounded on board. Exhausted, Heather stumbled up the steps and plopped in a back row.

Malcolm was acting sluggish, too. He kerplunked into a seat up front, across from the bus driver. He wanted nothing more than to curl up in Heather's lap for the long ride home, but he knew that could never happen. Heather's mind wandered along the same lines, wanting desperately to cuddle up with Malcolm. The notion plagued her so much that she finally gave in to sleep. And as she awoke she overheard herself mumbling, "I love you, Malcolm." But the figure hovering above wasn't Malcolm; it was her father and he was nudging her. Heather's eyes morphed into full moons.

"Oh, Dad, it's you!"

"Yes, honey. Who did you think I was?"

Thank the Lord, Heather thought, *he didn't hear me!* "Oh, nobody. I was just dreaming, I guess."

"That you were. A rather deep sleep, too. Your teammates said they tried to wake you up, but even tickling didn't work. That's when I came on board. You ready to go now?"

Heather gazed past her dad. She didn't see Malcolm anywhere. Maybe he'd hopped off the bus already. Maybe he was keeping his distance. Maybe en route home he'd dummied-up and totally changed his mind about her…about them. Whatever the case, he was gone!

"Still half-asleep there, eh Heather?" Ted asked, reaching for his daughter's overnight bag. "Why don't I take you home so you can get your fill of z's."

Staring off into oblivion Heather uttered, "Okay, Dad. Good idea."

The next week at school Heather felt ill at ease, unsure of herself. Apparently others noticed because at a point her English teacher inquired of her, "Is something wrong, Heather? You seem out of sorts."

The worst of her anxiety fomented just before last period every day, when she had to go to Poli Sci. Her heart raced as she entered the room. Her stomach knotted and made embarrassing noises as she sat through the class. Instead of raising her hand and vying for attention, she did everything possible not to get noticed. She even avoided eye contact with her teacher who was again Mr. Hawthorn. He was not in any way, shape or form, her lover, Malcolm.

This change of demeanor and spirit threw Malcolm for a loop. He did not understand what had changed so drastically. Was Heather so flighty that she'd lost interest in a flash? Was she so flippant that she might consider him a one-night stand? His heart hurt, but there was nothing he could do. He had no one to talk to. It was now his little secret to endure.

Two months later Heather figured out she was pregnant. Her queasiness evolved into retching and finally vomiting. Usually the nausea occurred first thing in the morning, before school. That was okay because she could hide her morning sickness, saying as her mom slept in late and her dad was always out the door by seven o'clock. At one point, though, the need to vomit happened at school and Heather had to race out of class when the volcanic urge erupted. She made her way to the girls' bathroom just in time, coughing up an explosion in the far stall that the janitor would later find and shout obscenities about.

After school, Heather fell to her bed. "No," she wailed. "I can't be having his baby. He doesn't love me anymore." Curling up in a fetal position, she cried herself to sleep.

That night her father asked why she'd been crying. Heather lied, saying she'd gotten a "C" on her Econ test.

"But you were all A's with History and Poli Sci. Same teacher, right? What's changed with Econ?"

"Beats me. I don't understand why we have to switch to studying economics when there's so little time left in the school year. The other subjects were no-brainers. But Econ...well, it's bogus."

Ted laughed. "I couldn't stand the subject either." He patted Heather on the back. "Don't worry. That one 'C' shouldn't affect your final grade too much."

But when Heather got her report card a month later, she wanted to cry all over again. Not because of the B+ Mr. Hawthorne gave her, but because the school year was over and she was pregnant. Nobody else knew and she felt horribly alone with her predicament. She still loved Malcolm, but couldn't approach him, not even to request a change in her final grade. The onset of summer had turned into pure annihilation!

For Malcolm, not hearing from Heather about what should have been a less than expected grade, gnawed at his inners. She deserved an A-, he knew. *She's usually such a fighter*, he told himself. *Why didn't she request a grade change? Yes, she would've had to meet with me. That was my goal, to talk and come to terms before summer arrived. But she's chosen to remain aloof. And icy. Why is she so unforgiving and unwilling to tell me what the hell I did wrong?!*

Malcolm taught summer school to keep his mind off Heather. Heather took the job at the movie theater again so she could hide in the darkness. When she wasn't busy working, she frequented the downtown library. She read every book she could get her hands on with regard to being pregnant, giving birth, and raising a child from infant to adulthood. It might as well have been an accredited class.

Though no one was doling out grades, Heather was once again an "A" student.

In her mind, she was keeping the baby. She cared deeply about her unborn child and felt a strong bond with the new life growing within. On a regular basis the fantasy she conjured up was that Malcolm would eventually come to her. He'd bend down on one knee and make a commitment for all eternity. She would then inform her beloved about her pregnancy. In turn, he would be elated and proud to learn that he was going to be a father, proclaiming that there was nothing in the world he wanted more. When the daydream was complete, Heather would return to reality and read more of Dr. Spock's *Baby and Child Care*, the book having become one of her favorites.

The week before school commenced who was in line at the movies again, but her teacher and his niece! *Mary Poppins* was the one-hit wonder of the year. The movie had been out a while, but families were still flocking theaters to see the show, usually for the second or third time. Apparently it was Holly's first time. Her excitement and enthusiasm were contagious, so much so that Heather didn't feel like retreating to the shadows to avoid Mr. Hawthorne. She wanted to hug Holly, hoping that some of the child's optimism might rub off on her. Heather was not taking tickets on this occasion. She was sweeping up a box of spilled licorice bits. So, setting her broom aside, she ran up behind Holly and gave her a squeeze.

Holly jumped, squealing, "Oh, it's you! You scared me."

"I would never scare you," Heather replied, tickling Holly. "I'm your friend."

"Are you going to watch *Mary Poppins* with us?" Holly asked eagerly.

"Not this time, sweetie. I have to work."

"You're not taking tickets today, though," Holly noted.

"No, but see that broom over there?" Heather pointed. "It has my name on it."

"Really?"

Malcolm bent down, saying, "She's kidding, sweetheart. She only means that it's her job to sweep right now."

Heather looked into Malcolm's eyes for the first time in months. His expression was somewhat sad. "Yes, your uncle's right. I have to sweep," Heather said.

"Well, maybe we can all go out for ice cream after the movie," Holly exclaimed.

Malcolm started to say, "I don't think Heather has time…"

But Heather interjected, "I'd love to!"

Standing tall again, head tilted, Malcolm asked, "Is that right? You want to go out for ice cream after the show?"

Playfully punching her uncle, Holly shouted, "Are you deaf? She said she'd love to."

Heather smiled, the memory of it glimmering in Malcolm's heart. "Okay. Okay," he said to Holly. "I'm psyched. Heather and you want to go out for ice cream after the movie."

"Hopefully you do, too," Heather replied, raising a brow.

Malcolm nodded. In jest, Holly slugged her uncle again and he choked, "Yes, yes, of course! Ice cream sounds good."

At the diner Heather ordered a banana split. She ate the entire thing and then finished Holly's chocolate sundae. Malcolm watched her, thinking to himself, *I've never seen her eat so much. She's gobbling everything down without a second thought, almost like she's trying to put on a few pounds.* He glanced over the rim of the table at Heather's mid-section. Hmm, looks like she's been successful. A real hotty, he decided, saying as last summer she looked like Twiggy. He thought back to her explanation for being stick-thin. She claimed she'd lost her appetite. Said she missed me so much that she couldn't eat anything. *Guess if she's gaining weight now she's not as miserable as I thought*, Malcolm mused.

Just then Holly noticed a mangy fly sitting atop Heather's last bite of ice cream. The youngster swung her arm around to shoo the bug away. The critter flew off, but Holly's follow-through landed a solid blow to Heather's stomach.

"Ohhh..." Heather grunted, contracting in pain. Then worried about the little one inside, with both hands on her tummy, she murmured, "You all right?"

"I'm sorry," Holly enthused. "I didn't mean to hit you." She leaned in and added, "Who are you talking to in there?"

Heather jerked her hands away from her belly, sloughing it off, "Oh, no one in particular. I just wanted to make sure my inners were okay."

Malcolm sized up Heather while reprimanding his niece. "Holly, you need to be more careful. When you playfully slug me I feel it. I can't imagine what that blow to Heather just felt like."

Endearingly to Heather, he asked, "Are you sure you're okay? No broken bones or punctured organs?" Suddenly it hit him, *Heather's pregnant!!!*

Chapter Twelve

Add a rich, organic compost

Malcolm could not say a word with his niece present. He dropped Heather back at the theater where her car was parked and politely said goodbye. Questions bombarded his brain, but not a single one could be posed. He desperately wanted to call Heather at home, but he didn't want to disturb the parents, especially saying as he was pretty sure she hadn't told them. If she had, certainly they'd have raised holy hell by now.

Sitting in bed with the light still on at two in the morning, Malcolm continued to ponder. *No wonder Heather's avoided me these past few months. What was she supposed to do, pin me down and ask me if I want to be the father of her child when all along I was the one who told her we had to keep our relationship a secret? And why? Because I might lose my credibility, my reputation, my job? How selfish was that! Oh, and then to tell her that my having made love to her might be considered rape?* "Asshole!" Malcolm swore aloud.

Realizing he had to mend broken bridges before the winds hit any harder, Malcolm returned to the theater that Sunday. This time Heather was behind the counter, taking orders for candy, popcorn and soda. Malcolm stood in line and waited his turn.

"Can I help you?" Heather asked in a professional manner.

"I need a favor," Malcolm said in a formidable tone.

"I'm afraid we don't serve that type of candy here, sir."

Malcolm looked forlorn, so Heather eased up. "Look, is there a place we can meet?" he asked.

Pretending to fill an order, Heather reached for a small bag of popcorn. Handing it across the counter she said, "I'm off at five."

"Can I come back and we'll go talk somewhere?"

"Just so long as we don't go out for anymore ice cream. I'm still stuffed."

Finally allowing a smile, Malcolm put some change down on the counter top.

"You don't owe me for the popcorn."

"I owe you for a lot more than popcorn," Malcolm said as he left.

It was five on the nose when Malcolm returned to the theater. He waved through the front doors so Heather would see him. She grabbed her sweater and as she left, tried to tie it around her waist. Malcolm noticed that it was a little too snug and that made him happy. *I think I'm liking this baby already*, he noted.

"Where should we go?" Heather asked with ease, like they'd been dating for years. Then she rephrased her query, "I mean where should we go so no one sees us together?"

Malcolm stopped in his tracks and pulled Heather around to face him. "I love you. And I don't care who sees us."

Heather gulped and replied, "Well now. That's a change. Mind if you fill me in?"

Spying a park bench on a small triangle of lawn nearby, Malcolm grabbed Heather's hand and guided her over to it. He gallantly helped her to sit down. Then he knelt down on one knee.

"Look, I've been a fool. I need to set things straight and do it right this time. I love you and I want to marry you." He bowed his head and added, "And though I don't have a fancy ring to put on your finger at this very moment, I need to know, will you marry me?"

Heather was speechless. A meteor could've slammed into the earth at that very instant and she wouldn't have been able to say "boo" about it. Staring at Malcolm, she was a Mona Lisa replica, a faint smile gracing her lips.

The silence was too lengthy, so Malcolm said, "May I defer to my niece's tactics? 'Are you *deaf*?!'" He laughed and then asked again cordially, "Heather, will you marry me?"

"You're serious?"

"Very."

"But when?"

"Does that matter so much? Listen, I don't want to get into the age thing again. It was stupid on my part to underline what you're already keenly aware of." Hemming a little, he continued, "Okay, so it doesn't make sense to wed until you're finished with high school. But we can be engaged. We can stick it out a year, don't you think?"

Heather gazed down at her belly, realizing that the term "sticking it out" was an appropriate one. How was Malcolm going to react when he found out about her condition? Surely he'd have a change of heart, knowing that there was a baby involved.

"Don't worry," Malcolm whispered. "I know you're pregnant."

"You do...but how...how did you find out?"

"Not sure. Intuition maybe?"

Heather brightened. "Yeah, right! It's because I'm fat."

"No, it's because you're beginning to show. I doubt you'll ever be fat." Malcolm then stood and took a seat next to Heather. "So, when were you going to tell me?"

"I don't know. I'm so confused. I probably should've had an abortion..."

"No! That's my child in there, too." Malcolm put his hand to Heather's belly. "Is the baby moving at all yet?"

Heather shook her head. "Not yet, but that should happen pretty soon."

Warily Malcolm asked, "Have you told your parents?"

"It came up a few weeks ago when some designer dress my mom had given me didn't fit any longer." Heather scowled and added, "I got the lecture about overeating and letting myself turn to flab. Then when I sat Mom and Dad down to tell them the truth, it was like Mom put in ear plugs; she totally ignored what I had to say."

"How did your father handle the news?"

"Oh, well...he's my dad. Obviously he was shocked and he wasn't real happy about things. But he's being supportive, unless my mother's around." Malcolm hesitated. Heather sensed his next question and said, "And, no, I didn't tell either of them who the father is."

Relieved, yet wondering, Malcolm had to ask, "And neither of them demanded to know who got you pregnant?"

"It's weird... Mom didn't insist on knowing because she immediately put the whole thing out of her mind. It's almost like what I have is an imaginary pregnancy."

"And your father?"

"No, he's not one to pry. He feels I'll tell him when the time is right."

"Hmm, wonder if the time will ever be right?"

Heather cast her gaze downward again. "I sure hope so."

Malcolm lifted her chin so she was looking deep into his expressive eyes. "I do, too, because you know now that I want to marry you. And that means this baby of ours was not a mistake; it was conceived in love. We can be a family, Heather. Maybe not today, but soon." Malcolm put his arms around Heather. "I want us to be together, got that?"

"Yes," Heather said, returning a sincere embrace.

But again, life didn't turn out like it did in flicks such as *Flipper* and *Mary Poppins.* Yes, everything *seemed* hunky-dory. Heather agreed to Malcolm's proposal. She agreed that the baby and he would make for a beautiful family and that they should wed at the end of her senior year. But then who knew how matters could spiral downward?

Toward the end of her sixth month, Heather's girlish figure was history. Her enlarged breasts gave her a maternal look and her belly grew bigger than a balloon. Her mother could no longer ignore the obvious. The calm before the storm was over.

"You need to have an abortion!"

"But I want to keep this baby. Besides, it's too late to abort."

"You have to take that chance."

"You mean that risk, Mom?"

"This is ludicrous! You cannot go to school anymore looking like you do."

"I look pregnant, Mom, because I am pregnant. What don't you understand?"

"How dare you talk to me like that?! Ted, get in here! You need to have a word with your daughter!"

Slinking in, Ted did his best to officiate. "Heather, honey, you need to show some respect toward your mother."

"Damn right she does! I will not stand here and let the fault of her indiscretion fall upon my shoulders!"

"What? I never blamed you!"

Ted raised a conciliatory hand. "Now, now. Nobody's blaming anybody. Heather, dear, just relax. And, Ivy, you need to calm down a little, too. You've known about Heather's condition. Why is it suddenly so upsetting to you?"

"Because it's going to come back as a slap in the face...*my* face!"

Heather could not refrain. "I'm the one who's pregnant!"

"Yes, but I'm your mother! I'm supposed to prevent these things from happening!"

"And just how are you supposed to do that when you're hardly ever around?"

Ivy's hands turned into fists. Ted stepped between his wife and daughter, managing to intervene and block the rage. "That's enough. Things are getting out of control." He stopped for emphasis and then continued, "I will think this through and figure out what's best for the family."

"Always the diplomat," Ivy grumbled as she stormed off.

Heather turned to her father and fell into his arms. "I can't have an abortion, Dad."

"I know, sweetie." Patting his little girl's head to console her, he added, "But I do think that maybe if we transfer you to another school for the duration of your pregnancy, that it'll be better for everyone concerned."

Nodding under the comfort of her father's hand, Heather whimpered, "Whatever you say, Dad."

The next week found Heather at a school called North Lake Interim. She abhorred the fact that she had to transfer there because most students referred to the place as the school for DDs, derelicts and dummies. For the most part students who held jobs while going to school enrolled there. But then others were sent there as punishment or banishment. In Heather's case the reasoning ended up being a bit of both. But she wasn't the only pregnant girl around. There were at least a dozen others. One whom she befriended was due any day, her stomach so round and stretched that her belly button protruded. And come to find out that this was her second pregnancy! The girl's name was Magnolia. From what Heather could discern she was sweet on the inside, but hard around the edges.

"Did you keep your first baby?" Heather asked her in the cafeteria one day.

"No, my dad would've killed me. The hunk who knocked me up was black."

Heather cringed. "Really? Did you love him?"

"Not really. Guess I should've been more careful. Felt kinda raunchy when I heard the rabbit died. But, man, Broderick was so cool and such a fox! He scoped me out and I was so psyched that we took it to the bone that very night! It was, like, heavy: I just couldn't keep my distance from that stud muffin."

"The man I'm with is black," Heather innocently divulged.

"Get outta here!" Magnolia tugged on the crop top she'd totally outgrown. "Wait, you say you're *with* him? Like how?"

"We're engaged."

"Dream on! Like what are you smokin'?"

"No, honest. We're in love and we're going to get married."

"In your next life maybe!" Leaning in as much as her full front would allow, Magnolia advised, "Look, sister, black men always want to shag pretty little white girls. Their pimpin' around makes 'em feel like they've conquered the odds; that they're righteous above all others. Let's be serious, white girls like getting down and dirty with black men because it's one of those wicked, forbidden desires. Oreo cookie shagging is so gnarly and bad that the idea alone is orgasmic."

Falling back against her chair, Heather sighed. "Wow, that's not how I see it at all."

"Then you're Snow White and you belong in a Disney cartoon," Magnolia quipped. Waving Heather off, she continued, "Bottom line; watch out. A black man will drop you faster than the match he lit his doobie with." Sitting forward again, Magnolia whispered loudly, "And forget about keeping that baby of yours. If you do, mark my words, you *will* be a single parent."

That night Heather went home and cried her eyes out. The next day Magnolia wasn't at school. She'd given birth to a baby girl that Heather heard through the grapevine had been put up for adoption. Heather couldn't help but wonder if Magnolia's second infant was mulatto, too. Maybe she had a thing for black men and maybe she was right about some of them, that they were great lovers, but not deserving or desirous of the title Dad.

Heather wanted more than anything to talk to Malcolm. She felt like when they were apart, she started to doubt his intentions and love for her. But when they were together his adoration was evident and she fully trusted him. When her senior year started, she didn't have Mr. Hawthorne as a teacher. But just passing Malcolm in the hallway was enough. His expression relayed volumes. She felt assured that he loved her. The fact that she now attended Interim High made it extremely challenging because she didn't get to see her man at all.

A few weeks before her due date, Heather's Grandma Lily called. It was the usual chit chat. "How're you feeling? How are things going?" Until her grandmother blurted out, "You know, I would be very happy to help raise that child of yours, dear."

Heather was blown away and didn't know how to respond.

Grandmother Lily continued, "Your mother said you're giving the baby up for adoption."

Heather gulped. She knew her mother felt that way, but as far as she was concerned she had no intention of giving her baby up.

"Your Grandpa Richard thinks I'm nuts, of course. But that baby deserves a loving family and a good home. And that's what we can provide until you're ready to take over." There still was silence on Heather's end so Lily rattled on, "Your father agrees with me. He doesn't seem to have an issue with me stepping in. But again, I have to be honest; it is very touch and go with your grandpa. He tends to side with your mother. He says we're too old to be parents. Maybe he's got a point, but I'm certainly capable enough."

Finally, Heather found her voice. "Grandma, you're the best. Really! But I think I've got things under control."

"You do?"

"Yes, the baby's father and I...well...eventually we want to get married."

"Really!"

Just as Heather was ready to fill her grandmother in, Ivy entered the kitchen, arms full of groceries.

"A little help would be nice," she grunted.

"Grandma, I've got to go now. We'll talk again, okay? Thanks for your offer. Love ya. Bye." Heather hung up the phone and lumbered over to her mother, taking a heavy bag out of her grasp. She set it on the counter and started to unload the items.

"And what was that all about?" Ivy asked in an acidulous tone.

"Oh, nothing much. Grandma just called to say hi.

"No she didn't. She wants to raise that baby of yours, right? That's why she called."

Heather faced her mother. "And is that so bad?"

Slamming down the can of beets she was holding, Ivy snarled, "It ain't going to happen, my dear. Your grandfather and I won't let it! That baby is not going to be a part of our family. The minute you give birth, it's up for adoption and that's that!"

"This baby is mine and I want to keep it!"

"Sorry, Heather. You're still living under our roof and the decision is not yours to make."

"Dad doesn't feel that way."

"He will when push comes to shove." Ivy sneered and added,

"So to speak."

Heather couldn't take it any longer. As the tears started to fall she turned away and trudged off with her mother calling after her. "Trust me. You'll thank me in the long run."

Two plus weeks of family feuds followed. Christmas was ruined and New Year's found everybody in a cantankerous rather than celebratory frame of mind. Even the weather turned ugly. The ice storms and chilling blizzards seemed to mimic the mood everyone was in. Heather was not only depressed, but frustrated. She knew her mother was winning out on the adoption issue and she had no means of fighting her. She considered contacting Malcolm, but what for? The timing was off. He'd agreed to marry her when she was eighteen, at the end of the school year; that way there wouldn't be any friction or discourse that might cause him to lose his job. Heather understood the rationale. But the gnawing thought that ceased to escape her was Malcolm had said he wanted to be the father of their child. And if he was hell-bent on keeping the baby, why hadn't he come forward by now? He had to know her delivery date was fast-approaching.

As it was, on January 8th, a mulatto baby boy was born. He weighed 7.6 lbs, was nineteen inches long, had a sizeable wail for a newborn, in prime health, and was readily put up for adoption.

Heather fell into a blue funk. It turned navy blue when she learned her father had succumbed to her mother's ultimatum and the family was moving out of Lake Forest. Having returned to the public high school the week after delivery, she still had not seen Malcolm. Now was the time and it was urgent! The very next day before classes began Heather sought and cornered her teacher, Mr. Hawthorne, in his room.

"Heather!" he said surprised. "When did you come back?" Eyeing her stomach a broad smile appeared. "You had the baby..."

Ready to breakdown Heather stammered, "Yeah...Yeah, I did. And where were you?"

"What do you mean where was I? Doesn't your mother relay *any* of your phone messages? Hell, I called at least a dozen times during your last trimester. I disguised my voice and became Jared and Mike and Bob. God, at one point I figured no boyfriends were allowed to speak with you, so I raised my voice and became Pansy."

Heather wiped a tear, shaking her head. "No, my mother didn't tell me."

"What about my letters? I got your address and wrote to you, too."

More tears fell. "No, I didn't get anything in the mail."

Crossing his heart, Malcolm pleaded, "You've got to believe me, Heather. Aside from barging into your house, I tried everything to get in touch with you. Honest!"

With her head down, Heather used the sleeve of her P-coat to wipe her runny nose. Malcolm handed her a Kleenex. As she dabbed, he asked, "Are you okay?"

"No, actually I'm far from it," Heather lamented. "Everything's so messed up."

"Is the baby okay?"

Heather looked up through flooded eyes. "What baby?"

She didn't need to utter another word. Malcolm knew the answer. Pacifying, reaching forward he pulled Heather to his chest, absorbing her remorse. Just then a couple of students stuck their heads in, saw the embrace and darted. That's when Heather pulled away.

"Timing's off…again," she murmured. "I'll come by and see you later when you don't have class."

"Don't wait too long, okay? I want to know everything."

"Actually, it'll have to be soon because on top of everything else, we're moving."

Malcolm's face contorted. "What do you mean you're moving? Where to?"

Heather blew her nose and said, "Who knows? Somewhere away from Lake Forest."

"Listen," Malcolm urged, "come talk to me today at lunch. I'll lock my door so we won't be disturbed. We're going to figure something out. I'm not going to let you go. No way, no how. I already lost our baby. I'm not giving you up. You're mine, Heather Simone.

And don't forget it."

Forcing a smile on lips that only felt like frowning, Heather waved and walked out.

Lunch was no better. She and Malcolm covered a plethora of plausible ways the two of them could stay together, but both knew it was useless. Unless they ran away together there was no getting around the fact that Heather was still underage and she did not have her parent's permission or consent. Plus, if Malcolm took Heather in, he'd lose his job and quite possibly end up in trouble with the law. Sadly, when the lunch hour was over, no resolve came with it. As they unlocked the door, a few earlybird students were standing outside with sheepish grins on their faces. Nothing was said, but oh, did the girls eye Heather.

One more time that week Malcolm and Heather met, this time after school. The students had all but vacated the premises, so the couple felt more comfortable in conversing and at a point, they hugged and kissed. The following day, Malcolm was asked to report to the principal's office. The stern and stout Principal Winston and the pitiless district superintendent were both on hand. A barrage of sticky questions were hurled at Malcolm and without so much as a warning, he was fired.

"I can't believe it!" he proclaimed to Heather. "It wasn't the students who ratted on us; it was the principal who just happened to be strolling by after school yesterday when I was kissing you." He threw up his hands. "This is so lame! I wasn't sexually assaulting you."

Heather remained calm. "No, but witnessing it through Winston's eyes…well, you know. Actually, both those admin guys live and breathe rules and regs. No offense, but you'd probably have done the same thing. It's their job." Heather strode up to her man and hugged him. "At least I can do this openly now. Let the world know, I love Mr. Hawthorne!"

"Lot of good it's going to do you. I'm now an unemployed Mr. Hawthorne with a reputation attached."

"And it's all because of me."

Malcolm brightened. "Hey, it takes two to tango." He placed his hands in dance mode.

"True. And from here on out we're going to be lifelong dance partners." Heather slid into Malcolm's positioned arms and they momentarily twirled about. After a few klutzy minutes of being stepped on, Heather said, "Maybe disco's more our thing."

Suddenly Malcolm suggested, "Let's get out of here."

"Okay, where do you want to go?"

"I have a cousin who picked up and moved to Hollywood about six years ago. Let's go visit him."

"Whoa! I thought you meant let's go do disco or something."

"No. I mean let's flat-out leave this place! Your family's going to pull up roots in Lake Forest anyway. Stand up to them for once. Tell them you're not going with them."

"But what about finishing high school?"

"If your family moves, you won't be finishing here as it is. I'm sure you don't want to start somewhere new with only a few more months of classes remaining."

"Of course not. But I do want to finish."

"Let's see, three to four more months is what you have left." Putting on his thinking cap, Malcolm toyed with some options. "I could talk to your teachers and gather materials so that I could teach you myself, sort of like home schooling. I could move out to Southern California and get settled, then bring you out this summer after graduation. Or we can just wing it and find the necessary coursework you'll need when we get there."

"To argue your points," Heather said like she was back on the debate team, "once my teachers find out about our relationship, I doubt they're going to give you an ounce of their time to help prepare materials so that I can graduate elsewhere. Secondly, I do not want you to leave me behind because that means I'll have to move to Wheaton and finish at a high school where I know absolutely no one. So, I guess the only alternative is that we wing it and head west together."

Heather threw up her hands and let them fall onto Malcolm's broad shoulders. He grabbed her and swung her around in circles. Elated to be continuing on together, Malcolm announced, "And on April 26th when you turn eighteen, wherever we are, we're going to the Justice of the Peace and I'm going to marry you once and for all."

But that didn't go according to plan, either.

Chapter Thirteen

Try nitrogen to stimulate growth

The note that Heather left her mother said, "If you'd told me about the phone calls and letters, I'd still have my baby today. I can no longer live under the same roof with you, Mother; therefore I am leaving. If it's possible for you to relay a message to Dad, please tell him that I love him and I'll contact him at a point when I get settled. So long, Heather."

Malcolm thought the message was a bit harsh, but he didn't say a word. Mixed emotions were at play because, having just been fired from his job, he was grateful that he didn't have an infant to provide for. But then again, he felt robbed of something very precious, something that was a living, loving part of the two of them. And now that was gone forever.

No turning back, though. The move was on. After taking his money out of the bank, giving notice to his landlord and paying off the monthly lease, Malcolm rented a large U-haul truck. He drove some of his furniture over to his brother's place and while he was there said a sad farewell to his favorite niece, Holly. He returned to his own apartment, reloaded the truck with the items he planned to take to California, stuffed his clothes in laundry bags, grabbed Heather's two suitcases and off they sped.

They took Interstate 80 and when they were too tired to drive any farther, they pulled off in some remote part of Clinton County,

Iowa. After downing greasy fried chicken and a plop of mashed potatoes for dinner, they retreated to their dingy motel room for the night. They cuddled up and made love like the last time they'd been together, the *only* other time they'd been together. As they lay breathless, savoring the indelible, molten reunion of their bodies, an unearthly quiet enveloped the room. The incongruous calm was followed by a sudden surge of incubi, paranormal and ominous. Malcolm rose and moved to the window. "Jesus Christ, Heather!" he yelled, "It's a tornado! And it's coming straight at us!"

Heather leaped out of bed into her bell bottoms and clogs. Throwing on her embroidered shirt, she shrieked, "What do we do now?!"

Jumping into his jeans Malcolm shouted, "We've got to get out of its path!"

"What about the bathtub? I've heard it's the safest place."

"Maybe in a house, but we're in a one bedroom shack. We'll be blown to bits. Come on," he ordered, "follow me!"

They charged outside where in the distance they witnessed winds tearing trees into shreds. One towering pine, ripped out by its roots, was swallowed up into the deadly funnel and then spit out like it was a toothpick discarded by some littering giant. Subsequent to the woody annihilation, an explosion of prickly needles and bark blew forth, slapping at their faces. Tottering, they tried to shelter their eyes, but there was no denying entry to the gritty, biting remnants.

"We need to find a trench or something below ground level," Malcolm hollered.

"But it's all farm land around here," Heather called back.

Just then a huge troth slammed into the shack they'd occupied. Metal shards were catapulted forward like a wave of angry arrows. Malcolm threw Heather down and fell upon her as a shield. When the tornado burped and lifted off the ground momentarily, he raised his head and noticed a creek bed nearby.

"Come on, it's our only chance!" He grabbed Heather's hand and pulled her along, the two cringing and stumbling like slaves being beaten and whipped by an impious lord.

"What are we doing?!" Heather cried out in distress.

"The creek...we've got to get to the creek!"

Just as they tumbled down into the trickling waters, the swirling gray monster careened into the motel, the attached diner, and the mini-mart. The area looked like a bomb had been dropped. But the menacing force still had an appetite, so it devoured vehicles in the parking lot, guzzling them up and puking their parts in every direction.

"No!" Malcolm wailed. "There goes our U-haul!"

Heather could not recall a time she'd been more frightened. Not wanting to see anymore she covered her eyes. But an instant later she had to cover her ears because the winds passing through were thunderous and deafening. And just when she thought things couldn't get worse, Heather spied a skyward Lazy Boy chair. The hulky piece of furniture passed over the trees near the creek which slowed its momentum some, but the force when the chair clobbered Heather was still colossal. The jarring impact thwacked her down like an ax splitting wood.

When she awoke she was in a sterile, white room. She felt a searing pain in her stomach and saw layers of thick bandages wrapped around her.

"What happened?" she asked groggily.

Malcolm was standing at her bedside holding her hand. "You got walloped by a Lazy Boy."

"Oh, yeah," Heather said, sorely recollecting. "One of those big, leisurely suckers."

Malcolm nodded. "For a while I thought I might lose you."

"Why's that?"

"If the impact of that flying chair had ripped you open any lower than the abdomen, like where your femoral vein is, you would have been toast. You would've bled to death before I could get you to the hospital."

Trying to recall, Heather asked, "How did you get me here? Didn't we lose our wheels?"

"Just the U-haul. What we were towing and the belongings in it are history. Luckily we weren't robbed of our car. If we had been, there wasn't an ambulance or fire truck, not a single emergency vehicle to be found. Phones were out, too, so I drove to Tipton and found this hospital."

"The tornado was a big one then?"

"Big? What everyone's saying is we just experienced a class F4!"

"Sounds serious," Heather said, her mouth drier than sand.

"Babe, that's the highest level of severity on the Fujita scale. The path this thing took…it spawned tornadoes all over the Midwest; forty-seven is what I've been told by the staff here."

Heather grunted in pain, "Guess we're lucky to be alive."

"Yeah, saying as the death toll is expected to reach a couple hundred, never mind the injuries."

Squeezing Malcolm's hand, Heather asked feebly, "And you're okay?"

"Couple of bruises, but nothing to write home about."

"Speaking of which…" Heather tried to sit up a little, but it hurt so she hunkered back down in the pillow.

"Hey, settle down. Don't worry about a thing. We're going to get you out of here as soon as we can. And when we do, we're driving straight to California. We're not going to let some dreaded tornado stop us. We're not going to head home with our tails between our legs."

Heather closed her eyes with a quivering smile upon her lips. She was relieved to know Malcolm was of the same mind set. Forge forward, no surrendering to misfortune and no retreating back to home base.

The next day while Heather rested Malcolm took the time to shop for a few items that had been in the U-haul. He went to the town's bargain basement and bought a few outfits for Heather and himself. He ducked into a nearby grocery store and picked up some drinks and munchies so they wouldn't have to stop en route for every meal. When he returned from his errands Heather was gone. At first Malcolm figured she had seen the doctor and was in the process of being released. As he set his bags down a nurse with a somber expression entered the room.

"Where's Heather?" he asked.

"I'm sorry to say she's in surgery, sir."

Malcolm was visibly shaken. "Surgery? What for? She was okay when I left."

"Please, sir, let me take you to the waiting room. A doctor will be able to speak to you there."

In a fog Malcolm followed the nurse through a maze of hallways. His mind was on full-throttle. *What could've happened in such a short period of time,* he wondered. *She was fine when I took off for the store. Ready to roll, ready for their adventure, ready for a new life!* As he took a seat in the cramped waiting room he wanted to cry. He hated not knowing. He wished he'd been the one hit by the flying chair. It was close to two hours before an official could speak with him, and by then he was a rattled mess.

"Are you the help for Miss Simone's family?" was the first question posed.

"Excuse me?" Malcolm asked with disdain. He held his tongue, but wanted to say, *Just because I'm black and she's white, I'm the help?* Glowering he relayed, "I'm her fiancé, for God's sake!"

"Please, sir. We're just trying to keep accurate records. And since Heather's under age policy dictates that the parents be notified of her accident and the subsequent surgical procedure performed."

"Heather doesn't want anything to do with her parents. She's with me now. And since I'm sitting right here and I'm the one who brought her to this hospital, don't you think it fair to tell me what's going on?"

The doctor sighed and looked at Heather's chart. "So, you're engaged, are you?"

"Would I get any info out of you if we were married?" The white coat didn't look up so Malcolm raised his voice, "Might there be a Justice of the Peace in this hospital?"

At a nearby desk a nurse readily picked up the phone and dialed. Malcolm figured she was calling security. And since he wasn't getting anywhere with the nurses or doctors, he stood and determinedly strode into the chambers out of which the doctor had just come.

"You can't go in there!" the doctor called out.

"Too late now!" Malcolm shouted back.

What he saw inside the room made him halt as though he'd collided into an invisible wall. There was Heather, on a cold, metal gurney with a slew of plastic tubes attached to her. The hospital smock she wore was wide open, revealing her naked body wrapped with even more bandages than before. Her hair was pulled back and her eyes were gently closed, skin glistening like she'd been sprinkled with dew. Malcolm couldn't get over how still and beautiful she looked.

"She's alive, isn't she?" he whispered to the doctor who was breathing down his back.

"Yes," he replied in a solemn tone. "Now come back to the waiting room where I can explain what's happened."

"Promise you'll treat me like next of kin? 'Cause otherwise I'm not leaving her side."

"Yes, I promise."

The two returned to the waiting room where they sat and calmly discussed Heather's condition. The medic told Malcolm that when Heather got up to get dressed that day, she fainted. Her blood pressure dropped to a drastically low level. When she regained consciousness she experienced intense sensitivity and piercing pain on the left side of her abdomen, just below the rib cage.

"We felt it was her spleen," the doctor reported. "Made sense the organ had punctured and there was internal bleeding in the abdominal cavity. We confirmed our diagnosis by drawing a sample of fluid from the abdomen which showed the presence of blood. Actually, as it turns out, Heather lost a good deal of blood. So in addition to her splenectomy, we had to give her a transfusion."

"How could this have happened? I mean she'd just been seen and released by the medical staff here."

"After a trauma injury, the spleen can appear fine. Then days, sometimes even weeks later, the rupture can occur."

"Lucky we were here when it happened," Malcolm uttered.

"Yes, it is, especially taking into account the amount of blood Heather lost."

"How long before she's well again?"

"Hard to say. Short term she will have to stay put here for about a week. Long term, well, there are issues that can occur when the spleen is removed."

"Like what?"

"In layman's terms, she'll be more prone to various infections because the spleen won't be around to help rid of them."

Malcolm lowered his head.

Finally, in a consoling tone the doctor said, "But she's young. She's a fighter and most importantly, she's alive. And considering 272 lives were taken by what they're labeling the Palm Sunday Tornadoes, you are one lucky man that you and your fiancée are around to talk about the ordeal."

Nodding in compliant comprehension, Malcolm then saw a man of the cloth hustling toward them.

"The nurse called me," he said out of breath. "Hopefully I'm not too late."

Confused, both Malcolm and the doctor rose and stood facing the priest. The priest turned and waved to the nurse at the desk to come over, which she did.

"Didn't you call me, saying I was needed for the last rites?"

The nurse nodded. "Why, yes, I did." She eyed the doctor. "What? Did I get that wrong?"

Grimacing, Malcolm interrupted, "Minor miscommunication. I was asking if the hospital had a Justice of the Peace."

"Oh, I thought you were hailing a *priest*. You sounded so desperate."

The priest was still stymied. "Why did you want a Justice of the Peace anyway?"

"So I can marry my fiancé who is a patient in there. That way I'll legally be considered her family or next of kin." Under his breath he added, "Not her *help*."

Without skipping a beat the cheerful priest said, "I can do that for the two of you."

The doctor interjected, "Well, his fiancée just had surgery. She's not exactly ready for the altar."

"No, but as soon as she's alert and feeling more chipper, I can marry them."

Malcolm momentarily considered the priest's offer and responded, "You know, I think that's a great idea. Heather and I have talked about this for a long while and every time we put it off something bad happens. She and I don't need another tornado on our horizon." Malcolm extended his hand and shook the priest's. "I'm going to take you up on your offer, Father. They say, 'There's no better time than the present,' so why not? Now is the time to finally tie the knot."

The priest turned to the doctor and nurse and asked diplomatically, "And would the two of you be willing to stand in as witness to this union?"

"If I'm not in surgery at the time," the doctor said, letting a smile emerge.

Giggling, the nurse said, "Oh, yes, count me in. I just love weddings."

The subsequent eve, propped up against a mound of cushy pillows with Malcolm sitting gingerly at her side, Heather wed her beloved. After the priest announced with an operatic flair, "I now pronounce you Mr. and Mrs. Malcolm Hawthorne," the couple romantically, but carefully, kissed. The attending nurse gleefully dabbed back a few heartfelt tears while the white coat jokingly exclaimed, "Just what the doctor ordered...love... it's the true panacea!"

Within the week Malcolm and Heather were back on the road again. Watching the scenery whiz by as their car settled into a manageable speed of seventy-five, Heather struck up a conversation with regard to fate. "Pretty amazing," she started, "that it took a tornado to get us married."

Malcolm laughed, responding, "I think it's pretty amazing you healed as fast as you did. It's serious stuff when you rupture your spleen."

"Okay, and maybe the fact that I beat the odds and got out of the hospital sooner than most is because we got married."

"Not sure if I get the correlation."

"You're the one who told the priest that our getting married might fend off evil spirits."

"I did not!"

"Well, not in those exact words."

"How would you know anyway?" Malcolm asked. "You were still on the operating table when I initially spoke to the priest."

"Just because someone is under anesthesia doesn't necessarily mean they can't hear."

"But through closed doors? No one's hearing is that acute."

Heather guffawed. "Oh, all right. I confess. When I was coming to, the priest was by my side, offering me words of encouragement. He told me what you'd said to him; that you thought our getting married might change our luck for the better."

"Well, it couldn't have gotten much worse," Malcolm retorted. "Heck, we give up our baby. Then your family decides to move. Then I lose my job, so we run away together…"

"And boom! We get kicked in the butt by a tornado."

"You end up with a ruptured spleen, nearly bleed to death…"

"Then you marry me…"

"And we live happily ever after," Malcolm concluded.

"Oh, I'm sure we'll have our share of ups and downs, but come on, you have to admit things are on the upswing right now."

"Yep, we're riding high," Malcolm said as he jacked up the radio to hear "Jailhouse Rock." Happily absorbing the highway ahead, he set his hand atop Heather's and tapped out the beat.

She was a magnet to the feel-good moment, joyfully singing, "*Let's rock! Everybody let's rock! Everybody in old cell block…is dancing to the jailhouse rock.*"

Their five-day road trip cross country was the most fun they'd ever had. But when they got to Hollywood, reality bit hard. Eric, Malcolm's first cousin, had recently been evicted from his apartment. When they knocked on his door after the final nine-hour leg of their trip, exhausted and ready to crash, they were informed that Eric was unable to pay his rent and so he was forced to move out. Malcolm begged to know where he'd gone, but the new renter had no idea.

Trying to assuage Heather's angst, Malcolm said, "Don't worry. At least I know where he works. We'll find out what happened tomorrow." But the next day when they went to the production lot where Eric claimed he had a job staging sets for *Gomer Pyle*, the pompous security guard there said he hadn't seen Eric in two days. In an imperious tone, he commanded, "Leave now. Tourists are not allowed."

"What could've happened to him?" Heather asked as she and Malcolm departed.

"I have no idea. He and I talked about our staying at his place right before we left the Chicago area."

Having eaten through Malcolm's savings and not knowing another soul they could reside with temporarily, Heather and Malcolm scrounged around Hollywood and finally succumbed to setting up house in a dumpy trailer that was abandoned on a back lot where Westerns had been sensationally produced and were now long forgotten. The hitching posts and frontier storefronts were still standing, but most everything else was dirt and dust. It was a headache coming and going, trying to stay out of sight. But the trailer provided a roof over their heads, and until they could secure employment and get settled, they felt fortunate to have the measly digs.

Though Malcolm was the one with the degrees and experience, Heather was the first to land a job. She applied for a position as a makeup artist with CBS. No schooling was necessary. The job entailed cosmetic applications for those who would be appearing before the cameras; sometimes it was a glamorous face, but more often than not, a professional face. Her first clients were newscasters, so that meant Heather had to report to work before sunrise. Her day ended about four-thirty, after she finished applying makeup for the evening crew who came on board for both the six o'clock and eleven o'clock news broadcasts. Heather liked the work a lot. It satisfied her creative side, all the while stimulating her intellect as she struck up conversations with the reporters about current events and national news. She had high hopes of finishing high school, but for the time being it was necessary that she bring in a paycheck.

It was August before Malcolm was assured of a job. He'd habitually visited various district offices on and off since late April, but the best they could do was put Malcolm on their sub list and, since there was no contact number that he could offer, they had no way of reaching him. When they did finally offer him full-time work, the position was that of a P.E. teacher for a local middle school. Malcolm wasn't sure which he liked least, the subject matter or the age group. As far as he was concerned all you needed was a booming voice and a barrel of patience to fulfill the position. It had nothing to do with shaping and empowering youthful minds in a contained, classroom setting. No, his would be all about harnessing energy on the playground before chaos ensued! But, what was he to do? He needed the work, so his response was an immediate yes.

To celebrate the fact that they both finally had jobs, Malcolm and Heather splurged and bought tickets to "Bowled Over," a Beatle's concert at the Hollywood Bowl. It was August 29th, a night to remember. The arena exuded energy and anticipation; comparable to something out of ancient Rome wherein the masses awaited the games to begin. The place was packed with loud and boisterous fans. Even when the music began the crowd was clamorous, never taking advantage of the actual seats they paid for. Heather loved the Beatles, and on this occasion, seeing them live, she was mesmerized. When the band played "I Want to Hold your Hand," she gripped Malcolm's with such strength, a few knuckles cracked. The entire evening was one memorable standing ovation, especially when a zany streaker broke protocol and skedaddled across the stage butt naked.

After the performance, as the masses were taking baby steps, funneling their way out of the Bowl, Malcolm spotted his cousin in the distance. He was in Army fatigues.

"That explains it," Malcolm said to Heather. "Eric got drafted."

"But I thought they said he couldn't pay the rent."

"Why bother paying rent when the government's going to be putting you up?"

"Or shipping you out," Heather added. Right then and there she said a little prayer for Eric. She'd heard how many draftees had been injured or killed in Vietnam. She hadn't met Malcolm's cousin, but suddenly she felt sorry for him.

In September of '65 new television shows were airing on CBS. One of the producers had taken note of the expert job Heather was doing to make the newscasters look their best; and thus he sent for her. The man had a reputation for being a little kooky, but Heather felt complimented that he liked her makeup mastery.

"I'm with *Lost in Space*," the stodgy man said. "Know the show?"

"I've heard of it."

"Better watch more TV, miss. After all, you're in the business."

Heather nodded in a professional manner.

"Want to work for us?"

Taken aback, Heather hesitated and said, "I imagine so."

"No imagining. We'll take care of that. What we need you to do is let loose of your creative skills. The crazier the better. We're talking outer space here. Can you do that?"

Heather nodded again. She knew sci-fi was not her forte, but thinking in terms of dollar signs, she answered definitely, "Yes. Yes I can do that."

"Good. Then you're hired. And, just so you know, you can still work for those morning newsies because we won't need you until later in the day."

"Yes, sir."

"Brush off the afternoon news crew, though, because we usually start about four and often work until damn near midnight." Adjusting his thick, horn-rimmed glasses, the man added, "We geeky space cadets like to go home in the dark…it's more like outer space to us."

Heather didn't get the guy's gist, but she didn't dare raise a brow. She wanted the job, knew the work would pay better, and she could still see about keeping her stint with the so-called morning newsies.

A month passed with Malcolm duly employed and Heather doubly employed, which meant there was finally enough money to rent. The couple was ecstatic to move out of the run-down, cramped trailer into a spacious sixth-floor apartment with a panoramic view. Life was starting to fall into place, but there was a drawback; the newlyweds hardly got to see each other. Heather left before dawn and got home after Malcolm was already asleep. She was exhausted, but plugged along with her makeup artistry positions. Malcolm was busy, but lonely. He missed his bride. He prepared breakfast and dinner for himself and ate alone. He did most of the household chores so Heather wouldn't have to. Cleaning the toilet and mopping floors were his least favorite. But he didn't mind folding laundry because he could do that at night while watching television. He faithfully tuned in to *Lost in Space*, but aside from admiring his wife's handiwork, the show was not his thing. He was a loyal fan of *Hogan's Heroes* and *The Wild, Wild West*, fun military and cowboy stuff, totally guy-ish, not ghoulish.

Weekends blew away the doldrums and ushered in happier times. Malcolm and Heather slept in until the hour they fancied. They cuddled, wrestled, snuggled, and made love under the sheets, on top of the sheets, on the couch, on the floor, in the shower; wherever the spirit moved them. Sometimes they set out for a long walk. Other times they' shop and browse. Going to the movies and restaurant-hopping were favorites. One day they saw the blockbuster *Jaws*. They dined out and ordered shark for dinner. Sometimes, though, the couple didn't so much as get out of their pajamas all day. They lived for their weekends; and gradually drained themselves Monday through Friday to get there.

By early spring Heather slowly succumbed to the stress of her work overload. She looked ragged. A flu came along that toppled her into bed, corpse-like; the lack of a spleen kept recovery at bay. By the fifth day Malcolm called in sick and drove Heather to the hospital. After being examined, the doctor told the couple that Heather had a miserable case of Swine flu and that it was more severe than most because of Heather's reduced immunity and the fact that she was pregnant.

Chapter Fourteen

Potash to ward off floral diseases

The doctor's diagnosis with regard to the flu fell on deaf ears. The only word Malcolm and Heather heard was "pregnant." Like a well-rehearsed comic routine, they both jerked their head to look at each other and with eyes bulging, in synchronized harmony, they sang out, "Pregnant?!"

"You didn't know?" the doctor asked.

Turning their attention to the medic, again they answered in unison, "No!"

"Well, I'd say you're about three months along, in the early stages." The doctor checked the couple's expressions and then felt comfortable saying, "Congratulations."

Malcolm and Heather were speechless.

Worried he wasn't on track the doctor asked, "You intend to have this baby, right?"

The two nodded enthusiastically, but the words were still frozen.

"Do you have an ob/gyn?"

Finally Heather found her voice. "No, no I don't. Can you recommend someone?"

"Yes, I'd be glad to. After you get dressed I'll give you Dr. Burlington's card and a prescription for the flu symptoms you're experiencing."

Malcolm jumped in, "But Heather can't take any medicine. Pills might hurt the baby."

The doctor smiled. "Already the fretful father. Don't worry, what I plan to prescribe can be taken by pregnant women."

What a day! Ailment transformed into acclamation. And because of the flu a riveting surprise had been unveiled and there was hope of giving birth to the product of their love. It was tough to say who was more excited. Both Heather and Malcolm celebrated the news. Both came to terms on how essential it was that they transition into the proper parental mentality and behavior. Changes in lifestyle needed to occur. Heather's long hours required lessening. And even though Malcolm was already pulling his own weight on the home front, he was aware that he'd have to do all the more once the baby was born.

After returning to work from a week of sick leave, Heather approached her superiors and explained the circumstances of her condition—how her spleen had been removed due to the tornado incident; how she now had a reduced capacity to fight infection; and most importantly, how she was pregnant and thus she needed to be extremely careful with her health. She asked if her hours with the television show could be reduced, that the long hours into the night were not conducive to getting enough rest. There was an in-depth discussion amongst her superiors, but the outcome was not what Heather expected. She was told that she could cut her morning hours with the news team, but they could not afford to have her go part-time with the popular outer space show. A final appeasing offer was made, that Heather could work part-time in the afternoons for the other new program on CBS, *Green Acres*. Though she regarded the sitcom as ho-dunk and inane, she knew it would not be taxing and thus she signed on the dotted line.

One month later, Heather was distraught over having made any changes at all in her work schedule. On a Tuesday afternoon she had gut-wrenching pains and by Wednesday she was informed by Dr. Burlington that she'd miscarried. Two pregnancies and, pathetically, both lost causes.

Malcolm took the news even harder than Heather. He moped around for weeks. Trying to perk him up, Heather made his favorite comfort meals like flank steak and grilled potatoes, or lamb shank with roasted onions. One weekend when she had more time, using a recipe from *Bon Appetite*, she baked a crème brule for dessert. She set a candlelit table and served in her lingerie. Meager smiles were revealed, but nothing genuine.

The following year Heather decided it was time to finish school, so at night she attended a six-month course that satisfied the three months she'd lost her senior year of high school. Returning to the classroom and delving into her studies brought back fond memories. She'd forgotten how much she loved to learn! The six months of night school wasn't enough and thus Heather signed on to take college coursework. The hours of her classes worked out well. Except for Wednesday nights she was home in time for a late supper with Malcolm. And Malcolm, who had recently been asked to teach two periods of history in addition to his duties as a P.E. teacher, was always home correcting papers and preparing for his next day of classes. Heather would waltz in at seven, prepare dinner, they'd eat by eight and afterwards she'd join her husband at the work table. Though Heather wanted to watch *Lost in Space* and *Green Acres*, neither she nor Malcolm had any spare time for television.

With work and going to night school it took Heather five years to get her college degree. She and Malcolm celebrated by booking a brief coastal excursion to romantic Carmel by the Sea. They stayed at the highly touted Highlands Inn. It was a honeymoon destination and in their case it was the honeymoon they never got to take. They pampered themselves with an in-room massage and treated themselves to breakfast, lunch, and dinner in bed. They were so content they couldn't bear to leave their suite. Their oceanfront view was exquisite, a prized portrait of masterful waves and sun-bleached sands. The sky and sea wore harmonious blues, with a sprinkling of sea birds to offset the two. Malcolm said he even dreamed of the panorama their first night. "Between you and this view, Heather, I thought I'd died and gone to heaven. I had a hard time waking up."

Their final day, Heather insisted they put a hold on their bedroom antics. She was hungry for a stroll along the beach. That languid stroll turned into a lengthy trek. There was so much natural beauty to absorb that the couple spent hours sauntering along the coastal trails and beaches, and later the charming streets of artsy Carmel. Neither wanted to depart late that afternoon, but they promised each other a return visit in years to come.

Three years later when Heather secured her law degree, Malcolm rented a house in Pebble Beach and surprised his wife with a one week trip to peninsula paradise. On this particular trip the goal was to get pregnant. Heather was twenty-six and Malcolm was already in his thirties. They felt the sandy granules of life's hourglass slipping through all too quickly. Time was advancing and having to repeatedly turn that hourglass over was bewildering at best. Thus, instead of being carefree and lustful, their week away was a carefully plotted baby-making retreat. But having gone through the motions of attempting every feasible position of lovemaking, toying with the time of day and hour of night, eliciting a host of moods and even passion foods, nothing gelled. Sadly, conception was not in the cards. Carmel was beautiful, but not obligingly memorable.

When conception did occur, the couple was busier than ever. Malcolm had shed his playground persona and was now a full-time history teacher and vice principal. Heather was a lawyer with a reputable LA firm. She thrived on being a trial attorney, rising in front of a courtroom assertively arguing her case. The work reminded her of the days on the debate team. But she also needed her creative fix. So she managed to keep her part-time job with the morning news crew. Putting on a professional face, not just her own, but the makeup for three or four others, kept her vocationally and artistically sated. Each morning when she left the CBS newsroom, even with the ghastly traffic in Los Angeles, she had plenty of time to make it to the law offices where she worked or the courthouse she regularly visited. Heather had a full and busy life, and because she loved what she did, stress no longer plagued her.

The couple couldn't pinpoint when they'd conceived because romancing hadn't been a priority. But with the onset of a new year came the confirmation that, once again, they were expecting.

Elation was all-consuming. But at the end of her second month, disappointment was back to wield another merciless blow. Dr. Burlington didn't have a medically erudite answer to offer Heather as to why she couldn't carry a child to term. He simply blamed her misfortune on the absence of a spleen. Then, with the miniscule amount of hope and optimism he could garner, he suggested the couple keep trying. "Maybe one day it will happen," he said with a consolatory shrug.

Again Malcolm lived out the blues. He dove deeply, almost as if he was searching his own inners for a place where he might carry a baby to term. Feeling totally inadequate, Heather tried her best to put on a happy face. But even with her talent for applying the right makeup she could not produce a credible smile. Why, after all these years, can't we have a baby? No, Heather underlined, why can't *I* have a baby?! This is all my fault!

A few months later the gray slate of their life was giving way to patches of pearly white again. Heather had been assigned an important case that for the first time required some travel. She didn't like leaving Malcolm, but the opportunity presented itself and she snatched the offer up faster than paper money floating in the wind. If she won the case, her reputation would solidify. The fact that her superiors requested she take on the case was a concrete indication that they trusted and supported her. Seemingly they knew she'd be passionate about the fight and desirous of a win.

The only drawback to Heather's travels was the destination. She was headed back to the city of Chicago for a week. A slew of thoughts kept nagging her and eventually churning in her core: *Should I go to Wheaton while I'm there? Try to hook up with Dad? But then, can I see him without seeing Mother again? Maybe he and I can meet downtown for lunch. How about calling on Grandma Lily? Who even knows where she is. Should I try to rekindle the years we lost?* Then the hauntingly vivid, biting query she'd tried to ignore all along, but couldn't because it continued to sink its claws into Heather's being: *Should I try to find out what happened to the child I gave birth to? The only seed that Malcolm and I successfully planted, took root, grew, and hopefully flourished. And if*

I were to find this living soul, could I then dig him or her up and endeavor to transplant? Might that not damage the roots irreparably?

Heather lowered her head and tried to focus on a desk full of prep work. She read page upon page, line after line of depositions, stark black words upon thin white paper. What she really wanted to do was read between the lines. Conduct a subtle search beneath, through and around that which was in black and white. Sort out and ascertain what she was truly looking for; comprehend the importunate void she'd endured so that she could come to grips with what in life she desperately needed.

The week prior to leaving for Chicago had been all-consuming. Heather knew in her heart that she hadn't given Malcolm the time of day or a night of whim. Thus, the evening before departure she stopped at a favorite restaurant and picked up a gourmet supper to go. She brought the meal home and lured her husband away from the work table. While he got them a glass of wine, she set a formidable table in their kitchen. She put out cloth napkins and china plates and lit several votive candles with sultry, hypnotic scents. Having set the mood, even she was ready for a taste of frolic before food. Seductively taunting Malcolm, Heather ushered him back *onto* the work table where the monotony of correcting tests and composing lesson plans became the farthest thing from his mind. Though their meal got cold, they got steamy; and pent-up anxiety was purged.

That night when her head finally succumbed to the pillow and her body surrendered to sleep, Heather dreamed of her grandma. She saw the creases of her sagacity stretched across a wide brow. She absorbed the compassion in her contemplative expression, the tenderness of a soft smile and the kindness that lingered in her eyes. *Where are you Grandma?* Heather's subconscious begged to know. *Do you still want to watch my baby? Will you keep my child a while? Keep my little one safe and warm? Happy and loved? I so want to be a mother. I just need time. I just need time…*

When she awoke her dream had made an imprint on her "to do" list. She rose and even before showering, Heather called her father. She purposely didn't tell him about her pending trip because if she made plans to see her father, inevitably it would include her mother. That was not going to happen. Instead, Heather merely asked for her Grandma Lily's phone number, chatted briefly with her dad and said she'd call back soon. After downing a mug of Hills Brothers, gifting a mushy kiss to Malcolm as he left for work, turning on the news to learn that Haldeman and Ehrlichman had received a sentence of between thirty months and eight years imprisonment for their involvement in the Watergate scandal, Heather made a mad dash to primp and pack. She had a full day ahead of her that would entail a final assessment of her caseload. At a point, she'd have to squeeze in a phone call to her Grandma Lily, to let her know she planned to drop by for a visit. A cab would arrive at five and she'd head straight to the airport to catch her O'Hare-bound flight. Everything was expected to go as planned and play out in an orderly, if not torpid fashion. Oddly, that numbing normalcy was precisely what Heather had high hopes of mitigating during her stay in the Windy City.

Chapter Fifteen

Leaves and stems, green appears

Lily was an emotional pretzel. Earlier that evening, fraught with concern over Presley's whereabouts, her heart had pumped blood at such a velocity that her veins felt like swollen rivers. She'd picked up the phone and out of nowhere her darling granddaughter had called to say she would be in Chicago for a week and she'd like to stop by for a visit. *Could life be any loopier,* Lily had to wonder. Later that night, upon finding sleep, she dreamed of her granddaughter, special little Heather who had achingly given up her newborn for adoption. Sweet Heather who'd never gotten a glimpse of the baby she'd brought into this world. Lily's subconscious mourned the loss. She sensed a deep and vicarious separation, one that connected her to Heather and created an impenetrable bond between them. When she awoke the next day, Lily had to wipe away tears she didn't recall shedding.

Still in a dither over what Grenade and his gang expected him to do at dusk the next evening, Presley focused his sights on making some changes to his schedule. That next morning while he was at Silver Trails putting in his one hour before breakfast, he decided to ask Rosie if he could set the tables for dinner as soon as he got home from school rather than later in the day. After tending to his busboy chores he'd run upstairs and explain to Lily that he couldn't start guitar lessons for a week because his mom was mad at him for being late and she'd grounded him. He hated lying, but there was no other way.

So far you've got things under control, Presley confidently told himself. But then a jarring thought struck. *What about walking the dogs? I still have to do that. This time it will be Boomer's turn. And I will be late bringing the dog home. That's going to make Violet and Dickie pretty darn mad. They'll never trust me again. And what if something terrible happens to Boomer? I don't want him to get hurt.* Presley wanted to cry, recalling how mean Grenade had been to Chimp and Squirt; how he'd threatened to kill them.

Tragically, Presley felt there was no way out! He had to comply because Grenade had forewarned him that he'd hunt him down if he failed to serve as his dog walking, druggie delivery boy. Presley was stuck in a nightmare of maleficent botchery with no escape.

The next afternoon Lily was only somewhat upset when Presley explained that he had to hold off on taking guitar lessons. "It's all right, young man. I know we'll get you and Blossom together soon. I'm just disappointed you won't be here to meet my granddaughter. She's coming to have dinner with me tonight."

"Your granddaughter is coming to visit you?" Presley asked, finally feckless.

"Yes, she called last night. She'll be here for a week on business. Can you imagine, I didn't even know that she's an attorney! I'm so pleased. Turns out she did just fine for herself after leaving here and going to California."

"That's so cool," Presley said. "She must really be smart."

"Yes, but I'd say she's more savvy than smart."

"Is that word spelled with two a's or two v's?"

Lily laughed. "Ah, another word for the spelling bee?"

"Could be. I missed one like that once before, the word 'vacuum.' I spelled it with two c's when it should've been two u's."

"Some words are tricky, aren't they? Well, just so you know, savvy has two v's."

"Okay," Presley said, "thanks. I have to go set tables now. Have a great time with your granddaughter. Maybe I can meet her the next time she comes over."

"Yes, let's plan on that."

Presley grinned as he took in Lily's felicity. He could tell how thrilled she was to be having her granddaughter come for a visit, worth more than gold itself. *Funny*, the boy thought, *how younger people mean so much to older people. Seems like most seniors are either really lonely and we're good company for them or maybe they just want to be young again and they're hoping our youth rubs off on them.*

Continuing down the hallway to get Boomer, Presley's nerves started to act up again. He'd conjured up a little white lie about bringing the dog back later than usual, and now his hope was that Violet and Dickie would buy into his ploy. Luckily it was Dickie who answered the door. He could be kind of grumpy at times, but he was more gullible than his wife, which allowed Presley to feel a tinge of relief. The cumbersome wheelchair Dickie practically lived in took up the whole doorway, but Boomer, with tail wagging like a hummingbird's wings, scooted under and through into the hallway, jumping all over Presley with icky, licky kisses.

"He sure knows who you are," Dickie said in an unusually robust way.

"Yes, we're old pals, aren't we Boomer?" *All the more reason I don't want anything to happen to him*, Presley thought.

"My goodness, his energy is boundless today. Mind if you take him for a little longer walk? I'll pay you extra to get him really good and tuckered out."

Presley's spirit rose like the sun, radiant rays of beatitude beaming. "Sure! That's no problem at all, sir. I'd be glad to take him for a longer walk. Is that okay with your wife?"

"She's in Elk Grove Village for a few days. Got a sister there that's taken ill with pneumonia."

"Sorry to hear that, sir."

"Might be why Boomer's so rambunctious. He's not used to Violet being gone." Dickie rolled backward in his wheelchair, ready to shut the door. Then as an afterthought he asked, "Sure your parents won't mind if you're out later than usual? Gets dark kind of early these days."

"No, sir. They won't care."

With that the boy tugged on Boomer's leash and the rollicking dog hopped to, prancing alongside Presley, down the hallway, out the doors of Silver Trails and into the hapless perils of Cabrini-Green. Paranoid, but methodically, Presley forged across the street, retracing his steps from the previous night. He made one wrong turn, but the alley he took still brought him to his destination, the deserted garage Grenade had ordered him to return to. Nobody was there yet. Presley hoped that it was all a practical joke he'd fallen prey to. Kids at school were always teasing him about being smart and being a goodie-two-shoe. Maybe Grenade was getting his jollies doing the same sort of thing. Unfortunately, Presley had to dismiss the notion because there in the distance was a dark hooded figure with a band of motley compatriots bringing up the rear.

"Primo, bro," Grenade called forth. As he approached he said snidely, "Glad my little dog walker didn't choose to disappoint." Then he looked down at the wiggly wart jumping all over his new boots. "Not much into dog training, are you, kid? Get that turd off me!" Grenade gave a brutal shove. "Down, you little shit!"

"I told you not to hurt my dogs."

"Better them than you, eh?" Then getting down to business, Grenade pulled out a satchel, this one larger and heavier than the last. "Here's the goods. Take this to Mangiatti's and make sure the owner gets it. Same gig, dig?"

Without a word, Presley reached for the bag.

"Make it smoooooooth, Ex Lax."

"Okay, but then I'm going home."

"No way, Jose! You're coming back here and reporting to me!"

"Why should I? I'm not taking any money from you."

Grenade nodded to his heckling gang. "Powerful. That's crazy, isn't it bros? All the more for us to split." Then he directed his wrath back at Presley. "I don't care if you take a dime, little delivery boy.

I want you back here just like before. Know why? Because I have to give you your *next* drop-off."

"I can't keep doing this."

Grenade hocked a loogy at the boy's feet. "'Fraid you have no choice, dog walker!"

Presley felt a reservoir of frustration ready to burst into a flood of tears, so he tugged on Boomer's leash and started to walk away.

"And just like before, Ace," Grenade yelled after him, "you need to be back here pronto...or else!"

The sun sank behind concrete slabs of neglect, the sad remnants of a bourgeoning era turned sour. Like taunting ghosts, creepy shadows came out to play. They slid in and out of the alleyways, causing both boy and dog to quiver. "It's okay, Boomer. Don't worry. I'll protect you."

Just as Presley's words fell on the dog's trusting ears, there in the distance was the figure of a beastly man lumbering toward them. His features blended in with the dusk, making them indecipherable and fearsome.

"Hey!" the figure hollered. "Hey, you!"

Making an abrupt about-face Presley pulled on the leash and started to run.

"Stop!" the deep command came. "Stop, I say!"

His feet would not obey the order brandished!

"Stop! Presley, stop!"

Hearing his name the boy halted. But Boomer didn't and thus the jolt forward on the leash caused Presley to tumble to the ground. Still the sinister ghoul in the shadows loomed closer. Who knows my name? Who's after me? Presley freaked.

"Stay where you are! It's me..."

Peering through the onset of night Presley struggled to see.

"Don't move. It's your father."

Though near tremulous collapse, Presley managed to get to his feet. "What are you doing here?" the boy choked.

"I should ask you the same, don't you think?"

Stammering, Presley unloaded, "I...I'm taking Boomer for a walk. His...his owner told me to tire him out."

"I'm sure he doesn't want you walking in these parts. You're lost, right?"

"No, at least I don't think so."

"Well, if you're not lost then you're downright stupid! This is a dangerous part of town, son." Grabbing the boy's arm, the father declared, "Come on, I'm taking you home!"

"But I can't go home."

"Look, Presley, it's not even safe for that dog you're walking. I'm sure the owner would be furious if he knew you were out here." Spying something on the ground and picking it up, the father asked, "What's this?"

Presley shuddered. "Um, nothing. It's…it's just a bag."

"I can see that! Tell me what's in it?"

"I don't know. I found it."

"You found it. Where?"

"On my walk."

The father untied the knot and poured out what was in the bag. "You're lying to me, kid." Turning the pills over in his hand, the dad growled, "You into drugs?"

"No…honest, I'm not."

"Then why do you have these?!"

Whimpering Presley fessed up, "Because I have to deliver them."

"To who?"

"A store owner."

"Which one?!"

Presley froze.

The father leaned in, his ire escalating. "I said which *one*?!"

"If I tell you, they'll kill Boomer."

"Who will?"

"I can't tell you."

Pulling away and putting the pills back in the bag, the father eased up slightly. "Do you know what you're doing, Presley? Do you realize you could be arrested for this?"

"Yes, sir, I know. But I don't have a choice."

"All right. Here's what we're going to do."

But before the father could speak, the boy sputtered, "We can't go to the police."

"I know that. This drop-off would be peanuts to them anyway."

Presley nodded, finally somewhat trusting his father.

"Okay, here's the plan. I'm going to take this pouch for you. I'll deliver it and tell the jerk who's expecting you that you're out of the picture from now on. They can find another do-gooder for their drug trafficking scheme."

"But...but what if they come after me again when I'm walking dogs?"

"So, it's not just the store owner we're dealing with here?"

"No, there's a gang of them. They nabbed me yesterday and made me do this delivery for them. They say I have to keep doing it or else!"

"Well, I've got news for those punks," the father seethed. He knelt down beside Presley. "Okay, let's start with the store owner. Where am I taking this?"

"To Mangiatti's."

Shaking his head the father said, "No kidding. How 'bout that? I just spoke with that asshole. He used to come to the gas station where I worked. Knew I was out of a job and said he needed someone to cover the register at night because he had other business to tend to...business that's bringing in more profit than the bottles of booze he sells."

"Do you think he wants to hire you because you're my father and he figures you won't rat on me when I show up?"

"Could be. But he's got another thing comin' if he thinks I'm going to let my kid fall into something like this. It's against the law and it's downright dangerous!"

For the first time ever, Presley felt like hugging his foster dad. Sadly, he didn't.

"You stay here," the father instructed. "Don't move a muscle, got that? The store's across the street. I'll be right back."

Moments later the sound of gunfire severed the stillness of night.

Chapter Sixteen

Buds begin to bloom

From the front door of Silver Trails, after having just waved farewell to her granddaughter, Lily noticed a patrol car pulling up in front of the neighboring apartment complex. There was no siren and the lights were not flashing so she wasn't overly concerned until she spied Presley getting out of the front seat with Boomer in his arms. She'd never left her residence without permission, but she just had to see what was going on. As she neared the police car, she could see that Presley was writhing in sobs. Hastening her feeble stride, she made a beeline for the boy and embraced him in a protective, tight squeeze.

"Presley, what's the matter? What's happened?"

The officer put a hand on the elder's shoulder, saying, "He's been through quite an ordeal this evening, ma'am. You need to give him some breathing room."

"That's okay," Presley gasped. "She's my friend."

The policeman tried to absorb the age difference and then said, "He's got a mother that he has to talk to, so you'll have to excuse us, please."

"But I'm like a mother to him…or at least a grandmother. Can't I know what's going on?"

"I'm afraid not. Only next of kin…"

"My father got shot," Presley blurted out.

Lily contracted like she, too, had been hit.

"Come on now," the officer said, separating Presley from the woman, "we have to go."

"Can't I tag along?" Lily pleaded, childlike.

"No, the two of us can handle it, thank you."

"But I want her to come," Presley cried.

After further bickering, it was apparent that the old broad was not going to take no for an answer. The policeman sighed and finally agreed to let the meddling senior accompany them. "But no interrupting," he admonished. "Stay behind the scenes." To which Lily replied, "I'll be quiet as a church mouse."

When Presley's mother answered the door, at first she was livid. "What the…What did you do, Presley?!" Then she addressed the officer. "Has he done something illegal?" Then she eyed Lily in the background. "He's always futzing around at that old folk's home. Did he steal something from you, ma'am?"

Unable to contain herself, Lily answered, "No, of course not. He'd never steal from any of us! I'm only here to support the child."

The officer stepped in front of Lily and said, "May I come in?"

"Of course. All of you, please come in. Except for that," she croaked, pointing at Boomer. "I'm allergic to dogs." In canine protest, the dog began barking maniacally. "Oh fine, but you hold on to him, Presley. I don't want his dander spread all over our floors."

Staying his course, the officer relayed, "I'm afraid we have some bad news ma'am."

"Father's been shot," Presley declared, his tears welling, ready for weeping.

The mother's face contorted in horror. She, too, began to cry. "Who did it?" she gasped. Who shot him, Presley?"

"The owner of Mangiatti's."

"But why? Your father went to talk to the man about working there. How did he end up getting shot?"

The policeman interrupted, "Are you sure he wasn't already working for the man?"

"What do you mean? No, I would know if he'd been hired on at the deli."

Shrugging, the officer said, "The shooting was drug-related."

Indignant, the mother flicked away a surge of tears. "There's no way! My husband may have been down on his luck, but he'd never stoop so low as to start pushing drugs."

Both Presley and Boomer squirmed.

"Sorry, ma'am, but from the evidence, that's what it looks like. Your husband got caught holding the bag."

"Then why'd he get shot if he was supposedly doing his job?"

"A fight over his share of the profits maybe. There was a scuffle. Only one gun, but both your husband and the store owner were found dead. Hard to know what really happened when there are no eyewitnesses." The policeman looked to Presley. "When we arrived your son came running from the shop with the dog close at heel. He said he didn't see who shot who, that he came in after the gunshots were fired. He didn't have any more info for us and we can't ask the dog, so we don't have too much more to go on."

Searching her son's face for answers and finding none, the mother surrendered to her sorrow. Contracting in angst and grievous disbelief, she slumped forward, sobbing.

"Don't worry; we plan to send a forensics team to the scene of the crime. We'll gather necessary data like fingerprints and what not. If we find anything new, something that will help us better understand what happened, we'll let you know."

"All right," the mother uttered, then pleadingly unloaded, "Why? Why my husband?"

"It's a rough neighborhood, ma'am. Be glad your son's okay." Then to Presley, the officer said sternly, "Take my advice, young man, find a safer place to walk that dog of yours and do it before the sun goes down."

With Boomer licking at his tears, Presley said, "He's not my dog, but thanks. I'll do what you say next time."

Then the officer stood and said to Lily, "Need an escort home, ma'am?"

At first Lily shook her head. But then she eyed Presley's mother and taking in her grief and need for solitude, she stiffly rose to her feet and said, "Thank you, officer. And why don't we take Boomer home so that you can stay here with your mother, Presley."

Not wanting her to leave, but knowing she had to, Presley placed Boomer into the policeman's arms. "Hold him tight," he said, "he likes to wiggle." Then quietly he asked Lily, "Can I come see you tomorrow?"

"Sure you can," Lily replied, hugging the boy. She smiled at the mother and said, "I'm so sorry for your loss. Please call me if there's anything I can do."

The mother nodded and through swollen, glazed eyes signaled a polite thank you.

Presley comforted his mother, but told her nothing. The riveted boy barely slept that night and when he arrived at Silver Trails the next morning he was the first to show up.

Waddling up the pathway, removing her woolen scarf, Rosie noticed the shivering boy and whispered, "What are you doing here so early, young man?"

"I couldn't sleep, so I came over to get my hour of work in as soon as possible."

Upon getting closer, Rosie spied the boy. "Sleepless nights at your age? There's got to be more to it than that." She patted Presley on the shoulder and then used her key to open the heavy door. "Sure you don't want to tell me what's going on?"

"Nah, it's kind of secret," the boy said, lowering his head. He truly dreaded telling Rosie any kind of fib, but he knew he had to tell her something because she wasn't budging. She was parked in the hallway like a hefty piece of furniture. "Okay, I'll tell you." Heaving a breath, Presley allowed, "My father left us."

Rosie slumped with a sigh. "Aww, poor thing…"

"It's okay," Presley continued, "I'm going to be all right. I need to set the tables and get back to my mother, though. Give her a little more help before the school bus comes."

"Yes, darling. Of course you do. And if it turns out your momma needs you this evening, I'll have someone else oversee your duties."

"No, I'll come by. We need the money. I think my mother will be better by then."

"Well, just so you know, the seniors have missed seeing you the past two evenings. And you know what else? They keep asking me when you're going to sing again." Seeing the boy's smile grow, Rosie added, "That's right. You'd better start those guitar lessons soon, so you can entertain us at one of our upcoming happy hours. The holidays are nearing. Maybe you can learn a few Christmas carols."

"I'll try," Presley said, his smile fading at the notion of a holiday waiting in the wings.

"Good… Now you'd best get going. Just set the usual amount of tables. Doubt any newcomers or visitors will be here for breakfast today." Rosie quickly grabbed Presley for one more squeeze and said, "I'm sorry about your foster dad, Presley. But don't worry. You have a big family here that loves you a lot."

"I know," Presley said with a grateful nod. Then he scampered off to the cupboard that housed the table linens.

Though it wasn't even seven o'clock yet, before leaving Silver Trails, Presley felt compelled to talk to Lily. He simply had to share what he knew about the killings or he was going to explode. After two attempts of gently knocking on her door with no response, Presley turned to leave. He was nearly all the way down the hall when he looked back to see a groggy grandma standing in her jammies ready to whistle at him. Presley raised a hand to gesture "don't do it" and then he quietly hustled back to the room.

Lily ushered the boy in and as soon as the door was closed she started to jabber. "My goodness. What hour is it anyway, my dear boy? Look at me. I'm a mess. Actually, *don't* look at me." Lily grabbed her robe and wrapped herself in it. "Can't recall the last time someone saw me without my eyebrows penciled in. No rouge on my cheeks, either." Lily glanced over at her dresser mirror and squawked, "Oh, dear! Where's the undertaker!?"

Presley chuckled and said, "You're funny."

"Yeah, just looking at me, I *am* a barrel of laughs."

"I think you look fine." Then putting on a serious face, Presley said, "I know it's early and I'm sorry that I woke you up, but I had to talk to someone."

Taking a seat on the edge of her bed, Lily leaned forward, intent and focused. "Tell me, dear. How can I help?"

Thirty minutes later Presley had to dash. He didn't dare miss the school bus. Lily was left behind to worry if he'd ever come back. The circumstances were that dire. Scrambling for the phone she called the Dalton Hotel and asked to be connected with Heather. The operator hesitated, waiting for a last name. Lily paused, too, and then tossed out, "Can you look under Simone please?"

Moments later the operator replied, "Sorry, ma'am, I have no one listed here with that last name."

"Well, look at their first names. I mean how many Heather's can there be?"

There was another brief pause. "I'm sorry, ma'am. I don't see that name at all on our guest list."

"Well, for heaven's sakes, she's staying there. Why else would she have given me this phone number?!" Slamming the phone down, Lily let agitation consume her. Then she told herself, "Calm down, ya old coot. Now think. What did your granddaughter say her married name was?" She clunked her head. "Serves you right for not paying attention."

It was after work when Heather finally called. "Hi, Grandma," she started.

"Heather…oh, Heather! It's you. Thank the Lord!"

"What's the matter, Grandma? You sound like something horrible has happened."

"It has. Trust me it's been a very unnerving day. I couldn't reach you. I had the hotel number, but I stupidly forgot your married name. All I had to go on was Heather Simone and the receptionist said they didn't have anyone listed under your first or last name."

"Oh, Grandma, I'm sorry. I'm registered here under the name of Mrs. Malcolm Hawthorne."

"That's your name?"

"It has been for nearly a decade."

"Gees, my head's been in the sand that long, eh?" Lily groaned. "Oh, well. Now I know. So, Mrs. Malcolm Hawthorne, you're a full-fledged attorney and you certainly know more about the law than I do… Can I ask you a few questions?"

"Are you in trouble, Grandma?" Heather asked jokingly.

"No, but I know someone who's going to be. And if the law doesn't get him first, the bad guys very well could. He's confided in me and I'm the only one who can help him. I really need some advice. Do you have a minute, dear?"

"For you, Grandma, I have all the time in the world."

Lily fretted through breakfast and then through lunch. By late afternoon when Presley was supposed to show up and didn't, her emotions were Jello. Wanting to unload the mounting concern she carried, but unable to tell a soul, Lily wore an air of nonchalance as she strut down to the kitchen to check on the boy's whereabouts. She stuck her head in through the revolving door where wafts of beefy meatloaf engulfed her.

"Anybody seen Presley?" she called in.

In oven mitts up to his elbows, Tony abruptly turned around almost dropping one of the hot Pyrex dishes he was holding. "Ma'am, I'm sorry. But you're not allowed in the kitchen. Besides, you could lose your head in that door if one of us came bustling through the other way."

"Sorry, just lookin' for Presley," Lily relayed as she pulled away from the door.

Tony knew enough not to upset the elders in his midst, so he removed his oven mitts and stepped out into the hallway. "It's Lily, right?" he asked as he approached.

"Yes, that would be me."

"I apologize for sending you out like that. I didn't mean to be rude. It's just that we have rules we have to follow around here." Tony slicked back his thick, dark waves and tried to stand taller than his height of five-five. "Usually Rosie's around to answer any questions you might have, but she had to step out for a few minutes. Told me a policeman needed to speak with her."

"A policeman?" Lily asked with alarm.

"Don't worry, Rosie didn't do anything wrong. The officer just needed some information regarding a pack of kids that have been dealin' drugs around here."

Just then Rosie strode through the back door and down the hallway, her feet landing like they were cement bricks. She looked to be a frenzied mess.

"Everything all right?" Tony dared to ask.

Rosie shook her head. "Knew that boy was too good to be true."

Lily chimed in, "Do the police think Presley's involved?"

"How'd you guess?" Rosie asked.

"Oh, no," Lily sighed, putting her hands to her head. Then she jerked to attention. "Do they have Presley in custody?"

"No, but they're looking for him. Guess that's why he didn't show this afternoon to set tables. For months he was so trustworthy and now this."

"Yeah," Tony said. "He's been a good little worker. What could've happened?"

Lily put her hands to her mouth, but she couldn't hold back. "Suddenly everything's happened to Presley and I'll have you know, none of it's his fault!"

Both Tony and Rosie looked on in awe. They'd never seen Lily so upset.

"I'm not at liberty to tell you all the details. But trust me, Presley is a good boy and he needs our help."

"But how?" Rosie begged to know. "How can we help him if we don't even know why the police are looking for him?"

"Or where he is?" Tony added.

"Hi, everyone," Presley called forth, as he waved from down the hallway. "How many are we expecting for dinner tonight? Sorry I'm late. My mother stayed home from work today and she needed my help after school."

Lily threw her hands up in total relief. "Oh, my gosh. You're safe. You're here."

Still befuddled, Rosie gestured a Hail Mary and said, "We've all been so worried. The police were here looking for you."

Presley's face fell. His eyes begged Lily for help. "The police? They came here?"

"Yes," Rosie confirmed. "They think you're running with a band of hoodlums."

"It's all right, dear," Lily said, "I just finished telling Rosie that you're not the bad guy. Now go set the tables and take care of your chores. Then you and I will talk."

"And what about us?" Tony said like a little kid wanting more.

"Once we get all the facts," Lily told him, "we'll straighten this mess out in no time. My daughter's an attorney. She's going to handle Presley's case."

"Well then," Rosie interjected, "I best tell you this now... The reason the police came to see me is 'cause Willie told them to."

"Willie Waggers? The homeless man that set off our fire alarm?" Presley asked.

"The one who stole all my muffins?" Tony scoffed.

"Yes, that Willie," Rosie replied. "Turns out he was in the Laundromat next door when the owner of the deli got shot."

"What was he doing there?" Tony queried.

"It's evidently his new hangout at night. I don't know, maybe he sits by the warm dryers after people leave with their laundry." Rosie raised a brow. "Anyway, he told the police he heard two gun shots, just moments apart. Then shortly after that he saw you, Presley, running out of the deli. He recognized you and told the police that you're a busboy here at Silver Trails."

With chagrin Presley told Rosie, "The police already know that part of the story. It was a policeman who brought me home after my father was shot."

The news slammed into Rosie like a wrecking ball. "Wait! You're father got killed last night? But you told me this morning he'd left you and your mom."

"I couldn't tell you the whole truth. I wanted to, but..."

"The police asked him to be quiet about things for the time being," Lily explained.

Rosie crumpled to her knees. Tony stood next to her agog.

"Shame on us for thinking you were involved," Rosie evinced, "I should've trusted my gut."

"There's still more we have to do to get Presley off the hook," Lily relayed. "I probably shouldn't tell you this, but Presley's fingerprints were found on the gun."

"Oh, no," Rosie bawled, "not a gun. You're too young for all this."

Tony cut in, "Don't worry, we won't tell a soul. Not a word about this, right?"

Rosie made the sign of the cross and Tony gestured a scout's honor. At that moment their promises were about the only thing Lily and Presley could be certain of. It was seven o'clock by the time Heather touched base with Lily. Engrossed in her job, she'd lost track of time and had missed the opportunity to dine with her grandmother at Silver Trails. *They all eat at five-thirty anyway*, Heather reminded herself. *That's a late lunch for me.* Thus, on her way out of the Wrigley Building, having spotted a pizza parlor, she ordered a small size veggie and headed back to the hotel. While gobbling down bell peppers and globs of cheese she set her mind to task, switching gears from the case she'd worked on all day to the one her grandmother had asked her to tackle. Heather mulled over the facts. *Two men had been shot. The incident was drug-related. And the boy that her grandma knew was at the scene, his father having been one of the victims shot.* "Need more than that to go on," Heather said, picking up the phone.

There was only one ring. "Hello? Heather, is that you?"

"Wow, you're quick, Grandma. You must've had your hand on the receiver."

"Actually I did; I've been waiting for your call. Did you figure anything out?"

"Well, no, not really. I was busy all day. Have they even charged the boy yet?"

"No, not yet. But something new has come up, something that may be rather incriminating. They found his fingerprints on the gun."

"Did you ask your little friend how they got there? More importantly, would this boy have had a motive to kill his foster dad?"

"His father abused him verbally on a regular basis. But I only know of one incident where he physically abused him."

"Not likely a motive for killing someone. So, did the child say why he touched the gun?"

"He said he removed the gun from his father's hand."

"I gather his dad was dead at that point?"

"As far as he could tell."

"Was the other man dead when he found his father?"

"He said the owner was face-down and wasn't moving."

"Well, it sounds like the two men shot each other. Most likely they had an argument over the drugs they were dealing."

"But the child claims his father wasn't dealing drugs. The dad only went into the deli to drop off what the child was being forced to deliver and to tell the owner to leave him alone. The boy feels awful that his father took a bullet on his account. He swears that his foster dad didn't shoot the store owner. He's pretty sure there was someone else in the rear of the store because when he ran into the building he heard the back door slam shut."

"So he thinks there was a third party?"

"Yes. And what I worry about is retaliation. The punks who forced him into delivering their drugs, they might go after him. Or if there was someone else in the store that night, somebody who would kill for drugs, there could be even more serious danger lurking about."

"Is the foster mom aware of the situation? Is she doing anything to protect her son?"

"Not to my knowledge. She's never been a doting parent. Seems like she pretty much comes and goes as she pleases. Having said that, she's got to be upset over losing her husband. And now she'll be all alone with a youngster to provide for."

"You seem to know a lot about this child and his family."

"Let's just say I've kept a close eye on them. This youngster is special to me and I want to make sure he's taken care of."

"Grandma, I don't mean to change the subject...but hearing the love in your voice, the concern you feel for this child, I have to tell you the real reason I returned to Chicago."

"I thought you came back because of this big case you're working on."

"Yes, for the most part. But I also came back to talk with you, to get your gut feeling on something, whether or not I should try to locate my…my…"

"…Your baby? The child you put up for adoption?"

"Yes, Grandma," Heather said with resolve.

Lily paused and then said, "Is it too late for you to catch a cab, darling?"

"No, Grandma. If it means a heart to heart with you, nothing's too late."

The discussion Heather and Lily had that evening lasted until the wee hours of morn. Heather finally caught a cab back to her hotel at three in the morning. She crashed, hoping to catch some power z's before heading to the office at eight. Lily slid under the sheets, hoping that she'd wake up in time for Presley's first guitar lesson that afternoon. She couldn't remember the last time she'd pulled an all-nighter! *Had to have been eons ago*, she told herself as she succumbed to slumber.

When she awoke it was to a pounding at her door. She eyed her bedside clock. It was twelve-thirty.

"Yes," she called forth sleepily.

"You all right in there?"

She recognized the voice. "Yes, Sal. I'm fine. I slept in is all."

"Until noon?" he shouted.

"No, until this very instant…when *you* managed to wake me up."

"Well, I was worried. You don't usually play hermit and hide in your room."

Lily achingly rose from bed and in slow motion wrapped herself in her terrycloth robe. She swept back a clump of frazzled gray hair and said as she opened the door, "I'm glad there's someone who worries about me. But as you can see, I'm fine."

"You don't look fine."

"Well, of course I don't," Lily snorted. "I was up until three this morning."

"Couldn't sleep?"

"No, I slept just fine…until a certain *someone* woke me up." Lily grimaced and added, "If you really want to know, I was up talking to my granddaughter all night."

"Oh, the one who was here two nights ago?"

"Yes, that one." Lily swelled with pride. "Actually, Heather is my only grandchild. And I'll have you know, she's a big-time attorney."

"Really? Did you call her here because of Elvis?"

"No, no. She's here working on some prestigious case. Although I did get her legal advice with regard to *Presley*."

"Does she feel he might be in trouble with the law?"

"Not at all. If anything, like me, she worries that someone might come after the boy."

"Why? Does Elvis know who killed the two men?"

"No, but *Presley* saw certain things that might help the police with their investigation."

Sal hemmed and hawed a little, but finally offered up, "I don't want to alarm you, but when I looked out my window yesterday, there was a stranger standing in the alleyway. Oddly, he stood there frozen, looking at the flower beds. Then he peered into Elvis's apartment. Then back at the empty planters. I'd never seen him before. Probably should have reported the incident, but at the time I figured it was a relative of the father's who'd been shot. He was big and beastly like Elvis's foster dad. Could've passed for his brother. Anyway, he finally left. So, I didn't give it too much more thought. Until now…"

"Do you think he's after Elvis?" Lily then clenched a fist and grunted, "Darn it! See that, you've got *me* calling the boy Elvis!"

Realizing he'd upset Lily, Sal sloughed it off. "I doubt the guy was after anyone. He was probably a hobo or some weirdo roaming the streets. We see so much of that around here these days."

"Well, all the same, be on the lookout," Lily warned. "We can't be too careful. Oh, and thanks for being my alarm clock, Sal. I'd better get a move on so I'm ready for Presley when he comes by for his guitar lesson."

"But he's not out of school until three."

"And he won't be here until three-thirty. But that's about how long it's going to take me to get ready. Hey, what're you looking at me like that for? I'm no spring chicken anymore. I can't exactly hop-to like I used to."

Sal laughed. "Nor can I, Lily."

When Presley arrived that afternoon, he was crying. Lily asked if he was still sad about losing his dad and he said, "No, my mother's sending me back to Care and Family Services."

Chapter Seventeen

Flower power

Heather gathered the final pieces of evidence that she needed in order to present her case. Her flight would leave that evening and thus she had a free afternoon to spend doing a different kind of research. After talking at length with her grandmother, spilling her guts out about how desperate she was to connect with the baby she'd given up for adoption, Heather decided that after ten years it was time to dig into the past and determine once and for all—where is the child Malcolm and I created?

After two hours of scratching the surface, being referred by this organization to that organization, she learned that the Department of Care and Family Services was the agency that generally helped to find permanent homes for unwanted babies born in Chicago and the outer lying suburbs. Immediate remorse returned. The term "unwanted" wrapped around Heather's chest like a boa aiming to constrict and crush ribs. Catching a cab she sped off to the agency. The instant she stepped through the front door she wished she'd stuck with the phone instead. Never before had she witnessed such administrative anarchy. Even though there seemed to be countless employees on board to assist, all they could offer her was the clichéd standard, "Take a number and have a seat."

When Heather was finally able to speak with an agent, the first thing the woman asked was, "Are you looking to adopt?"

"No, I'm looking to find the child that I put up for adoption," Heather replied.

"Is that child now eighteen years or older?"

Heather paused and said, "No, why?"

The afternoon was a loss, though not a total waste. The meager information Heather was able to procure was that she'd given birth to a boy who had been adopted at the age of two months. The agent said the child was no longer with the original adoptive parents, that he'd been living in foster care for a while. When Heather begged for an address or phone number so that she could contact her son, the agent could not oblige. "Its policy, ma'am, I'm sure you understand. If the child was aiming to find you, that'd be different."

Standing in pensive silence, Heather finally said, "Then please jot down my name and phone number. If this boy is ever in need of assistance, please notify me. I'm his birth parent. And I'm totally capable of caring for him now. Both his father and I want him back. We're married and we want this child to be part of our family."

The agent nodded with showy empathy. Heather could only hope it was heartfelt. On her way to the airport she called her grandmother and filled her in on the particulars.

"Well, dear, at least you know he's alive and in good hands," Lily said. "Remember, miracles do happen. Some day you might just have that little boy to take home."

"Yes, Grandma. I'll keep saying my prayers."

"So, when are you coming back, Heather, dear?"

"I'm not sure. This case I'm handling might avail me another ticket to Chicago before we go to trial. Don't worry, I'll be in touch. And thank you so much for everything! I loved seeing you." Heather listened, waiting for a farewell response. She heard dulcet music and singing instead. A little louder, she asked, "Grandma, do you have your radio on?"

"Isn't it lovely, dear?"

"Yes, but I'm trying to say goodbye and I can hardly hear you, Grandma. Can you turn the volume down?"

"Actually, dear, it's not the radio. It's my little friend. I just gave him his first guitar lesson and he's already strumming the strings like a pro. And his voice…isn't it mesmerizing?"

Heather listened some more. "He's really good, Grandma. Is he playing Blossom?"

"Sure as shootin'. Blossom has come out of her case and I couldn't be happier!"

"I remember how you used to play for me, Grandma. I miss it."

"I miss it, too, dear. But now I have someone who can take over where I left off. Next time you're here, I'll have my friend serenade us." Lily then cupped the phone and whispered loudly. "After all that's happened to this poor child, he just found out his foster mom is giving him up for adoption soon. So I'm going to see about taking him in."

"You're what?! They're not going to let you take care of a youngster, Grandma."

"Oh, my, yes. We both had such a nice visit," Lily said, ignoring Heather's comment. "Call me when you get back to California, dear. Love you, too. Bye bye." Then she promptly hung up the phone, shuffled over to Presley, and gave him a pat on the back. "Good job. With those three chords I taught you today, C, F, and G7, you can play a slew of songs."

Lily watched as Presley molded his hand around the neck of Blossom, pressing three of his fingers down onto separate strings along three different frets. "You're a pro at playing that guitar, young man. I can't wait to book your first official gig with the seniors. Next time you come over I'll teach you an Elvis tune. That way you can wow us old bitties and baldies all over again."

Presley smiled, but it wasn't his usual. There was no denying his fear of the unknown, what family he'd be placed with next and where. Disappointment, dismay and dread… interwoven distress that, to a boy of ten, equaled disaster. Lily empathized, losing her smile to quivering lips. She rummaged through her sheet music, giving her star student the song she'd written, "The Daisy Field." Humming the tune once through, she then told Presley, "It's an easy one. Look over the lyrics and we'll practice it next time."

Saturday was going to be a fun day. When Thomas learned that Presley's father had been shot, he had it in his sights to bring the boy a little happiness. His own father had been killed when he was a teen and Thomas felt that an upbeat distraction might help diminish the doom and gloom that suddenly sets in when death dismembers a family.

"I'm taking you to see the Harlem Globetrotters," Thomas decreed in an excited, higher than usual pitch. "See here, I got us tickets for Saturday's game. You'd better be comin' with me, Presley. I had to dip into my savings to buy these. They're some of the best seats in the house. And I'm told Meadowlark Lemon is going to be playing."

Presley smiled faintly and said, "Thanks, Thomas. I wouldn't miss it for anything."

But then *anything* didn't include getting kidnapped.

It was nighttime. No moon. They were waiting in line outside the Chicago Stadium on Madison. Thomas was engaged in a friendly conversation with a gentleman his size, another coach who was a huge basketball fan. The cavorting jabber of the countless people making their way into the arena was dissonant. A multitude of bodies in constant motion lent itself to snatching one out of the mix. With Thomas' back turned, the opportunity was ripe and thus taken. Suddenly out of nowhere a dark clothed figure lunged forward and grabbed Presley. Though the child let go of a faint squeal, no one noticed.

When Thomas turned around, the boy was gone. His yells and shouts for Presley proved useless. As the seconds ticked away, his heart ran a pounding marathon. Those around Thomas appeared disturbed; they were primed for frolic not frenzy. And so, getting out of line and pushing his way through the masses, Thomas finally located a police officer. The patrolman wasn't able to leave his post, but he offered to assist if the boy was still missing once all the fans were inside the stadium. That was nowhere soon enough for Thomas! He knew damn well that Presley was not one to wander off. The boy was not just missing; he'd been stealthily seized and abducted. Darting in all directions, Thomas scoured the neighboring streets and alleyways. When he came up empty-handed he sat on the curb and sobbed.

Thomas was not the only one crying that night. Presley was, too. He'd been yanked away by a ghastly gorilla of a man, captured and thrown into a van with a bag over his head, and hauled off to an unknown place of terror. The drive was brief, which gave Presley a smidgeon of hope. *At least I'm still in Chicago,* he resolved. When the van doors swung open, again he was strong-armed. He heard two voices, cussing and threatening. Oddly, he sensed one of his captors. Upon being shoved into a cold, cement basement and the bag being removed from his head, he was able to confirm what he felt sure of—Grenade was there!

"Ah, so we meet again. What 'sup, my little dog walker?"

Incensed Presley screamed, "I am not your dog walker!"

"Now is that any way to talk around the head boss man?"

Presley shot his gaze over to the burly beast. "You killed my father! You're the one who shot him!"

"Tsk, tsk..." Grenade chided, "We were afraid of that...a nark on the loose."

"Why'd you do it?" Presley choked. "Why'd you have to kill him?"

The apish gestapo broke his silence, stammering in a bass staccato. "He...he saw me...take out the...the store owner. Had to kill... kill him, too."

"So you put the gun in my dad's hand...like he did it? You coward!" Presley wailed.

Grenade raised a fist. "Jump back, dog walker! Nix tossing out bogus names, 'specially when you know zilch about what's going down. This man here is The Boot. Head honcho in charge of honcho affairs. He's the baddest bomb around! Don't *ever* call him a coward!"

"Yeah!" the gorilla trumpeted. Then he stupidly admitted, "I...I used my piece to kill both dweebs. Th...the store owner first... 'cause he started it. He was going to whack me, so I pulled my...my piece out. Then the other bro…he comes in the store…and…and it was like sick! Had to n…nail him, too, or the dude woulda ratted on me. Back at ya, narkies!" The Boot bellowed. "Yeh, then after slammin' 'em I…I picked up the owner's gun with the sl…sleeve of my…my jacket and I…I put it in the other dude's hand. Rad, huh? The fuzz can't pin Jack squat on me. No prints, no..."

Grenade continued, "When The Boot gave me the skinny on what went down, he said he saw a punk barge into the store as he was truckin' out the back. It had to be you, dog walker, because you were doing the drop-off that night. But just to make sure we got the right kid, I cruised around your usual dog walking turf until The Boot pointed you out."

"And yep, y…you're the nark," The Boot said, aiming his trigger-tugging finger.

"So, little dog walker, you blew it. You botched things up royal. And now it's your turn to pay."

Presley lowered his head, defeated and tremulous. A single tear fell as he awaited his bullet.

"Aw, shucks. Lookie there," Grenade teased. "He's actually shaking with fear." The druggie raised his hands to show that they were empty. "Did I say I was going to shoot you, little dog walker? You think I'm that bad, that restracto?"

The Boot howled, evoking base echoes.

"Nah, you're too cute, too nice, too much of a wuss to kill off pronto." Grenade said in a sissy voice, "Ewww, I'd have nightmares of you whining in my ear… 'Don't shoot me. Don't shoot me.'"

"So what's the p..plan?" The Boot asked eagerly.

"This hellhole you're in is like solitary confinement," Grenade explained to his captive. "Nobody's going to find you. You can scream your guts out and even the pig patrolling this section of The Green won't hear you. Sure, it's a drag down here. And you'll probably die of hunger…maybe freeze to death…either way you *will* expire." Grenade exaggerated a yawn. "But don't have a cow. Shine it on. That's life."

The Boot gurgled with excitement. "Yeh, p…power to the people, Grenade! Y…you tell 'em!"

Glowering at Presley, Grenade said with finality, "Sorry, kid. Can't say we'll be seein' ya 'round the block, but it's been nice knowin' ya…my little dog walker."

As the definitive sound of a door being shut and bolted resonated throughout the stark, frigid parameters, Presley shivered and snapped, "I'm *not* your little dog walker."

❀

When Thomas finally shook off the throes of tumult and shock, he hailed a cab and returned to Silver Trails. Only Rosie was there; the rest of the staff had gone home for the night. Spilling his guts, writhing in guilt and begging for forgiveness, he pleaded for presto-resolve. Waving his big mitts like a lunatic he repeated, "What're we going to do, Rosie? What're we going to do?"

"First we're going to call the police. This is no accident, no fluke kidnapping. Presley was taken by those druggies, the same ones who shot his foster dad."

"But how are the police going to find him? There are no eyewitnesses. I didn't see anybody snatch the boy. And it happened right under my nose! They're pros, Rosie." Thomas put his beefsteak palms to his brow. "Oh, my God. He may already be dead. What have I done?!"

"Now don't go thinking like that, Thomas. We've got to stay positive. Presley's still alive and we're going to find him. Don't beat yourself up. Even if you did turn your back for a split second, you're not the bad guy. Whoever nabbed Presley is! And we've got to see that he isn't struck down like his father. Come with me. The phone in the hallway's for emergencies."

The police came in a hurry, but like Thomas figured, there was little to go on. They drove back to Madison and searched high and low. When the basketball game let out, fans were questioned as they departed, but nobody knew anything about a missing ten-year-old boy. Shortly after eleven o'clock Thomas suggested they revisit the deli where the store owner and Presley's foster dad were killed. The shop was boarded up. No one was loitering about. Another dead-end, or so it seemed, until a mangy homeless man shuffled out of the Laundromat next door. "Willie!" Thomas called forth.

Groveling, Willie repeatedly bowed like a bobblehead. "Oh, hello, tall friend. Hello, officers. How are you three doing on this star-studded evening?"

Shunning the maggot's greeting, one of the officer's said, "You been here all night?"

"Why yes, officer. Right here doing laundry."

The policeman eyed the disheveled man and said, "Doubtful."

"So, did you see anything strange going on?" the second officer asked.

Willie considered the question and noted, "There're always strange things happening around these parts. So strange, in fact…I should write a book."

The officer twirled his nightstick and said, "Let me be a little more specific…did you see anyone shady hanging out by the deli or anyone rustling a young boy around?"

Thomas interjected, "You remember the busboy at Silver Trails, right? The kid by the name of Presley?"

"Oh, yeah. I already told the police about him. He was around when the two guys next door got whacked."

"Right. But now he's been kidnapped. Probably by the thug who killed his father."

"Oh, well, I haven't seen the kid; haven't seen that dog of his neither." Willie scratched his bristly chin. "Felt sorry for that wiry mutt. After hearing the gunshots, it flipped out. Ran around like somebody cut its tail off. In and out of the deli, barking, yapping, then in and around the Laundromat. It was weird…almost like it'd seen a ghost. You know, you might do yourself a favor by getting that dog to help you search for the child. If that busboy is anywhere near here, that dog's sniffer is sure to track him down."

"You're a genius!" Thomas proclaimed, giving Willie an over-zealous pat on the back. He reached in his pant pocket and pulled out a couple of bills. "Here, you've been a big help to us. Don't spend it all in one place." Then gesturing to the policemen, Thomas said in no uncertain terms, "We've got work to do, gentlemen!"

But midnight put the search on hold. The policemen dropped Thomas off at his apartment and agreed to meet him back at Silver Trails the next day. In the meantime Thomas plotted a strategy triggered by Willie's brilliance. He would ask Dickie and Violet to borrow Boomer and for Sal to loan him Squirt and Chimp. With their fine-tuned senses certainly canine intervention was in order. Watch dogs, search dogs, rescue dogs...dogs for the handicapped... they'd made careers for canines because of their keen sight, smell, and auditory perception. Why not bring the three pooches to the plate and put their natural abilities to the test? As Thomas lay in bed, hoping to find repose, he thought to himself, *I just hope if the dogs can find Presley, that he's still alive.*

The next morning Presley's foster mom was banging on the door of Silver Trails. "Where's the boy?" she hollered.

Rosie who was all the way in the back of the building heard the pounding and hurried to the front door. "What're you doing out here making so much noise? It's Sunday morning. Our residents sleep in."

"Where's Presley? Are you hiding him here?"

Rosie secured her hands on her hips in the don't-mess-with-me stance. "No, ma'am, he's not here."

"Isn't he supposed to set tables this morning?"

"Yes, but he hasn't shown up yet." Rosie scanned the mother's face. There was a hint of concern lingering there, so Rosie continued, "Actually, we're a little worried. Apparently he's gone missing again."

"Missing? But he can't be missing. I'm taking a half day off so I can drop him back at DCFS tomorrow."

"So, that's your only worry?" Rosie seethed with disgust, "Never mind that Presley might be in serious trouble or maybe even dead?"

"Who'd want to harm Presley?"

"Maybe the monster who killed your husband!"

"My husband was in the wrong place at the wrong time."

Rosie scolded with a furious finger. "You don't deserve to be a parent, know that? It's one hell of a shame that Presley ended up in your care."

"I did my best."

"No, you didn't. What you gave that child in the way of love and support was meager at best. You're the one who reaped the rewards. Presley cleaned and cooked for you. Tended a beautiful garden outside..."

"Oh, those flowers. Nobody asked him to plant those..."

"He worked here so that he could help out with the family finances. He protected you by trying to keep the peace between you and that drunken husband of yours... "

"I think I've heard enough." Turning her back to leave, the mother said, "If he shows up, tell him to get his butt home in a hurry."

"What home?!" Rosie said, shutting the door forcibly.

Along with a gusty wind, at eight o'clock sharp, Thomas blew in. He raced to the kitchen and, while tending to his chores, filled Tony in on what had transpired the night before; then in the same breath relayed to Rosie his plan to locate Presley. His excitement was contagious. Tony pleaded to join him in the search while Rosie agreed to hold down the fort. All of a sudden the kitchen crew was stirring up a rapturous recipe for rescue.

"First, we have to speak with the dog owners," Thomas began.

"I'm sure they'll be fine with you borrowing their pets," Rosie insisted, "Especially if it means finding Presley."

"What about the police?" Tony asked. "Have they already given up on the search?"

"No, they're meeting me here," Thomas noted. "But truthfully, I think they're better off looking on their own. I worry about the kidnapper spotting a cop car patrolling the area. It could work against us."

"Well, then," Rosie said, "You get the okay on using the dogs and I'll explain to the police when they come that you're out conducting a canine search."

"It's a deal!" Thomas confirmed with a bark. "Come on, Tony, we'll talk to Sal first."

Sal was still in his toasty flannel pajamas when Thomas and Tony appeared at his door. "Ah, to what do I owe this early morning visit, gentlemen?" he asked sleepily.

"We're hoping you'll let us borrow your dogs, sir," Thomas said politely.

"At this hour?" Sal asked, his expression askance.

Tony chimed in, "Yes, sir. You see we need to find Presley and your dogs…"

"Wait a minute," Sal gasped. "You mean to tell me Presley is missing *again*?"

"Yes, sir." Thomas replied, trying to maintain his composure. "Last night while we were waiting in line at the Chicago Stadium he was kidnapped right out from under me. I searched everywhere and the police helped me, but we still didn't find the boy. Then Willie, that hungry vagabond who comes 'round here begging for scraps, he shows up outside the deli and suggests that we get the dog that was with Presley the night his father was shot."

"But that was Boomer, Violet and Dickie's dog."

"Think about it," Thomas said, now an astute 007 agent rather than a bumbling Maxwell Smart. "Your two dogs also know Presley well. They were with him that first evening Presley didn't come back on time. Maybe these two incidents are related. Either way, I think your dogs can help us. Their senses are so much better than a human's."

"And if we take them along Presley's usual walking routes," Tony attested, "and then all the way over to where the shooting occurred at Mangiatti's, perhaps they'll pick up on his scent."

"Well, of course you can take Squirt and Chimp. But I want to come along, too."

Thomas cast his gaze downward. "No offense, sir. But I think it would be better if you leave this to Tony and me. We don't want anyone getting hurt."

"Plus I'll probably hold you up," Sal acknowledged. "Dang, I wish I wasn't so old!"

"Don't worry, sir," Tony appeased. "You're helping us out immensely as it is. We can handle the rest."

A jolting notion rocketed through Sal. "Wait, it just occurred to me! I told Lily this, but I didn't report it to the police like I probably should've." Intent, Sal relayed, "A few days ago, right after the shooting, I saw a big man loitering around in the alleyway. He kept peering into Elvis's apartment and then back at the flower beds. I found it odd that he cared anything about the daisies because at this time of year, there's next to nothing in those planter boxes. I assumed the man was either a vagabond or hobo looking for a spot off the street where he could rest, find a little shelter from the rain. Or else he was some drunken bum on a binge. But then, lands, he could've been a criminal who was casing the joint." Sal lowered his head. "Damn, what an idiot! I should've picked up the phone and called the police right then and there!"

"That's okay, sir," Tony said. "Can you tell us anything more about the man?"

"It was getting dark out so I couldn't see a whole lot. He was big, though..."

"How tall do you think he was, sir?" Thomas asked.

"About six feet...maybe a few inches more. Your height, maybe."

"And when you say 'big,' did he have a muscular build?"

"No, more stocky than muscular. He had dark clothing on and was bundled up in a parka, but you could sense that he was wide around the gut and broad at the shoulders."

"Black, white, Hispanic?"

"Don't know. Never saw his face and he was wearing a ski cap so his hair was covered. I'm sorry. I wish I could offer more."

"No, really. Thank you," Thomas said. "We'll be on the lookout and we'll let the police know about your sighting, too."

Sal turned and reached for the leashes. As he did, Squirt and Chimp charged forward, jumping and licking and yapping. "They sure love to walk. Keep 'em going as long as you like. As long as you need..."

Tony noticed Sal's eyes were tearing up. "Don't worry, sir. We'll keep going until we find Presley."

It took Violet a while to respond to the knocks on her door. Finally opening up, she rubbed her swollen, gritty eye lids and groaned, "What time is it?"

"We're sorry to bother you, ma'am. But we have a favor to ask of you," Thomas said.

"So early? What's today?" Violet wondered, her hands now patting down spikes of hair that had her looking like a gray rooster.

"It's Sunday," Tony responded, knowing full well that he and Thomas were tight-roping a fine line between rousing the residents and letting them get their rest.

"But we don't have to be down for breakfast until later on Sunday mornings."

"Right, ma'am. But this has nothing to do with breakfast," Thomas said. "We need to borrow Boomer."

The conversation went on as it had with Sal. Once Violet woke up a little and was able to absorb all the particulars, she willingly offered up her pet as yet another canine search and rescue avenger. And thus they were off—Thomas, Tony and the three duty-driven dogs! Before hitting the streets, Tony made a prudent observation.

"I think before we start we should get something of Presley's that the dogs can sniff...sort of reacquaint them with his smell and alert them to what they're looking for."

"Good idea. I saw them do that on an old episode of *Rin Tin Tin*. They gave the German Shepherd a missing girl's sweater, which helped the dog find her."

"Funny, I remember that show, but I thought it was *Lassie*." Tony paused and then asked, "What time is it? I wonder if Presley's foster mom is even up this early."

"You'd think she'd be pacing the floors praying for the boy's return. Forget her!"

"Agreed. Hey, I know. Didn't Lily give Presley a guitar lesson recently?"

"Yeah...on Friday."

"How could I forget," Tony said, grinning with a vicarious memory of the afternoon. "Presley burst into the kitchen after his lesson and rattled on about that guitar Lily gave him for…oh… maybe ten minutes. I think he called it Blossom. Man, was he jazzed! Even after he went into the dining room to set tables, he was still babbling on about that instrument." Tony tugged on the leash he was gripping and suggested, "I think we should go back upstairs and knock on one more door."

"Wake up another resident?" Thomas said with a worried scrunch to his brow.

"Yes, Lily loves that boy. I'm sure she wouldn't mind us waking her up."

And Lily didn't. Lickety-split she pulled the guitar out of its case. As she held Blossom nice and close, the three dogs yelped and got their sniffs in. "Here," she ordered. "Here's the sheet music Presley was holding. Smell that. Oh, and this is the pick he used to strum the strings. It's little, but come take a whiff." Looking up at Thomas and Tony, discouraged, the senior said, "I wish I had something more, like a jacket he left behind."

"That's all right, ma'am. I think the dogs got enough of a smell," Tony noted.

"Oh, wait! He left a comb here so that he could tidy up before going downstairs to help with dinner." Holding the plastic piece so the canines could get their fill, Lily smiled and said with certainty, "That did the trick. They know what they're looking for now." Handing over the comb she pleaded, "Find him…please!"

As a team, Tony and Thomas declared in unison, "We will!"

After six hours of searching, they were proven wrong. Presley was nowhere to be found!

Chapter Eighteen

Watering at night, an invitation to blight

Chomping on a peanut, Presley set his mind to what he was going to do when he had nothing left to eat. Talking to himself he said, "I'm lucky I stuck these in my pocket to take to the basketball game." He looked down at his salty hand and then at the nearly empty bag. "Man, there's only…one, two…" Counting in silence, he added them up and said aloud, "…eleven left. Then what am I going to do?" He broke open one more shell and popped the two bitty pieces in his mouth. "No more. I have to save some in case I'm down here a while."

Then he remembered something from one of his history lessons, about the Native American Indians. How they lived off the land and when necessary, for survival's sake, ate whatever they could find. Earlier in the day Presley had seen a lizard and a few pill bugs wandering about the cement room. He thought to himself, *it'd be super gross to eat them, but if I get hungry enough, guess I'll have to.* Frowning, the boy got up and walked over to the wall where he'd spotted the lizard. "What I really need is a blanket," he said. "I think I'll freeze down here before I starve to death." He pulled the sleeves of his parka over his bare hands. "Wonder why my hands hurt so much. They should be numb. Maybe its frost bite." Then Presley ordered, "Keep moving! Don't stop!" He proceeded to do jumping jacks. "That's what Mr. Kendall tells us whenever we go out for PE on cold days. 'Get your hearts pumping, kids! Keep that blood moving! Don't stop or you'll freeze!'" Presley counted his jumping jacks and jerked to a halt at one hundred. "That's it. I can't do anymore." He returned to the step where he'd been sitting, placed his head in his hands and cried. "Why can't someone find me?" He started to holler. "Help! Help! Please, someone…anyone…I'm down here! Let me out! Heeeelllppp!!!

Rising and walking the borders of his cement confinement, Presley continued to shout. He continued until he had very little voice left. Woeful, he sat again, this time licking his tears, thirsty enough not to mind their saltiness. Then bundling up into the fetal position, Presley tried to fall asleep. His head, though, was too close to his stomach and it kept gurgling, reminding him of how famished he was. Finally, he sat up and reached into his pocket for the remaining peanuts. Instead he pulled out a piece of paper. "Wrong pocket," he noted. But then through the dim light he eyed the crumpled paper. "Oh, yeah. This is the song Lily wrote." He tried to remember the tune. The voice he had left was a raspy crackle, but he sang anyway. "*He was in the daisy field. Everything there seemed so real. He could laugh, talk, cry or sing. He could do most anything…in the daisy field…*" He repeated the song like it was a lullaby. Then curling up into a little ball, Presley finally found sleep.

❀

"What do you mean you didn't find him?" Sal blasted. "For God's sake, you were out there damn near all day and you've come back empty-handed?"

"We're just as upset as you are," Thomas revealed, running his fingers like they were razors through his curly black hair.

"No clue at all where the boy is?" Sal pressed. He shuffled in fretfulness and then added, "So our dogs turned out to be a total waste of time, is that it?"

"Actually, sir," Tony said, "your two dogs went berserk at a point. They were growling and tugging and turning their heads.

We thought they were on to something…"

"And?" Sal asked with his body aligned like one big question mark.

"We think the dogs may have recognized this one guy who happened to be behind us."

"Were you being followed?"

"Could be," Thomas replied. "But when we turned to face the guy, he fled."

"Was he big like the fellow I said I saw outside Presley's apartment?"

"No," Tony reported, "he had a small build. Young, too. Probably in his late teens or early twenties."

"Why didn't you follow him?"

"We tried to," Tony assured, "but he literally vanished. We backtracked half a block and looked down the alley, but there was just a bunch of kids hanging out, wrestling. They were loud and obnoxious; and one of them kept shouting the word 'grenade.'"

"That was a little too weird," Thomas cut in, "so we got the heck out of there."

"Maybe they're all part of some gang," Sal suggested.

"You might be right," Tony said, "but at that point we didn't exactly feel like taking on the pack."

"Probably smart," Sal agreed. "But if I were you, I'd go back to that location because, my dogs may be yappers, but they don't growl and bark in an uppity way unless something is really wrong."

"Do you want us to go back there now?" Thomas asked. "It's getting dark out."

Tony regarded Thomas with concern. "Hey, bud. It's not safe out there during the day. Why are we going to chance a confrontation at night?"

"You're right, probably too dangerous," Sal said. He paused and decreed, "So, I'll go with Thomas!"

"But, sir…" Tony griped.

"Nope, done. I'm going this time." Sal crossed his arms and gave a compelling nod.

"He means what he says," Thomas confirmed. And as an aside to Tony, he said, "Don't worry, we'll do just fine. That brave old goat and I have tackled the after-hours search before."

"Well, I wish you luck," Tony said with a worrisome sigh. Then so Sal could hear, Tony decreed, "If evil is at play tonight, hopefully you'll be able to crush it before any harm comes to either of you."

"The bigger hope is that we find the boy," Sal said with purpose. Shuffling over to his closet, he pulled out a heavy overcoat, a pair of gloves, and a woolen beanie. "It's freezing out. That poor boy...after last night and now tonight...we simply have to find him! Thomas, grab that throw off my bed. I'll put it around my shoulders. When we find Elvis we can wrap him in it."

Thomas did as instructed while Tony looked on thinking to himself it was doubtful Presley was still alive. Feeling miserably inadequate, Tony returned to the kitchen to inform Rosie that they'd not only be minus their busboy, but their extra cook. Picking up speed while bustling about to cover everyone's bases, Rosie bowed her head and mumbled a prayer.

Downstairs, Lily stood rooted by the front door. She'd gotten word that Sal was intent on joining the search effort. Donning the expression of sending a loved one off to war, she lightly kissed Sal on the cheek and then offered her trusty, compact flashlight, the one she used for late-night reading. Softly she said, "You probably won't want to draw attention to yourselves, but just in case you have to light the way..." Lily then paused to gather herself. "Be careful. And bring our Presley back."

✿

Night had already fallen by the time the determined search duo and their dogs arrived on the scene where, earlier that day, Thomas had seen the group of teens mulling about. Much to their dismay, the alley and back lot were empty. Not even a distant hum of voices could be detected in an area that was usually a magnet to clamorous eruptions. The pervading stillness was a direful signal that disturbed the dogs. They didn't bark or act up as before, but instead slunk low to the ground and pulled on their leashes to leave. As Thomas and Sal retraced their steps out of the vacant lot, they saw a car parked on the street that hadn't been there before. Inside the vehicle a darkly clothed figure sat waiting. With gnawing suspicion Thomas nudged Sal, gesturing that they might be better off retreating *into* the back lot rather than toward the street. That's when Boomer went berzerk, barking and not just growling, but snarling like a savage beast.

Suddenly a monstrous brute got out of the car. As he lumbered forward, Sal recognized him as the man he'd seen outside Presley's apartment. Boomer recognized him, too, because his feral inkling to attack ignited. Sal seethed with loathing. His agitation boiled and he craved assault.

"Stay where you are!" Thomas yelled forth to the menace. "We don't want any trouble."

"Oh, n…no trouble," the threatening hunk stuttered. "It won't be any trouble k…killing you."

Sal pulled out the flashlight and pointed it directly into the encroacher's eyes. "You son of a bitch, tell us where the boy is!"

"He's d…dead by now," the thug stammered, his hands fighting the glare. "Just like you're g…going to be if you don't t…turn that freaking fl…flashlight off."

"You said you're going to kill us anyway, so screw you!" Sal hollered, locking the glare in place. Bending down, he let Boomer off his leash and the dog charged forth with malicious intent. Biting the hoodlum just above the boot, Boomer tasted blood and hungered for more.

"Let the other two go!" Sal shouted.

Thomas unleashed Chimp and Squirt into the pack mentality, both dogs leaping and ripping at the man. An outburst of terror bit through the silence, enticing the werewolf canines all the more. When the ruffian finally buckled over, Thomas took the upper hand.

"Where's Presley?!" he yelled, pounding the assailant to the ground. "What'd you do with him?!"

"We had to get r..rid of him." After being slugged some more, the thug grumbled through his pain, "He was an eyew…witness, okay? W…we had to do it."

"Do what?!" Sal bellowed. "Spit it out! What did you do with him?!"

Suddenly out of nowhere, Sal was forcibly shoved forward. He wasn't able to brace himself, so the fall was fast and ferocious. As he hit pavement, there was an audible crack. A groan of agony escaped, but no further bodily movement followed.

"Take that, you old fart!" Grenade howled as he kicked Sal in the upper back.

Thomas looked on in horror. And because of his hesitation, the man he was wailing on rolled free from bondage, laying a heavy fist into his jaw. Losing his balance and falling backward to the ground, Thomas careened into the pack of dogs. They scattered, yelping in a pained frenzy.

"G…good job, Gr…Grenade," The Boot said with his heavy black boot now atop Thomas's head. "I knew I could c…count on you."

"Told you the dudes I saw earlier today were looking for that kid," Grenade boasted.

"You were r…right."

"So, what're we going to do with them?" the gloating teen asked.

"K..kill 'em and throw 'em in the r…river."

Grenade hedged. "Ya know, Boot, I'm tight, man, when it comes to dealin' for ya, but I'm not much into whacking narks. Maybe we should just lock 'em away like we did the kid."

"Maybe if we'd k…killed the kid we wouldn't be here with these two worthless p…pansies." The Boot jammed his foot down as Thomas let go of a painful grunt. "I say we do 'em in! Hell, that old fogey there, h…he's on his last leg anyway."

"How 'bout I leave the final dirt for you to pound?" Turning sheepish, Grenade said, "Hey, I'm your bro. I've been loyal, right? I deal the drugs and watch your back. I can be bad, Boot, but I'm just not into killing people."

The Boot frowned. Grenade didn't need to see it; he could feel it. Making amends he added, "How 'bout I whack the dogs for you?"

"Okay, but…but you have to do it in fr…front of them."

The dogs' intuition kicked in. Boomer readily transformed into a wimp, cowering a few feet from Thomas. When Grenade took a step toward him, the mutt turned and bolted toward the street. Squirt who was licking Sal's face and Chimp, who was nudging him with his nose, froze in terror. Grenade gingerly tiptoed toward the petrified dogs. He was able to snatch up Squirt, but Chimp scampered off into the darkness of the abandoned lot.

"Not very g…good odds. One d…dog out of three."

"Yeah, well, if you take out those two narks and if I silence this one dog…that's three out of five. Not half bad."

"Don't do it," Thomas muttered in pain.

The Boot crushed his head into the cement again. "Sh…shut the hell up!"

With a death grip on Squirt, Grenade asked, "Got your piece, Boot? Can I borrow it to pump a plug in this here mutt?"

"Yeah, I g…got it on me."

Grenade stepped over Sal who lay in a lump. As he reached for Boot's pistol, Squirt squirmed out of his arms. Dropping the dog, he missed grabbing the gun. The weapon fell to the ground and went off. Suddenly the sound of screeching tires penetrated the street. From the back lot, flashing lights pulsated through the charcoal night.

"It's the fuzz!" Grenade shouted as he fled in panic.

The Boot didn't move. He was dead.

Chapter Nineteen

Eliminate the weeds

Police flew forward through the darkness, swarming like moths to a floodlight. One of them hustled to Sal's side, bending down to check his vitals. Another hovered over Thomas who had puncture wounds from being sandwiched between a boot and the gravely pavement. A second pair ran after Grenade and in no time tackled him, wrestled him to the ground, slapped the handcuffs on, and strong-armed him back to the scene of the crime. The two officers in the car, who had squealed to a halt to avoid hitting Boomer, hurriedly got out and chased the confounded dog. The skittish canine kept running in circles. From afar, the chase appeared comical, like a fractured flicker of old. But nobody was laughing. The vexation was profoundly intense because along with the fallen Boot, Sal lay motionless.

"We need an ambulance," one officer shouted to his compatriots in the street. "Forget the dog! Call for help!"

Just then Boomer jumped in the police car, a gesture of concurrence. The phone call was made and seconds later the shriek of sirens tore through the dire stillness.

Thomas got up achy and slow. His head felt like a watermelon that had been thrown to the ground and split open. But he sensed the severity of Sal's situation, so he rallied and stumbled over to the immersed vigil taking place.

"Sir, don't worry. Help's coming," Thomas assured. "You took a nasty fall, but you're going to be okay. Don't give up on us, sir."

One of the officers shooed Thomas away. "We've got it covered," he said in an authoritative tone. "Let us do our job. Stand back."

Sal finally opened his eyes and mumbled, "He's my friend. I want him here."

Thomas gingerly lowered next to the senior as if he was in church, kneeling in prayer. "I'm glad you're okay, sir. You had me worried."

"Think I'm going to take off on you when we haven't fulfilled our promise yet?" Sal said, gasping for his next breath.

Thomas grinned and gave a thumbs-up.

"Did they get the bad guys?" Sal asked, his quivering lids slowly shutting again.

"The big guy took a bullet. He's a goner. The teen's in custody."

"Are they questioning him?" Sal coughed out, writhing in pain.

Thomas cringed as he absorbed the seriousness of Sal's predicament. He steered himself over to where Grenade was being detained. Informing the officer there, Thomas said, "This kid is the only one who knows where Presley is." He paused, glaring at the teen. "You said you're not a murderer. But if you don't fess up, you will be."

Grenade spat at Thomas's feet. "Get lost. I'm not ratting."

"Who're you trying to protect?" Thomas asked, leaning in. He pointed to The Boot and relayed, "If you hadn't noticed, your fearless leader's dead. It's obvious he's the one who killed your contact in the deli. So who's left in your little drug chain?"

Snide, stubborn silence was all that Grenade would offer.

"Okay, kid," Thomas said. "Guess you'll be arrested for murder, then, because if we don't find Presley tonight, he's sure to be dead. You want that on your conscience? Killing an innocent child?" Thomas stepped back. "What did he ever do to you?" Returning to Sal's side, Thomas reported, "The kid's not talking."

Turning corpse-like, Sal uttered, "Tell him if we don't find the boy, I'll die, too."

"What? No, you're not going to die," Thomas lamented, kneeling again.

Just then a shrieking ambulance pulled up. Carrying a stretcher and a load of medical paraphernalia, the emergency response team descended upon the ailing senior. As they smothered him with first aid, Sal urged with what voice he had left, "Tell the kid I'll die, too, if he doesn't talk."

Jolted, Thomas stormed back to the teen. He grabbed Grenade's arm and shook him. "See that over there? You're responsible. You're going to have two murders on your record. Two deaths to haunt you for the rest of your pitiful life! Know why? Because that old man there is not going to survive the shove you gave him if the boy isn't found. He said so himself. So, what're you going to do?!" Thomas tightened his grip. "Look, kid, dealing drugs is one thing. But killing's another. They're going to lock you up and throw the key away! Got that? You best talk…and *now*!"

Jerking away from Thomas's stronghold, Grenade surrendered. "Okay, I'll talk."

By the time Sal was strapped on the stretcher and being wheeled off to the ambulance, Thomas had the information he needed to rescue Presley. He hustled over to tell Sal, wanting to give him something more to live for. As the doors to the ambulance were being closed, Thomas cried out, "We know his whereabouts. We're going to him now!"

Unable to talk because he'd been strapped with an oxygen mask, Sal raised a triumphant fist.

Thomas mimicked the emboldened gesture and evinced, "We'll find him, sir!"

When Thomas and the accompanying policeman arrived at the designated locale Grenade had divulged to them, they felt overly anxious. They couldn't help but wonder if the area was a thug-infested drug haven where deals that went sour resulted in torturous tragedy. After all, strewn about the dilapidated building were shreds of torn clothing, a pair of smashed sunglasses, an empty cardboard box that'd contained razor blades, broken liquor bottles, brass knuckles, a blood-stained piece of rope and a long chain. When the policeman lowered his flashlight to the cement stairs, there were dark red drippings spattered about and the base of the stairwell was a rat-befouled sewer. The air reeked like it was death-infused. The atmosphere screamed of vulgarity and corruption.

"God, I hope he's still alive," Thomas said, fraught with concern.

"This should be the door," the officer said. "We'll soon find out." Like the stairs, the door was speckled with dried blood. The policeman found an unscathed spot and pounded his fist against it. There was no answer. He tried again. Still no response.

"Here, let me try," Thomas said. He stood as close to the door as possible and hollered, "Presley, are you in there? It's me, Thomas." Silence prevailed, so Thomas continued, "Presley, we're here to rescue you. Please answer me. Are you okay?"

Not hearing a sound, Thomas turned to the officer and snarled, "I wonder if that Grenade lied to us. Maybe this isn't the right place."

"Shhh," the policeman said. "I think I hear something."

Sure enough, when the two listened closely they could hear singing. It was faint and distant, but Thomas knew the voice.

"That's him…Presley!" He started banging on the door. "Presley, it's me, Thomas! We're here to get you out!"

Presley stopped singing. He lifted his head and listened. When he heard thumping on the other side of the thick door his hope was reawakened and he scurried toward the clunking sound. Putting his head against the cold metal block that separated him from his saviors, Presley squealed, "Help me, I'm in here! Please…get me out!"

Thomas was so jazzed he did a jig. The officer looked on in amused disbelief. "That must be the rescue dance, eh?"

"Oh, man, you have no idea how happy I am! And how happy the folks back at Silver Trails are going to be." Thomas kept up with his silly antics, singing, "*Praise the Lord. Oh, praise be our Savior. Blessed is He. He is good. He is kind. He's the grooviest…*"

Finally the policeman, who was already working on breaking down the door, suggested, "A little help would be nice. You can praise God later, okay?"

With Thomas's almighty assistance, within the hour, Presley was freed!

On the way back to Silver Trails, Thomas wrapped Presley up in Sal's coverlet. The child was next to frozen, his fingertips white, his body shaking off hypothermia. The policeman and Thomas were sweating because the car heater was on full blast, but poor Presley continued to shiver.

"So," Thomas praised, "you're some kind of walking miracle, my man. What'd you do to stay alive in there?"

With his mouth frigid and his teeth chattering, he answered, "Three things."

"Really. Want to tell me what they were?"

"Eating peanuts. Practicing my spelling. And singing a song Lily wrote."

Walking through the doors to Silver Trails was going to be like passing through the pearly gates into heaven. Presley was elated to be returning to the place he considered more welcoming than home. Thomas called ahead to alert those anxiously awaiting the boy's arrival. When the patrol car pulled up, there stood Rosie, Lily, Violet, Dickie and Tony huddled together in big overcoats braving the midnight air. Their arms were open and eager to engulf Presley. The homecoming was jubilant, but a splinter in the celebration remained. Lily was the first to get pricked.

"Where's Sal?" she queried, looking in the direction of the police car.

Thomas's smile fell. He wasn't sure how to put it, but finally relayed, "He got hurt."

"Hurt?" Dickie asked. "Like how?"

"Some creep gave him a shove and he fell."

"Is he going to be all right?" Lily asked fretfully.

"Sounded like he may have broken a hip," Thomas replied.

Everyone gasped. Then Rosie said, "Damn those drug dealin' kids! They're nothing but trouble!"

"Do you know where Sal is now?" Lily pleaded.

The policeman stepped forward. "Don't worry, ma'am. The ambulance team took your friend to the hospital. He's in good hands. They'll fix him up and he'll be back in no time."

Thomas absorbed Lily's anxiety. "The officer's right. Sal will be okay. He's really the hero in all of this. He and the dogs helped nail the two main drug dealers. And that led us to finding Presley. If it weren't for Sal, Presley wouldn't be here now."

Joining the bandwagon, Presley eagerly asked, "Can we go see Sal?"

Lily put her arm around the boy, assuaging him. "You've been through enough for one night, son. We'll call in the morning and see when he can have visitors."

"But who's going to watch his dogs? We can't leave Squirt and Chimp alone."

Dickie wheeled himself forward. "I've got it covered, young man. Don't you worry about the dogs. Boomer considers Chimp and Squirt his buddies. They've been through a lot together. They're welcome to stay with us until Sal gets back."

"But can I still walk them?" Presley begged.

At that point, everybody got a good chuckle. Already things were returning to some level of normalcy and that was essential for the child who'd been through hell and back and still had a rocky journey ahead.

That night when the police officer escorted Presley back to his apartment, there was no answer at the door.

"Does your mother work nights?" the officer asked.

"No, sir. She's usually home by six. But don't worry; I know where she hides the key."

"Look, son, if she's not home, you're coming with me. I'm not leaving you alone, especially after what's happened to you the past few days."

"But I've been home alone before, sir. I'll be okay. She's probably at her friend Olive's."

"Trust me, if she's not home at this hour, she's not coming home. At least not tonight."

"Then can you take me back to Silver Trails? Please? Lily will take care of me. I know she will."

"Sorry, son. If you're in foster care, then you have to go back to Care Services until they can find your mom or another family who can take over."

Fessing up, Presley blurted out, "My mom doesn't want me. She already told me that. I'm going back to that adoption place soon anyway. Don't make me go now. Please, sir, Lily wants me. She'll take extra good care of me."

When the policeman shook his head, Presley was once again dissolved in tears.

The next morning came a little too early for everyone concerned. Having only snagged a few hours of sleep, Rosie and her kitchen staff were exhausted. When Presley didn't show up to help with breakfast, Rosie dismissed his absence, saying, "Thank goodness somebody's getting some rest around here." But then when the child didn't show up for his late afternoon shift, she got very concerned. "What more could possibly go wrong with that boy?" she mumbled under her breath.

Tony heard her and said, "Want me to go next door? Make sure he's all right?"

Rosie nodded. "Please do. I just got to know he's safe."

When Tony returned to say that there was no answer at the apartment and the place looked vacant, Rosie dropped her apron and charged out of the kitchen. She didn't usually move quickly, so anyone who spotted her barreling down the hallway did their utmost to clear a path for her. Upon getting to Lily's door, Rosie banged hard, hollering, "Ma'am, it's me, Rosie! I need a moment. Please open up!"

Lily was roused from her power nap, frazzled and drowsy. "I'm coming. Just a minute." Upon opening the door, Lily knew immediately that something had gone wrong...*again*. "What is it now, Rosie? Is it Sal?"

"No, ma'am. It's Presley."

"Well, he wasn't at breakfast, but surely that's because he's home resting and getting back to normal."

"No, ma'am. I'm afraid not. Tony just went over there and nobody's home, the mother or the boy."

"I knew I should've stepped in sooner!"

"Me, too!" Rosie said in a huff. "That mother of his, turns out she's been no help at all. I know she lost her husband, but not to care for the boy? If you ask me, that's bullshit!" Rosie abruptly covered her mouth.

"Don't worry. I couldn't agree more! Let me get on the phone, Rosie. I'm going to phone that department of wayward kids or whatever they call that agency. Been meaning to do it for a few days now. It's just that lately everything's been cattywampus around here. Don't know if I'm coming or going. But I do know this...I want to adopt that child!"

Rosie was agog. "Really, you do? But how? Will they let someone like you adopt?"

Lily chuckled and said, "You mean someone *my* age?"

"I didn't mean it in that way, ma'am."

"I know you didn't, Rosie. I'm just joshing with you. And, hey, the only way to find out if they'll let me adopt, is for me to ask."

Standing alert and taking a deep breath, to the point she nearly burst a button, Rosie announced, "And if they don't let you adopt, then maybe they'll let me. I haven't played Mommy for a long time, but I'm sure I could take care of Presley. That boy has managed to find a warm spot in my soul. He's more than welcome to do the same in my home."

"We might have to fight over him," Lily said with a determined grin, dukes up.

"You'd have me down for the count in no time," Rosie jested. "Nah, they'll be no fightin' over Presley. That child's seen enough trouble and misery to last a lifetime."

"Yes, what he really needs is stability." Lily whisked back her bed-head hair and said with authority, "And I'm going to find that for him." Hurriedly hobbling over to her bedside stand, looking like she'd suddenly downed a dozen cups of coffee, the energized senior grabbed her reading glasses, picked up the phone book, and speedily flipped through the yellow pages. "Here it is!" she exclaimed pointing a knotted, arthritic finger at bold print. Dialing at warp speed, she sang out, "Get ready 'cause Granny's comin' at ya!"

Gradually the enthusiasm Lily exuded waned. Having been put on hold for over ten minutes, she finally covered the receiver and told Rosie, "You best get back to the kitchen. I'll fill you in later. Who knows how long this is going to take."

Rosie trudged back to her duties downstairs, clucking like a sassy, sauced-up chicken. "Something good better come of this!"

It was late in to the supper hour when Lily finally showed up in the dining room. She was last to be seated and last to be served. Rosie tended to the task because there was no busboy on board to help.

"What did they say?" Rosie asked as she poured Lily some water.

"Can you believe after all that time on the phone, I know little more about Presley than the fact that he's safe and presently in a group home."

"And what about your adopting him?"

"They asked if I was a relative and I said no. I think the woman thought I was a grandparent at first. Anyway, then the lady listed a litany of things. She said I'd have to make an appointment and an agency rep would come to my home to determine if foster care or adoption was the right thing for me and my family. Of course, I didn't divulge that I live in a senior residence surrounded by a bunch of over-the-hillers. So, the gal blabbed on about applications and medical forms that each of my family members would have to fill out. Once those are analyzed, and if you pass "go," then there's a criminal background investigation to include fingerprinting and reference checks. And finally, if all the necessary criteria are met, then you get to enroll in training classes. The whole process can take up to six months!"

"Doesn't sound like we have a chance in hell," Rosie said.

"Well, maybe not. Nonetheless I'm going to take a cab over there tomorrow and speak to someone in person."

"But you've never left Silver Trails alone before."

"I won't be; you're coming with me. I plan to stop by the hospital to see how Sal's doing, too."

"But how am I going to get the time off?"

"Don't worry; I'll arrange it with Mr. Taylor. After breakfast is cleaned up, Tony can take over in the kitchen. You get gussied up and meet me in the front hallway at ten o'clock. That should give you plenty of time, right?"

"Yes, ma'am!" Rosie said, honored to be included.

He'd been in the group home less than twenty-four hours, and though he was being treated kindly, Presley felt depressed and abandoned. He had to wonder, *what did I do to be subjected to feeling miserably alone all over again? Wasn't the dungeon punishment enough for me?*

"Why can't I just go home?" he asked, badgering the representative who'd been assigned to his case. She was cute and nice, but just too perky for the mood he was in.

"Because there's no one *at* your home," the rep repeated for the umpteenth time. "And we cannot leave you with a family that isn't properly caring for you."

"I know, I read your brochure while I was sitting outside. You call it abuse or neglect. But, ma'am, I'm not talking about the home or the family you think I am; I'm talking about Silver Trails."

"I'm sorry," the agent said, glancing down at a manila folder lying atop her lap. "I see nothing in your file regarding a place called Silver Trails. Perhaps that's the name of your housing complex? Or is it perchance a favorite amusement park you frequented with your foster parents?"

Presley slumped forward, deflated. "Never mind."

Raising her chipper voice a notch higher, the rep said, "Don't worry, we'll find you another home soon. And we'll make sure the family is reputable and devoted to taking care of your special needs."

"But I don't have special needs. I just want to go back to Silver Trails."

Presley sighed, but the agent wasn't listening. Her bouncy, can't-sit-still legs had toppled the boy's folder to the ground. Bending down to gather up the paperwork she noticed an index card paper-clipped to one of the forms. The notation on it read, "Heather Hawthorne…birth mother." A phone number was scribbled below the name and then the note instructed, "Call if a return-home ever becomes a possibility." The agent who'd written the message had jotted down her name and extension also.

"Well, now," the rep said, rising like a helium balloon headed skyward, "Looks like we have a little leg work to do before we send you anywhere, young man."

Chapter Twenty

Stakes and other supports

Heather had endured a hectic day in the courtroom when she got home to find her phone ringing off the wall. She was tired and did not want to answer, but finally had to succumb because the ringing was headache-driven and frantic. Chucking her purse on the kitchen counter, she grabbed the receiver and anchored herself on a barstool.

"Hello!" she barked.

"Is this Mrs. Malcolm Hawthorne?" a cordial voice asked.

In a less predatory tone, Heather said, "Yes, this is she."

"Hello, ma'am, this is the Department of Care and Family Services in Chicago, Illinois."

Heather's heart flipped over and over like a little poodle doing tricks for treats.

"Ma'am, are you there?"

"Yes, yes, I'm here. Do you have my son? Is that why you're calling?"

"Well, we have a note in our files that indicates you were here asking about a certain child."

"Is he all right?" Heather pleaded to know.

"Oh, yes. If we're talking about the same boy, yes, he's fine. He's between foster families, that's all. Looks like his first adoptive parent turned him back to us and now there have been issues with his second foster family. We aim for early permanency, which includes a child's return home, adoption, or guardianship. Obviously, the ultimate goal is to return a child to his or her birth parents, as long as they are willing and capable of caring for that child."

"Oh, trust me, my husband and I are perfectly willing and capable."

"So you are married to the boy's birth father?"

"Yes. We got married after I gave the child up for adoption." Heather felt like she needed to connect the dots. "It was a huge mistake on my part to give the child up at all. But at the time we weren't married and I was a teenager. I had no means of properly caring for the boy." There was no response, so Heather underlined, "Giving up our son was the biggest mistake I've ever made in my life! I was young and foolish. I've regretted it ever since and if there's even the remotest chance of our connecting with our child again, I'd...I'd do *anything*!"

"I can tell from your voice, Mrs. Hawthorne, that you mean what you say. But before we're able to release the child into your custody, we will need to meet with you in person. You're on the West Coast, correct?"

Heather was practically panting. "Yes, but I can book a flight out as soon as possible. I'm positive my husband will want to accompany me. So, we'll both come."

"That would be ideal," the agent said, exalted. In her three years at DCFS only once had she been lucky enough to reunite a foster child with his birth parents. It was the quintessential highlight of her job and she couldn't wait to do it again. "Please ask for me. My name is Laurel Williams. I really look forward to your reunion with Presley."

"Me, too!" Heather exclaimed. As she hung up with the agent, her fingers were poised and positioned to dial Malcolm. When her husband picked up, Heather broadcast as though she had a megaphone, "We're getting Presley back!"

Malcolm could tell it was exciting news, but confounded he asked, "Presley? Is Elvis back in town?"

"No, silly! Presley…our *son*!"

When Malcolm walked in the door later that evening he had an armful of peach-colored roses.

"Oh," Heather gushed, "for me?"

"They're your favorite. You're my favorite. Life is starting to bloom and it's time to celebrate!" Malcolm set the long-stemmers in the sink and turned to embrace his ebullient spouse. "Know what? You are radiant tonight. Absolutely glowing. I don't think I've ever seen you this happy."

"Well, who wouldn't be? We're about to become a family. A *family*…just saying the word sends me into a tizzy!"

"So when do we leave?"

"I booked us a flight to Chicago early tomorrow. We can visit Grandma Lily over the weekend and be at the front door of DCFS first thing Monday morning."

Malcolm ushered Heather into the family room. He settled down on the couch and gestured for her to sit on his lap.

"What's up?" she asked, slightly worried. "You can get the time off, right?"

"It's not that." Malcolm hesitated momentarily as he gathered his thoughts. "I've been mulling something over for a while and I think now's a good time to bring it up." Looking deep into Heather's eyes he said, "I think we should move back to Chicago."

Lily and Rosie were first in line when the doors of DCFS opened. Even still they were told to take a seat in the waiting room. Looking around, most everybody was at least a decade younger than Rosie and that meant thirty-plus years less than Lily.

"Guess they don't get too many grandmas wanting to adopt," Lily whispered.

"Don't mean to offend," Rosie responded, "but you could be a great-grandma to Presley. I'm more the grandma age. And I've got the gray hair to prove it."

"At least your hair's not white yet. Between my skin and hair color they could lose me in a snowstorm."

Rosie chortled from the gut, which drew curious stares. Annoyed that the two of them were being sized-up, Lily finally stared back, removing the glued gazes. About five minutes later a young lady toward the back of the bustling room, rose from her desk and approached them. "Hello, my name is Laurel. I'll be the one helping you today. Please follow me." Turning around the rep trotted off like a horse out of the gate.

"Can't walk quite that fast," Lily alerted.

"Oh, I apologize," Laurel said, slowing down. "I'm used to people racing through these hallways."

To Rosie, Lily noted, "We're older than antiques."

Laurel glanced over her shoulder and smiled. "That's all right. There's no age limit and you're more than welcome here." Arriving back in her corner of the department, Laurel gestured for Rosie and Lily to have a seat. She daintily slid into her chair. "So, how can I help you two ladies?"

"My name is Lily. This is Rosie. And we'd like to adopt."

"Both of you?"

"Well, if you won't let me 'cause I'm too old, then Rosie here said she'd be willing."

"And what has stirred you to come in? Have you always wanted to adopt?"

Rosie sat taller and said, "This isn't about adopting just any child, miss. We have a specific boy in mind."

Lily added, "Yes, we've come to know him well. He practically lives at our home."

Laurel looked perplexed, querying, "You both live in the same place?"

"No, I don't live there," Rosie offered. "I work there." Under her breath she added, "Sometimes it feels like I live there, though."

More confused, Laurel stated, "Okay, so you, Rosie, work at the home where you, Lily, live. Is there anyone else that lives or works in this home of yours?"

Rosie looked at Lily and shrugged. "I think at last count we totaled forty-seven residents and eleven employees."

Laurel's eyes grew planetary. "That many?"

"Yes," Lily continued, "and they all know and adore this young man we're referring to. He's been a gift to all of us."

"Where does the boy live?"

"He used to live next door," Rosie started.

"But then his father got shot and his mother no longer wanted the responsibility," Lily finished.

Laurel put her hands to her head. "I'm sorry. I'm so confused."

"Don't be," Lily said. "It's all pretty simple when you know the whole story."

Laurel leaned to the side, looking down the hallway into the already crowded waiting room. Then she glanced at her watch. "You've got five minutes. Give me the scoop."

For the next five minutes Lily regaled the rep with tale after tale of how special and important the boy they wanted to adopt was. When Lily finally mentioned Presley's name, Laurel jerked forward in her chair.

"Wait a minute! Presley? That's not a very common name."

"No," Lily said, "and Presley is not your usual child. Like we've been saying he's unique and very dear to us."

"I'm sure he is. But what I mean," Laurel gasped, "is I just finished talking with Presley's mother. There can't be two children by the name of Presley in our system."

"You're not referring to his first adoptive mom, are you?" Lily queried.

"No, not his second foster mom, either," Laurel offered.

Suddenly Lily slouched down in her chair. "His real mom, eh? So why, after all these years does the real mother want Presley back again?"

"She claims she never wanted to give him up in the first place." Noticing her clients' sudden disappointment, Laurel continued, "It happens more often than you might think. Especially when the birth mother is a teen and she has no way of caring for her baby. In this case, the birth mother and father married later on. They're still together, wanting to reclaim the only child they've been able to have so that they can be a family."

"Well, their story sounds real," Rosie quipped. "But it'd better be because this boy has already been through so much. He can't possibly take any more hurt."

"Yes, I agree. Enough's enough. When I spoke with the child yesterday he seemed fairly distraught. Now that I think about it, he kept repeating that he wanted to go home. And then he said, '… back to Silver Trails.'"

"That's us," Rosie enthused. "It's a senior assisted residence. I'm the head cook at the home. Presley's our busboy."

"And I live there," Lily added.

"Okay, now it's all starting to make sense. No wonder the child wants to go back. Sounds like he's got a very supportive, loving family there."

"That he does," Lily confirmed. "So, when is Presley going to be returned to his real parents?"

"They're flying here to meet with us first thing next week."

"And where is Presley going to stay until then?"

"Where he is now, in one of our group homes."

Lily grabbed Rosie's hand. The two exchanged knowing glances. Then resolute, they said in unison, "We'll take him."

"But I just finished explaining…"

"No," Lily interrupted. "Not for good. Just for a day or two. Or at least until his real parents come for him."

"But I can't let you have…"

"Why not?" Rosie pressured. "He knows us. He wants to be with us. He *needs* us."

"And we need him," Lily emphasized.

"But there's a mound of paperwork and reference checks and training…"

"You already told me that on the phone…" Lily broke in.

"That was you I spoke to the other day?" Laurel asked. "I thought I recognized your voice."

"You mean my old grandmotherly tone? Yep, that was me," Lily said.

Laurel heaved a sigh. "Well, it's very apparent that you deeply care about Presley and have his best interests in mind. I'm not sure, but let me discuss this with my superior. Perhaps because Presley has his busboy job at Silver Trails and he's already spent so much time there, maybe we can make an exception."

"Maybe for the time being, our group home can serve as an alternate to *your* group home," Lily suggested. "Bottom line, we're talking about a brief stay. Quite frankly I wish he could move in permanently. But just to have the boy back in our midst for a few days will be a blessing."

"That's right," Rosie agreed. "Everybody's been so worried about him. They'll be glad to know he's going to be reunited with his real parents, but they'll be even happier if they can give him a proper farewell."

Laurel stood with resolve. "All right, ladies. I said I was here to help and that's what I'm going to do. I shall return!"

They weren't sure how their superstar rep was able to finagle matters, but by midday Lily and Rosie had a beaming Presley sandwiched between them, holding his hands, and leading him out of the departmental hustle into a cab headed for their next stop...the hospital.

"There's a candy store half a block from Northwest Memorial," Lily told the cabbie. "Drop us off there, please."

"Candy?" Presley said, smacking his lips.

"Yes, I want to get Sal a little gift. I think he'd much prefer gummy bears than a bouquet of perfumed roses," Lily said, rubbing up against Presley. "Besides, I kind of figured you might like a treat, too."

"Can Rosie pick out something she likes?" Presley asked thoughtfully.

"Sure she can! Today *everybody* gets a treat!"

"What's your favorite, Presley?" Rosie asked.

"I've never been to a real candy store before. I've only had the kind that comes in wrappers, like the stuff you get at Halloween."

"Do you like chocolate or caramel or sour-tasting sweets?"

"I like it all, but my very favorite is what they put in chocolate chip cookies."

"Oh," Rosie said. "The bittersweet chips?"

"Yes! When our baker, Poppy, makes those at Silver Trails, I sometimes take a cookie and pick the chips out. They're yummy!"

"Then let's look for something just like that," Lily said. "If need be, we'll stop on the way home and get an entire bag of them at the grocery store."

Licking his lips, Presley said, "Oh, boy!" Then hugging Lily, he said sincerely, "I wish you were my grandma."

Rosie tickled the child, teasingly chiding, "Hey now, what about me? I should be the grandma. That there should be your great-granny."

Beaming the boy enthused, "You're both great!"

Arriving at the front desk of the hospital, candy bags in hand, the three visitors asked the receptionist for Sal's room number. They were told he was on the fourth floor in a semi-private room, just to the right of the elevators.

"Room number 44," the receptionist read-off.

"I like that number," Presley acknowledged. "Sounds kind of lucky."

Lily said, "Maybe it's lucky because you're with us, Presley."

"That's right," Rosie said, "And after what you went through with Sal, he's going to rejoice knowing that you're safe and sound."

"He's my hero," Presley said. "He broke his hip trying to save me."

"You tell him that," Rosie recommended, "I think that'll make him feel good."

But Sal wasn't remotely close to feeling good. His pain was agonizing. As the three visitors entered the hospital room, they could see that their friend's fists were tightly clenched. A groan escaped his lips and his eyelids twittered.

The gentleman behind the curtain next to Sal's bed bellowed, "Ah, hush up! You've been moaning ever since they brought you in here. For Pete sake, why can't they move the old coot out?!"

Presley shot a fiery glare that could've seared a hole through the curtain. "He's not an old coot. His name is Sal and he got hurt. And he did it to save me. He's a hero and you should be glad you're sharing a room with him."

Hearing the boy's proclamation, Sal opened his eyes slightly. "Is that you, Elvis?"

"No, but it's Presley," Lily answered sweetly.

With a moan Sal raised his arms. "Come here, young man. Let me see for myself." Presley moved forward and stood rooted by the bedside. Sal achingly turned his head and sighed. "Well, now, glory be. It is you. I thought I was dreaming." Sal lowered his arms back to his chest, drained of energy. "I was so worried. Thank God, you're safe."

"You're my hero," Presley announced, reaching for one of Sal's hands.

"My goodness. Yes, I heard you tell my friendly roommate that." Sal felt privileged and touched by Presley's proclamation, but he didn't have the strength to return the boy's grip. Feebly he let his hand fall limp at his side. "You know," Sal wheezed, "I'm grateful to have been a part of your rescue, but I'm not the only one who helped. Thomas went out of his way to bring you back."

"Yes, and the dogs, too."

"Say, how are my pooches?" Sal asked, allowing his crinkly lids to rest shut again.

"Violet and Dickie are taking care of them until you're better."

A sigh followed another groan and then Sal muttered, "Hopefully they can watch Squirt and Chimp a while because my doctor says I have to go to a rehab home before I can come back to Silver Trails."

Lily stepped forward and gently patted Sal's shoulder. "Not to worry. We'll take care of the dogs, however long it takes you to recover." She nodded to Rosie and Presley that it was time to go. "We're glad they fixed you up, Sal. We'll come back tomorrow to check on you. Get some rest now, okay?" Lily leaned over and planted a docile peck on Sal's cheek.

Rosie added, "We're all saying our prayers, sir. Take care of yourself, ya hear."

Sal whispered back, "Thanks for stopping by." And with a monumental effort, he lifted his hand, located the boy's, and squeezed it. "I'm relieved you're okay, *Presley*. Now I can finally get some rest."

That evening Sal's rest became permanent.

Chapter Twenty-One

Deadhead spent flowers

When they landed at Midway, Malcolm and Heather hustled to baggage claim and hurriedly steered themselves and their luggage to the car rental agency. Time was of the essence. They only had half of their Saturday and all day Sunday to find a house. Ultimately it'd been Malcolm's idea to move back to the Chicago area. He'd secretly wanted to for the better part of five years. Knowing now that their son was still in the area and that they could settle there as a family, the mere mention of his notion had Heather catapulting on board.

"You're brilliant!" she'd exclaimed the night Malcolm broached the subject. "Your idea makes total sense. We're both from the area. We had our son there. He's still there. Securing work won't be tough. Some of my law firm's biggest clients are in Chicago. Maybe instead of flying lawyers back and forth from the West Coast, I can start an office for them in the city. And, Malcolm, it'll be a cinch for you to find a job. You're not only a credentialed teacher, but now you have administrative experience as a vice principal."

"Yeah, so long as I stay away from Lake Forest, we'll be fine."

"Ya know, I think you should apply there. Screw 'em! We're married. Been married. And now we're reclaiming our child. You did everything right. They should know that."

Malcolm patted Heather's head like she was a little girl. "Babe, it doesn't matter. They're not going to care and, as they say, 'Why open that can of worms?'"

"Ya know, that's exactly what they are...*worms*."

"Maybe, but eh, it's a huge city with lots of bordering suburbs. What I like most is that, compared to California's suffering system, education in Illinois reigns supreme."

"What I like," Heather said excitedly, "is that we'll be able to afford a three-bedroom home. Actually, with what we can get for our digs in LA, we might be able to snatch up a four-bedroom house."

"But we don't need four bedrooms. It'll just be Presley and us, with a guest room for your Grandma Lily if she decides to stay once in a while." Malcolm reflected momentarily. "Wonder if she's going to get along with our son? Hell, she's never even met me. You've never told her I'm black, right?"

"No, but unlike my mom who'd have a heart attack, Grandma's open-minded. If I love you, she'll love you. The fact that our son is mulatto, she won't give it a second thought. Trust me, after my grandma having an only child that's a daughter, and not a very nice one, and then me as an only grandchild..."

"A granddaughter and a *very* nice one," Malcolm interjected.

"She'll be so excited to know she has a great-grandchild that is a boy."

"And hopefully a very nice one."

"Oh, come on," Heather guffawed. "If he's part you and part me, he has to be *more* than nice."

Malcolm nodded and said, "I'm sure he's perfectly nice."

"And smart. And witty. And cute. And..."

"...And *perfect*."

Heather suddenly changed course. "I hope so, Malcolm. But you know...Presley's had to live with two different families already; families that tossed him back into the system. I wonder if he is what we'd call perfect. Maybe we're kidding ourselves. Maybe he's a problem child who lashes out at authority and that's why he was sent back to DCFS. Or maybe he's some stressed-out kid that has serious issues and can't function properly. Or depressed to the point he can't tolerate what life has doled out for him."

"Why are you suddenly positioning yourself on the pessimist's platform? What happened to that gleeful optimist I know?"

"I'm sorry. I guess I just don't want to be disappointed." Heather gesticulated with her hands like she often did in court. "If we had raised our son from day one, we would've instilled the behavior, the values and qualities we believe in and find admirable. But let's face it; our son, who is turning eleven in January, has already had *two* pairs of parents. Who knows what kind of example they set; or how effective they were in laying the groundwork for what we'd consider a suitable upbringing?"

Malcolm took one of Heather's waving hands and held it. "Stop, you sound like an attorney more than a parent. Don't get so agitated. Come on now. Let's go back to being thrilled about bringing Presley into our lives. Certainly some of who he is as a person is genetic. If there are characteristics or behaviors that need modifying, we can tackle that later. We'll rub off on him in no time. You'll see."

"I knew there was a reason I fell for you," Heather said, kissing Malcolm. Then showcasing a Travolta move or two she sang out, "Let's boogie, babe. I can't wait for our adventure to begin!"

The first place the couple decided to visit was Skokie. The town was reasonably close to downtown Chicago, which meant wherever Heather landed within the city limits, the commute wouldn't be overly taxing. Housing was affordable. The neighborhoods were well established and safe. The schools in the area had earned high marks. As a teacher or VP, if Malcolm was unable to secure a job in Skokie, there were neighboring communities like Lincolnwood or Niles where the schools were equally good.

After driving around for a spell, reacquainting themselves with the area, Heather and Malcolm confirmed that the town would be a comfortable spot to begin and so they pulled up at a local realty office to have an agent help them with available listings. It was one o'clock when the overzealous agent ushered the couple out to her

Mercedes and six in the evening when she brought them back. After five hours of playing lookie-lous, traipsing through a total of twenty-two homes, Heather and Malcolm were not only exhausted but dismayed. They'd seen two or three properties that were worth a second look, but not one screamed for a "Sold" sign out front. The hardcore realtor pleaded with them to "Come back tomorrow. I've got lots more to show you."

But Malcolm took the lead and said, "We've got your card. Thanks, but I think we'll look around a few other neighborhoods first."

After dinner at a pizza joint, Heather and Malcolm found a nondescript hotel and booked a room. Just before turning out the light, Heather said groggily, "Guess we'll call Grandma Lily tomorrow," to which Malcolm replied, "Oh, that's right. We didn't even call her yet." Then they crashed.

On Sunday morning, Heather and Malcolm were out the door by eight. Bracing themselves for yet another whirlwind day of house tours and the all-encompassing notion of where to even begin, both were wild in their thoughts and both forgot again that they should contact Lily.

"So, where are we going to start, Malcolm? You're driving like you know where you're headed."

"Honestly, I have no agenda. But I just saw a sign back there for Morton Grove. Thought we might give the place a look."

"Sounds good to me," Heather said. As Malcolm motored them through the township Heather saw a house with a "For Sale" that made her jerk around in her seat and order Malcolm to a halt. "Go back, okay? I really like that house."

As Malcolm pulled up in front of the stately two-story brick house, Heather hopped out and dashed over to the sign post where flyers were offered. She stood gawking for a moment and then jumped back in the car. "Do you like it?" she begged to know.

Unable to match her enthusiasm, Malcolm simply nodded. "It's nice. What's the listing say? How much?"

"Is that all you care about?" Heather protested. Reading the small print she reported, "Three ample-size bedrooms with a study off the master bedroom. Two full bathrooms upstairs and a half-bathroom downstairs. Formal dining room. Full kitchen with newly installed appliances. Family room opens up to a spacious deck and yard. Mud room with washer and dryer. Basement has a play room and lots of space for storage. Two-car garage…"

"And the price?"

Heather squinted to read and announced, "It's affordable!" Waving at Malcolm to drive on, she instructed, "Let's go talk to the realtor. I've got to see the house and *now*!"

Malcolm sighed and said, "Yes, boss."

By nine-thirty, the realtor had an appointment. Once the occupants went off to church Heather and Malcolm were allowed entry. As she got out of the realtor's classy sedan Heather twirled on the driveway. Taking in the surroundings, she praised, "Isn't it glorious? Look at these trees, how full and tall they are. Lots of privacy; I like that." Upon stepping into the home, Heather cooed, "Oh, these wood floors are to die for. They're so vintage, but hardly a scratch to be seen." As she was escorted throughout each room in the house, her compliments poured forth like a favored wine—savory, esteemed, and memorable. Finally, in the basement of all places, Heather exclaimed, "We need to live here, Malcolm."

Malcolm shrugged and to the realtor said, "Sold!"

They worked out an offer over lunch, explaining the details of their move, the fact that they'd have to sell their place in Los Angeles and find jobs in the area, and so on. It was close to three o'clock by the time Heather remembered to call her Grandma Lily. She was elated to share the good news, but there was no answer. She called again before dinner, but still no answer.

✿

Lily wept when she got word that Sal had died of heart failure only hours after they'd visited him. When Presley saw her crying he came to her side. "What is it? Are you okay?"

Lily drew the boy in and sat next to him on the edge of her bed. She dreaded telling Presley, but she had to. When he heard the words, "Sal has passed away," Presley burst into tears. "But we just saw him!" he bawled.

Everyone at Silver Trails was stunned by the news. The moping and mourning was contagious. Sal, who'd been somewhat of a recluse early on, but because of Presley had gradually turned gregarious and valiantly resolute, was going to be genuinely missed. At lunch the following day the topic of conversation was all about Sal. With his back to the residents in the dining room, Presley stood tidying up the buffet table. Dickie, who tended to speak loudly because he never quite accurately adjusted his hearing aid, was talking to his wife, Violet. Presley could hear every word the senior was saying.

"He was so strong and forthright. Can you imagine any other resident here going out after dark to look for Presley?"

Violet then replied in a mournful voice, "He really cared about that boy."

"Yes, his concern basically killed him."

"Aw, now that's not fair, Dickie. I wouldn't go so far as to..."

Presley couldn't stay to hear the rest. He was mortified. Slinking out of sight, he returned to the kitchen where he busied himself until Rosie queried, "Did you finish cleaning up in the dining room?"

"I can't be in there. Everyone's talking about Sal."

Rosie understood the sorrow Presley felt. She sensed his pain and was managing her own. Gently setting her hand atop the boy's shoulder she intoned, "At least we got to see him before he made his way to God."

Presley broke down. "But it's my fault. Don't you see? If I hadn't been lost, Sal would never have left here to come looking for me. None of this would've happened. I killed him!"

Rosie knelt down and looked eye to eye with Presley. "You did no such thing. What happened to Sal was not your fault."

"But he got shoved and broke his hip because of me."

"You were locked away in a basement at that point. How could that have been your fault?" Rosie paused and wiped away a stream of Presley's tears. "Sweetheart, look at me. Sal loved you. He was concerned for your welfare and didn't want anything to happen to you. I think he felt like he was your guardian angel. Or maybe the grandfather you never had. It was his choice, his need to go looking for you. Please don't blame yourself. He wouldn't want you to."

Whimpering Presley relayed, "He was my hero."

"Yes, and you know what? When you told him that in the hospital, I saw a light shine within him that could've turned night into day." Rosie hugged her little busboy and emphasized, "He loved you, Presley."

Shortly after lunch Lily knocked on the kitchen door. Rosie was glad she'd come by because she felt Lily should know about the deep remorse Presley was experiencing.

"We need to take his mind off of things," Rosie recommended. "He's having a hell of a time dealing with this."

Like the Statue of Liberty, Lily held her hand high, revealing two tickets. "Maybe this'll help. Mr. Taylor just gave these to me. Last minute, he and his wife can't go. He said Presley should be the one to go see Elvis. He asked if I could find somebody to take him. What do you think?"

"Might take his mind off things; cheer him up a little," Rosie said supportively.

Sighing, Lily said, "We only have him for another day and a half, Rosie. Selfishly I'd like to lock him in my room and let him play Blossom for hours on end. But that wouldn't be fair to the boy. Steal him away like that. You know, I think he'd love to see Elvis in person. How's about if you go with him?"

"You want me to have the extra ticket?"

"Not really. But it makes more sense for you to go. I can't handle a crowd that size. "

"Well, so long as I don't miss any more hours in the kitchen…"

"You won't. It's this evening after dinner. You'll have plenty of time to get there."

Rosie eyed Lily who appeared disappointed. "Are you sure you want me to go?"

"Trust me; if I were a decade shy of what I am now, Rosie, there's no way I'd miss the opportunity to take Presley to this concert. But there's no sense in tempting fate. I'm no longer a stable Mabel, especially when it comes to a concert hall of pushy people."

"All right, then," Rosie said, "hopefully Presley won't mind me being his date."

The tickets for Elvis rendered a smile from Presley, but his being remained downcast. Lily asked him if he'd like to come play guitar before his dinner duties and the show, and he nodded. Back in her room, as Presley held Blossom, Lily got the sense that some of the boy's sorrow was being released right into the instrument. He sang her song, "The Daisy Field." He sang it with such poignancy, such purpose that each of the lyrics leaving his lips was like a melancholy tear being shed. When Presley finished he looked up to see Lily's reaction. She was dumbstruck.

"I memorized it," Presley said because he didn't know what else to say.

Drawing a full breath Lily exulted, "That was absolutely beautiful, Presley."

"You know, when I was all alone in that basement…I sang your song because it made me feel like you were there with me."

"I was there…in spirit anyway."

"I know. I think that's why I lived. So I could see you again."

Lily felt her heart jerk. How could she bear not to have this child in her life? And how was Presley going to feel once his real parents showed up and separated him from the people he'd grown to love and trust? She got lost in thoughts that Presley must've read.

"Lily?" the boy muttered. "Do you know if my real parents live anywhere near here?" Not waiting for a reply he added, "Because I don't want to move far away from you. I'd really miss you. And Rosie and Thomas and Tony. I don't want to leave."

Her heart was now exploding. No matter how hard she tried to form the proper response, the words wouldn't oblige. She finally exclaimed, "Oh, Presley. Come here!"

Carefully setting Blossom back in the case, Presley charged into Lily's open arms. Not saying a word, the two embraced.

That evening after their dinner duties were complete, Rosie and Presley caught a cab to the concert hall. While waiting in line, Presley caught sight of Tony.

"Hey, look over there, Rosie. It's Tony! He came to the same show we did."

Rosie chuckled. "Well, I'll be…"

Presley then waved and called forth, "Tony! Tony, over here."

Seeing his workmates, Tony waved back and spoke a few words to the lady he was with. Snaking his way through the crowd, he maneuvered over to where Rosie and Presley stood.

"Golly, I didn't know you were coming to this. Where're you two sitting?"

Bringing forth their tickets Rosie said, "Beats me. These are Mr. Taylor's. He gave them to Lily and she insisted I take Presley."

Tony gazed at their tickets and exclaimed, "Man! You're in the second row! What great tickets!"

"Where are you sitting? And who's that?" Presley asked, pointing.

"That's Jasmine, my steady. Actually we're engaged, so technically she's my fiancée."

"She's very pretty," Presley noted.

"Thanks. I'll tell her you said so. I'd let you tell her in person, but I doubt you'll get a chance to meet her tonight. This is such a big place and it's going to be packed. Plus you'll be up front and we're *way* in the back. I mean miles away…"

"How come?" Presley queried.

"Our tickets are freebies. Got them through a high school chum of mine who does acoustical work for Elvis and his band. They're the bottom of the barrel, total bargain seats. But hey, I'm not complaining. I'm stoked! It's out of sight just to be here."

Suddenly Jasmine was hailing Tony, gesturing that she was fast-approaching the entrance.

"Well, I best be on my way." He nudged Presley and said, "Enjoy the show. Ya know that might be you up on stage one day."

As things turned out, that very night was Presley's debut.

Chapter Twenty-Two

Miracle-Gro® and mulch

In a way the incident was a fluke. But then again, Tony was somewhat instrumental in how things panned out. Upon entering the hall Tony saw his friend checking the band's equipment and various amplifiers on stage. Squeezing his way through the masses Tony got close enough to get his buddy's attention. The pal came to the edge of the stage and clasped Tony's hand in a fraternal grip. The guy was only able to chat briefly, but in that time Tony fed him tidbits of trivia about the kid who'd be sitting in the second row. "His name is Presley. He was born the same day as Elvis. And not only does he love Elvis's music, the kid can sing. I mean really sing!" Then it was, "Thanks again for the tickets. If you're around after the show, let's grab a beer."

The chum gave a thumbs-up, went back to work, and Tony returned to his seat in the back row next to Jasmine. That was that until the last set was played.

Elvis, in all his glory, donning a slick white-and-silver-sequined suit, was gyrating on stage and crooning, "*Return to sender. Address Unknown. No such number. No such zone.*" When he finished the song with a single forward thrust of his pelvis for emphasis, he strode to the edge of the stage, microphone in hand. He sheltered his eyes from the glare of spotlights and absorbed the applauding masses.

"Looks like I have some real fans in Chicago," he proclaimed. Thunderous applause followed and, raising a hand to quiet the crowd, Elvis continued, "Thank you all for coming out. It's my pleasure to be here with you tonight." Leaning slightly forward he stared down into the orchestra section and said, "Seems to me... heard it through the grapevine anyway...that there's a mini-Elvis in our midst."

The crowd fell silent. Heads turned and those in back lifted in their seats to look forward. "Yes, where are you, son?" Elvis asked. "Stand up so I can see you." Nobody stood, so Elvis knelt down to get a closer look. "We celebrate the same birthday. You love to sing my tunes. And from what I understand, my last name is your first name."

Rosie wiggled in her seat like a worm tortured by the hot sun. Urging the boy to his feet and then waving and pointing, she hollered, "Here he is! This is Presley!"

Elvis moved over on the wide stage so he was directly in front of Presley. "Nice to meet you," he said. "So, you like to sing?"

Still dumbfounded, Presley simply nodded.

"Know most of my songs?"

Again, a humble nod.

"Want to come up here and join me?"

Presley looked to Rosie who was already shooing him onward. He turned back to Elvis and gave a shrug.

"Aw, come on. It's not often I invite someone up here to accompany me."

With that the audience started to clap, some calling out, "Go, kid! Get up there!"

Finally Rosie exclaimed, "You can do it. Show 'em what you've got!" She patted Presley on the back, enough so that he made a move forward. As people in the row stood to allow the boy passage, Rosie hollered, "Remember, you're a star, Presley!"

The moment Elvis held out his hand to bring the boy on stage, the band struck up their intro to "All Shook Up." Elvis gave his mike to Presley and grabbed another one.

Once the singing began, Presley shed his jitters and started to jive. His moves were totally Elvis to the point Elvis mimicked *him*. With his high-pitched tone, Presley lent harmony, allowing the star to belt out his melody. It was a sonorous, adroitly orchestrated piece the two performed. In fact, the audience was incredulous, hard-pressed to believe the number was impromptu. The applause was nonstop, bordering on clangorous. Elvis gestured to Presley to take a bow. Then Elvis did. The crowd went wild. Then they bowed together and Presley finally returned to his seat.

Into the mike, Elvis said jokingly, "Are you sure you're not one of the Jackson Five come to spy on me?" When the audience's laughter simmered, Elvis pointed to Presley and noted, "Now folks, I'll have you know, that young man is a future star. And you all can say you were in the house when he made his debut. I'll be boasting about it, too." Acknowledging the boy one more time, Elvis said with sincerity, "I was honored to have you join me, Presley. Carry on and do me proud."

Presley stayed at Rosie's that night. It was all Rosie could do to calm the child down and get him to bed. She brought out a sleeping bag and laid it on her living room couch. She set a big, fluffy pillow down with a snuggly throw in case he got cold.

Pointing her finger, she instructed, "Now…it's past both our bedtimes. We both have to get up early tomorrow. So, as soon as your head hits that pillow, I want you to get some shuteye. Understand?"

Presley climbed in the cocoon-like bag and, closing his eyes, pretended like he'd fallen asleep instantly. Then he imitated snoring.

Rosie poked him and said, "No fooling around, mister. I mean it. Get some rest."

Just as Rosie was moseying off, Presley sat up and called her name. When she turned around, he imparted, "I'm really going to miss you."

With that, Rosie made her way back to the boy. Hovering over him she shook her head, saying, "You'd better watch out or you're going to have me crying all over you. You want to get wet? Is that what you want?"

Presley smiled and said, "Not really."

"Then you lay back down so I can give you a big hug goodnight." Rosie knelt down and smothered the boy in a hefty embrace. Presley grunted under her weight. When she straightened, Rosie joked, "See that? I'm a lot to miss, aren't I? Now get some sleep. We still have tomorrow to share and I want it to be a full day."

The next day couldn't have come soon enough. By the time Rosie appeared, Presley was dressed and groomed, and he'd even rolled up his sleeping bag in a caterpillar bundle.

"Good job on rolling up that bag!" Rosie spouted. "We should've had you making the croissants and jelly rolls for us at Silver Trails. Didn't know you had that kind of dexterity." Rosie hesitated, scratching her tidy gray coif. "Pretty sure that means skilled."

The compliment bypassed Presley, but the word didn't. "Dexterity. That was one of our spelling bee words." Then reciting from memory he said, "D-e-x-t-e-r-i-t-y. I'm pretty sure I got that right."

"I'll take your word for it," Rosie responded. "You're a master at spelling." Grabbing her coat off the back of a chair she added, "Ya know, young man…you do a lot of things well. I bet your parents are going to be so impressed. How lucky they are to have found you and be bringing you back into their lives!"

"I wonder why they put me up for adoption in the first place."

Feeling badly for broaching the subject, Rosie faltered a little in saying, "Oh, now, they're a lot of things that could've happened early on. I don't know the real reason, but I'm sure they'll be up front and tell you the whole scenario. The bottom line, though, Presley, is that they love you and want you to be with them. And there's nothing better than being part of a real family."

Lowering his head, Presley mumbled, "I guess so. But I still hope I don't have to move far away." Reflecting he continued, "I mean who's going to take care of the daisies this coming spring? Gosh, Mr. Taylor was talking about me planting a bunch more daisies at the other two homes he's in charge of. And who are you going to get for a busboy? And who's going to walk the dogs? Violet and Dickie have all three of them now. They're really going to need some help. And what about Lily? She wanted to give me guitar lessons. Who's going to play Blossom if I'm not around? Plus, I was supposed to sing at Happy Hour once in a while. Elvis even said I should keep it up. I mean, if I move away, I'm going to lose everything. Everything, Rosie!"

Lowering her head, too, Rosie said, "We'll have to hope for the best, son. That's all we can do. Trust in the Lord and hope for the best."

Catching the first bus that powered through her neighborhood, Rosie and Presley arrived at Silver Trails earlier than need be. They had an entire hour before breakfast was to be served. Tony was already in the kitchen, preparing his various muffins and Danish. Thomas was gathering the ingredients to make omelets and the various eggs to order. They both waved robustly as Presley and Rosie sauntered in.

"What a great show that was last night," Tony called out. "You were awesome, Presley. Everyone loved your singing! Even Elvis. I was telling Thomas all about it."

"I always knew you had talent! You're going to be a star!" Thomas proclaimed.

"Gee, thanks. To tell you the truth I was pretty scared at first. But when I got up there with Elvis and we were grooving together, it felt really cool. I hope someday I'll get to do that again."

"Oh, you will. In the meantime you'll get to serenade us here," Tony said.

"I don't know. Not if my parents come get me and move me to another state."

"What do you mean?" Thomas asked.

"Dearie me," Rosie said. She turned to Presley and reported, "They don't know about your leaving us."

"What?!" Tony bellowed. "Leaving us? What are you talking about, Rosie?"

Squeamishly Presley interjected, "Yeah, my real parents asked for me back. I've never even met them and I don't know how come this is happening all of a sudden. But since my adoptive dad got shot and my adoptive mom bailed on me, the people in charge say I should be returned to my real parents."

Wiping his hands on his apron, Tony came over to Presley and gave him a hug. Thomas stood confounded, looking as though his life was going to be turned upside down, just like the over-easy eggs he'd soon be frying.

Shedding her bulky coat, Rosie informed, "We're not sure about anything just yet. His parents will come for him tomorrow. We're keeping good thoughts that Presley won't be taken far because we'd miss him way too much. So, gentleman, say your prayers and get back to work."

Rosie didn't mean to be curt. It was just that, deep down, she was already struggling with the reality of losing Presley. And she didn't want to dwell on the thought. As she put on her newly washed apron, persnickety and fresh, primed and ready to greet the Sunday morning breakfast crowd, Rosie declared, "Presley, we have some spare time this morning, so you're going to try something new. Does that sound good to you?"

The boy stood at attention. "Yes, I'd like that."

"Remember how I said you should be rolling our croissants?"

"Because I rolled my sleeping bag like one?"

Rosie nodded. "It's Sunday morning and croissants are on the menu. See that mound of dough over there? Tony will demonstrate and then you take over, okay?"

"Yes, ma'am!"

Tony grabbed Presley's hand and led him to the sink. "Wash up, kid. It's time to rock and *roll.*"

By the time the residents shuffled to their various seats in the big dining room, Presley had taken care of all his chores *and* he'd rolled enough dough to make six-dozen croissants. Rosie claimed they could open a French café with the bounty they had to offer that morning.

When Lily wandered in, she immediately scanned the room for Presley. Rosie noted her need to see the boy and so she released Presley from his duties and told him to take a seat at Lily's table. It was the first time the busboy had ever dined with the residents, a bonus he'd gleaned that was now a timely reward.

"And before you go out there, young man," Rosie instructed, "take off your white jacket. You're not serving this morning. You're going to *be* served."

When Lily caught sight of her young friend coming out of the kitchen she stood up and waved. "Over here, Presley!"

Presley skedaddled over to his gussied-up friend with the white hair and pink lips.

"Oh, there you are!" Lily enthused. Giving the child a big kiss, she said, "I couldn't wait to see you. I rose so early this morning and had so much free time that I forgot and put my lipstick on twice!" Noticing the bright pink remnants she'd managed to leave on Presley's cheek, the elder added, "Oops, it seems I'm back to one coat now." Reaching for her napkin, she erased the smoochie smudge. "There, all better."

Politely pulling the chair out for Lily, Presley said, "Want to sit down?"

"Only if you can sit with me."

"Actually, I can this morning. Rosie said so."

"Smart woman, that one. You deserve a break, this being your last day with us." Lily slapped her own hand and reprimanded, "Quit reminding us!"

Presley smiled faintly and said, "That's okay. I keep thinking about it, too."

Just then Rosie, Tony, and Thomas burst through the kitchen door like a plume of vaporous heat escaping the oven. Each one carrying a plateful of steamy breakfast delights, they paraded through and about the dining room tables until they stood surrounding Presley.

"Sir Presley," Thomas exclaimed, "sit and let us serve you!"

Lily gleefully clapped as she took her seat. She pulled Presley down into his. "Come on, how often do you get this kind of treatment?"

Tony leaned over and decorously set his dish in front of Presley. Thomas set his in front of Lily. Rosie proffered hers, placing it in the center for all to share.

"These are hot out of the oven and right out of the frying pan," Rosie asserted. "Indulge to your heart's content."

Once the kitchen team departed, between taking bites of the best breakfast he could ever recall having, Presley regaled Lily and the elders at his table with tales of the previous night. "And I was invited up on stage with Elvis!"

One silver-haired dame asked, "Is he the one they call 'Pelvis'?"

Lily laughed and responded, "There's a reason for that. He's quite…how shall I say...an *exotic* dancer."

"Oh," the tittering senior said, "I do like him."

Presley giggled, gulped down a wad of his cinnamon roll, and continued to bask in the appreciative attention being showered upon him.

After dining with his senior friends, Presley insisted on clearing the table and continuing with his kitchen duties. Rosie kindly pushed him away, saying, "Just go have fun." But Presley felt comfortable in the kitchen and he wanted to spend as much time as he could with Rosie, Thomas, and Tony, too. When there were no more dishes to wash or put away, Presley decided to wander upstairs and visit the dogs. Only a few days had elapsed since Sal passed away. Certainly the dogs hadn't been walked since then. Quick potty outings, but nothing substantial, no real exercise. The child missed the canine companionship that Boomer, Chimp, and Squirt gave him. So, knocking on Violet and Dickie's door, Presley begged to take all three dogs out for a brief walk.

"I don't think that's such a good idea," Dickie said from the back of the room.

Presley's disappointment was evident, so Violet replied, "Aw, don't be such a worry wart. Presley's a pro at walking these fellas. It's broad daylight and there are no boogey men out there right now."

Dickie shook his head and raised a skeletal hand. "Oh, fine. But you be careful, son. We don't need anything happening to you."

Excitedly, Presley said, "Don't worry, sir. These three will protect me. We'll be okay. Honest!"

With that, Presley bounded forth to collect the three leashes and the three mutts. As he headed into the hallway, tangled in leashes, he exclaimed, "Thank you so much! This might be my last time with them."

Violet looked shocked. "Why is that, Presley?"

"Because my real parents are coming for me tomorrow. I might have to move away."

Dickie froze in awe. "Oh, my. We didn't know that." Looking to the dogs he asked, "And who is going to take care of Sal's dogs?"

Shrugging, Presley replied, "I don't know, sir. I sure wish I could take Chimp and Squirt. But I don't know if my parents like dogs."

Covering her mouth, Violet groaned, "Oh, dear. Three dogs and no dog walker."

"I'll ask if I can take them," Presley offered.

"Please do," Dickie said in a grumpy tone. "Otherwise we'll have to give them up. Call the pound to come get 'em…"

"Oh, sir. Don't do that! They'll put them to sleep."

Violet kindly took over. "Not to worry, Presley. Sal's dogs will not be harmed." She glared over her shoulder at her husband and whispered to Presley, "He's not feeling well today. Kind of in a bad mood. You run along and enjoy your walk with the dogs. We'll pay you when you get back."

"Oh, no, ma'am. I don't want any money. I'm the one who asked if I could spend time with them."

Violet nodded as she gently closed the door.

When Presley passed by Lily's room he knocked. He wanted to let her know he'd be gone for a short while. Upon opening the door, she chuckled to see the boy wrapped in leashes. "I'd say those dogs want out of here. You be careful. Stick to the safe side of the street. And when you get back, let's have one more guitar lesson, shall we?"

"Sure!" Presley resounded. "Good idea!"

When he returned from his walk, Lily was not in her room. Confounded, Presley scoured the house. He asked Rosie and the kitchen crew if they knew where she was. He dropped by Mr. Taylor's office, but forgot it was Sunday and said aloud, "Day of rest. Not in." He wandered the corridors, listening behind closed doors to see if he could hear her voice. Nothing! *Where can she be on my last day here,* Presley wondered. *She said she wanted me to play Blossom; give me one more guitar lesson.* Retreating to the kitchen, Presley asked if he could chop some of the peppers Tony had stacked in a pile.

"Promise you'll be careful?" Tony asked. "Don't want you getting too slicey-dicey with us your final time in our midst."

Taking the small knife Tony handed over, Presley said, "To tell you the truth, I'd rather be playing guitar right now. But I can't find Lily."

"It is rather strange that she took off," Rosie said from behind the sink. "Especially today. Maybe that numbskull daughter of hers finally decided to show up and take her for tea at the Drake."

"She only comes to visit once a year," Presley said, forlorn. "Why now?"

Like the peppers that got sautéed and the beef that got braised and the gingerbread that got baked, the afternoon simply melted away. It wasn't until Presley was dressed in his uniform, ready to serve the early Sunday supper that Lily reappeared.

Drowning Presley in a waterfall of apology, trying to catch her breath between outbursts, she poured forth, "I am soooo sorry, young man. This was not my idea. I wanted to stay here and play guitar with you all afternoon. Why today? They couldn't have picked a worse time…"

Rosie finally interrupted, "Who's they? Who're you talking about? Your daughter and son-in-law?"

Lily tilted her head, confounded. "No. They barely ever come to see me."

"Are you talking about my real parents?" Presley whimpered.

"No, I've never met them before."

"Then *who* are you ranting about?" Tony interjected.

"Sal's daughter!" Lily proclaimed.

Rosie threw up her hands. "Oh, *her*!" she said sarcastically. "And how the heck were we supposed to know about Sal's daughter?"

Lily gave it some thought and said, "Oh... I guess you wouldn't." Then at auction-like speed Lily continued, "Well, her name is Camellia. She's really quite lovely. She flew in from out of state and tried to leave me a slew of messages, of which I got none. So, she had a limousine bring her here. She knocked on my door and said she needed to speak with me, would I like to go for a cup of coffee down the street. At first I was hesitant, but then this Camellia told me it was about Sal's will. So, I agreed to go with her. I put my shawl and some lipstick on and I followed her out of the building. Do you know that her driver got out of the limo and actually opened the door for me? It was like I was a movie star or someone really special!"

"You are special," Presley noted.

Patting the boy on the shoulder, Lily rattled on. "Well, as it turns out...you're not going to believe this...none of you are...it's amazing...really..."

"Just tell us!" Rosie urged.

"Turns out old Sal was quite wealthy. After leaving Cabrini-Green he got into real estate. Owned some land up north and managed a slew of rental properties here in the city."

Tony drew in a deep breath, eyes glazed. "Do you stand to inherit a chunk of it?"

"No, silly! Not me. I could care less about Sal's money. I mean, come on, at my age? What would I do with his riches this late in life?"

"I could think of a lot of things," Tony said candidly.

Rosie waved Tony off and addressed Lily. "So, if you're not in the will, who is?"

Lily beamed as she turned and knelt down in front of Presley. "This young man."

"Me?" Presley asked quietly.

"Yes, you."

Presley looked to Rosie and Tony. They both had smiles wider than the Texas plains. Then he reconnected with Lily. "Why me?"

"Because Sal thought very highly of you. He really, truly loved you. While we were in the coffee shop his daughter read to me what Sal had written in his will. She said, 'He's as close to me as one of my own. He's the great grandson I never had.' Evidently he left instructions for Camellia to find me here at Silver Trails. He knew I'd be willing to work out the details with her."

Presley was speechless.

"Don't you want to know what Sal left you?" Lily asked excitedly.

The boy simply nodded and said, "I guess so."

"Okay, then, here it is in a nutshell. Wherever you decide to go to college your tuition will be paid for. Sal also left you a trust fund so that when you decide to record your first album, the money will be there. On top of that he is giving you a parcel of land in Door County where he and his wife used to vacation. Camellia said there's a log cabin on the property. Needs some work, but there's money put aside for that also. And most importantly, on that parcel is a huge field and every summer guess what it's covered with?"

Presley couldn't even imagine, couldn't answer. He was still stymied by the notion of receiving anything!

"The land that the cabin sits on is *surrounded* by daisies," Lily enthused. Tall Shasta daisies! Camellia told me one has never seen anything like it. It's one enormous daisy field."

Tony couldn't help but ask, "Doesn't Sal's daughter want the property?"

Lily stared at him and replied sternly, "No, she is honoring her father's wishes. Besides, she married into money. She could buy up any piece of real estate Door County had to offer. But when you have that kind of wealth, why go north when you can go south? Apparently Camellia and her husband have a place in Miami and one in Jamaica, too."

"So, Sal's daughter isn't mad that I'm getting this?" Presley asked timidly.

"Of course not," Lily proclaimed. "In fact, she can't wait to meet you. She told me anyone who could make her old pop melt like you have is worth his weight in gold!"

Confused, Presley said, "I think I weigh almost sixty pounds."

At that moment, everyone laughed, deliriously blithe to be sharing in the uplifting, joyous good news!

Finally Lily interjected, "And you know the only thing Sal requested; what his final wish was?"

Presley shook his head. "No, what?"

Lily leaned in and prompting the punch line, giddily announced, "He wants his ashes spread over that daisy field while you sing the song I wrote."

Presley gulped, then enthused, "It's called 'The Daisy Field.' That's why I'm supposed to sing it. He loved that song. He loved the daisies I planted, too. That's probably why he gave me the land where the daisies are. He knew I would take care of them. And keep them growing."

"Yes, Presley," Lily said. "You are all about that song and your daisies, too. Sal knew that. In fact, he knew a lot more than I ever gave him credit for. But most importantly, he knew how much your daisies mean to you."

"I do like caring for them," Presley said innocently.

"So, when is the funeral service?" Tony inquired.

"When are his ashes supposed to be spread?" Rosie asked.

"Tomorrow," Lily said succinctly.

Not a word followed.

Finally Presley said, "How can I sing tomorrow?"

Crumpling her brow, Rosie continued, "Yeah, how can Presley be in Door County when he's supposed to be at Care Services to meet his new parents in the morning?"

"Why do you think I'm so frazzled?" Lily said. "After hearing what Sal had to offer Presley, I didn't have the heart to tell Camellia he wouldn't be there."

"But Care Services dictated that we be there at nine tomorrow," Rosie reminded Lily. "It was a big deal that we were given temporary custody. We have to show."

Presley slumped and mumbled in a somber tone, "But I have to sing at Sal's funeral. It was his final wish."

"Is there a way of getting hold of anyone at DCFS?" Tony asked.

"I already tried," Lily relayed. "The department is closed until Monday at nine, the hour we're supposed to be there. There's an emergency line, but it's just to report abuse or neglect, that kind of thing. I don't know what to do. I really don't."

"You don't have the parent's phone number?" Tony probed.

"No. Wouldn't that make life easy?"

"All right," Tony said, taking charge. "Here's what we'll do. Right after breakfast Monday, I will hop in a cab and head over to Care Services. I will explain everything to them. You, Lily, take Presley to Door County..." Tony hesitated, pondering a moment. "How the heck are you going to get up there?"

"Camellia said she'd send a limo over to pick us up late this afternoon. So, at least we're guaranteed our transportation."

"Perfect. And she can arrange a ride back right after the service?"

"I guess she'll have to," Lily said.

"It's a long drive, close to six hours, but I think you can make it back to the city by evening, right?"

Lily gestured a response by crossing her fingers.

"If we can clear it with Mr. Taylor," Rosie interrupted. "I want to go with Tony."

"Good idea. They won't know me, but they'll recognize you, Rosie," Tony relayed.

Lily stood at attention. "So we're okay? Presley and I can go to Sal's funeral?"

"I think you should," Tony affirmed.

"I do, too," Rosie said. "I just hope we don't get our butts thrown in the slammer for not producing Presley tomorrow morning as promised."

"Well, if my parents are anything like I hope they are," Presley said, "they should be okay with it. I mean they've waited this long to come claim me. What's another day?"

Lily gave Presley a quick squeeze and hastened him, saying, "Let's get going. We have to practice the song one more time before the limo comes for us."

"I've never been in a limo before," Presley said jazzed.

"Neither has Blossom!" Lily asserted, giving the boy a nudge toward the door.

❀

The next morning things were fine in Door County, but they were not so copasetic in the offices of Care Services.

Laurel Williams was steaming mad when she learned that Presley was not going to appear, that Lily had whisked him off to Door County. "What was she thinking?" the department rep asked in a cantankerous stupor. "How am I going to explain to the parents that they flew here for nothing?"

"It's not for nothing," Tony started in.

"He'll be back this evening," Rosie finished.

"That's not the point," Laurel stressed. "We agreed that you would bring Presley here first thing this morning! I stood behind you. Told my supervisor that you could assuredly be trusted."

"This is something the child has to do," Rosie chimed in. "People are counting on him. And he wants to honor the man who passed away. Sal was a hero to Presley. He helped save him. On top of that, he left him a sizeable chunk of change. His parents should appreciate that...I mean the child's college tuition is already paid for!"

Laurel fudged a second and then said, "Tell me the deceased man's name again? I don't know why, but it sounds familiar."

"Sal," Rosie reported. He also lived at Silver Trails. He really took a liking to Presley. In fact, twice Sal went out at night to help find the child when he went missing. The second time, that's when he broke his hip. Died of complications a day or so later."

Laurel scanned Presley's file, running her index finger along as she attempted to speed-read the contents. Looking up, she said alertly, "Here it is. Sal's the one who called and reported that Presley's foster dad was being abusive."

Tony and Rosie could only stare.

"Says that the father was drunk and pressuring the boy."

"And how did DCFS respond?" Tony asked.

"Looks like we didn't do much of anything."

"And why is that?" Rosie pressed.

"In the report it explains that an agent called the apartment the next day to ascertain if there had been neglect or abuse and the foster mom said no. When the agent indicated that someone from next door had filed a complaint, the mother negated everything. She said that the person who placed the call was, and I quote, 'a grumpy old man.' And she assured the agent that her husband would never harm their son."

"And that was the end of it?"Tony queried. "No more follow-up?"

"We have certain policies and procedures that we adhere to. If there had been additional reports of abuse, we would've insisted on making a house call."

"Well, at least now you know who Sal is, or rather was, and you can understand how much he cared about Presley; why it's so important for the boy to sing at his funeral service today."

Laurel set Presley's file down, nodding. Moments later her phone rang. She listened and only replied with a perfunctory, "I'll be right there." Gesturing for Rosie and Tony to have a seat across from her desk she said fretfully, "The parents just arrived. Please wait here. I will try to explain what is going on. It might be that I'll need you as backup, but I'll do my best to handle matters without bringing you into this."

"I'd actually like to meet the parents," Rosie said.

"Please," Laurel pleaded, "just stay here."

❀

The day of Sal's service was a picturesque winter postcard. The morning air had a bite and, with the clouds having been ushered away overnight, the sky was as blue and pristine as an alpine lake. The terrain looked like a bunny's back, white and fluffy with small mounds of snow that resembled cottontails. There were no daisies in the field; the earth denied their arrival until at least May. So, to make up for their absence, Camellia ordered a truckload of hothouse daisies to be delivered.

While a buffet brunch for weary travelers was being set up in the cozy cabin, Camellia and the nurserymen were out back, situating the plants about the property. The backdrop they created was a magical illusion because the plastic containers were set down in the snow and all one could see were the daisies sprouting up—white snow, green stems and white daisies. When Presley caught a glimpse of the backyard, he cried out, "Jeepers!" He ran over to Camellia and praised her saying, "It's just what Sal would've wanted!"

Sal's family and friends started to arrive at ten. All total there were about forty in attendance. Camellia was pleased to see that so many had made the lengthy drive. Her eulogy ended with the statement, "Dad would be highly honored by your presence here today." After Sal's son, Michael, offered his poignant jaunt down memory lane, an urn of ashes was released into the frosty air, weightless matter flying free like the fluffy bits of a dandelion blown off in a wish.

When it came time for Presley to sing, he sauntered out holding Blossom like the guitar was a favorite toy or blanket. He took a seat on a cold iron-rod patio chair and shivered. The crowd caught his gist and snickered. They, too, were chilly; huddled together in heavy wool overcoats and furs, braving the brisk morning air. Once Presley sang his first lyric and strummed his first chord, the gnawing frigidity melted into a cool, soothing refreshment. Like a dripping icicle that might sate thirst, Presley's song filled a void that so many felt. The child had a knack for acting out a story through his vocal inflections and tone. There was such purity and sincerity in his singing that he completely owned his audience. Presley was an old soul at a very young age. And everyone in attendance sensed it. When the last lyric liltingly drifted from his lips and the final chord on Blossom was played, the crowd literally sighed. The reverence they were made to feel did not warrant applause, only grateful silence. It was Camellia who finally broke the awed stupor and releasing a foggy breath proclaimed, "Heavenly!"

Rubbing her mittens together, she announced, "Come on, everyone, there's a blazing fire inside and more than enough tasty treats to warm your inners. Come and enjoy!"

Lily couldn't wait to tell Presley how beautifully he'd sung the song she'd written and how masterfully he'd performed it. Cold as she was, instead of heading inside with the rest of the group, she made a beeline for the boy outside on the patio. "You are the most talented, heart-gripping, wonderful singer I've ever had the pleasure of knowing! You bowled them over, young man!"

Presley lifted his eyebrows, looking like an owl. "I didn't mean to," he said.

"No, silly. That's a good thing. I'm complimenting you."

"Oh, okay. I'm glad I sang your song the way you wanted me to."

"Better than that…the way Sal wanted you to. I know he's up there in heaven right now doing a jig and clapping his hands to beat the band! And you know what, Presley? After hearing you sing my song the way you did today, not only is Blossom yours, but my song is yours, too."

Presley beamed. "Those are nice gifts. And it's not even my birthday."

"Well, I'll tell you what…you'd better not let too many more birthdays zip by before you start that singing career of yours. I want to be alive to buy your first album when it's released. Deal?"

"I hope my new parents will let me keep singing."

"If they don't, you let me know." Lily saddled up for more… "I'll be your agent. I can go to bat for you and help get you out there in front of the crowds. I'll do whatever it takes. We can start tomorrow if you like."

Suddenly Lily felt a chill that wasn't from the cold. She looked at Presley and felt such profound love that her heart jolted. Staggeringly she said, "I sure hope you don't move away. I don't know what I'll do without you." Then Lily cried.

Chapter Twenty-Three

A bountiful manifestation

Laurel had a lot of explaining to do. She didn't return to her office for at least half an hour, which thoroughly worried Tony and Rosie. They sat nonchalantly shooting the breeze, trying not to display their concern. But in reality, both were fretting the legal actions that DCFS might invoke for not having produced the boy.

Her heels pounded heavily as Laurel marched back to her cubicle. She rooted herself at the door, arms crossed. "I never want to do that again," she said. "I'll have you know that you put me in an extremely awkward position."

Rosie dared to ask, "Are they okay with our bringing the boy back a little later?"

"No, they're not okay with it," Laurel snapped. "But what choice do they have? They came to get their son. They flew all the way from California. Their plane leaves tonight, but now they've got to change their flight because Presley won't be back in time. They're unnerved about everything right now. And to tell you the truth, so am I."

"Presley should be back by the dinner hour. Did you tell them that?" Tony asked.

Laurel glared right through Tony. "No, I'm afraid we didn't discuss the *dinner hour*."

"But they are going to stay?" Rosie affirmed.

"They both have work tomorrow. They plan to call in sick. Bottom line, we have totally inconvenienced them but, yes, they're staying until their son is in *their* custody."

"If they need a place to stay tonight, maybe we can find them an empty room at Silver Trails," Tony suggested.

"No, they have a grandmother they're trying to reach. They want to go see her." Laurel finally let her guard down and said, "But thank you for offering."

"So, what's the plan then?" Rosie asked. "Do you want us to bring Presley back here as soon as he makes it home?"

"Our doors close at five. So, that won't work. I think now that the parents are extending their stay, I think it best if Presley spends one more night with you all. But you have him here tomorrow morning at nine A.M. sharp. Not a minute after…got that?" Crossing her arms again, Laurel underlined, "This time a change in plans could land you in jail. Do I make myself clear?"

Rosie and Tony nodded emphatically.

Heather and Malcolm were more annoyed than angry with the glitch in plans. They wanted to believe that their son was doing the right thing by honoring a dead man's last wish. They were pleasantly surprised to learn their son had a decent voice and that he'd taken up guitar.

"The best laid plans…" Malcolm said as he pulled over at the nearest phone booth.

Heather hopped out with a handful of change. "I'll call the hotel and tell them we'll be staying one more night. Then I'll call and change our flight. *Then* I'll call and see if I can reach my Grandma Lily. I'd really like to see her, saying as we're in the city. Plus I still haven't told her about Presley. As long as we're staying another day, maybe we can take him to meet her."

"Horse before the cart, Heather."

"You're right. We best wait until we actually have him in our clutches."

It took close to fifteen minutes and more quarters from Malcolm's pocket before Heather finished her calls. As she returned to the car she snipped, "Darn it! Where can my grandmother be? I called twice yesterday and now this morning. She's still not answering."

"Maybe they have some marathon quilting group she's joined." Heather shot off a twisted grin, so Malcolm rethought and noted, "Yesterday was Sunday. Maybe she was at church when you called."

Heather plopped back in the passenger seat. "Not at three in the afternoon. I called later in the evening, too. I mean, come on, where would she be on a Sunday night?"

"Senior movie hour?" Malcolm said, lifting a thick eyebrow.

"Possibly. But just to make sure everything's all right, I want to drop by."

"Let's play tourists first," Malcolm suggested. "It's been ages since we spent any time downtown. We can drop by your grandmother's place later. We have no plans, nothing until the morning when we have to be back at DCFS."

Heather smiled and said, "Good idea! I've missed Chicago, too."

Uncharacteristically Malcolm burst into song, "*My kind of town, Chicago is...My kind of town...*"

Carefree and cavorting, the two of them sang to their hearts content as they motored their way through city streets until they finally reached the renowned Miracle Mile. Driving down Michigan Avenue brought back so many memories for both of them. Heather recalled the time her father nearly ran into a Salvation Army volunteer who was ringing his bell in front of Water Tower. She reminisced, "Yeah, Mom shrieked at Dad to pull over to the curb so she could hop out and get a jump-start on her Christmas shopping. Poor, Dad...instead of applying the brake, he hit the accelerator. Gees! Our car lurched forward, up onto the sidewalk, and that unsuspecting bell ringer nearly got mowed over."

After hearing his wife's story, Malcolm recalled the buggy ride he'd shared with his grandpa. Like he'd returned to the incident of old he told Heather, "Michigan Avenue was dressed in holiday style. Every boutique and store window was decorated. The trees that lined the mile-long street were flickering with millions of baby white lights. The entire downtown was lit up and it was so festive!"

As if he was partaking of the memory again, Malcolm laughed and continued, "So, my grandfather and I were bundled up under this scratchy woolen blanket that the driver had thrown over us. There was horse hair all over the thing and Grandpa started in with one of his sneezing fits. We went a total of four blocks before Gramps insisted the driver turn the buggy around and head back. I remember feeling crushed. I wanted that buggy ride to go on forever."

Heather patted Malcolm and said, "Name the day; I'll go with you on a buggy ride anytime, hon."

Finally, after driving along the stately thoroughfare, reacquainting themselves with the familiar sights and feeling like friends with each of the pedestrians passing by, the couple parked in a lot near Congress. They grabbed their winter coats and gloves and disembarked on a stroll along the lakeside. The chilly walk led to warm Rueben sandwiches at an Irish pub after which they sauntered over to the Shed Aquarium. Feeling like kids again they made funny faces at the turtles and sea creatures behind the glass partitions. Malcolm's lips were plumper than Heather's. They allowed him to pucker-up and masterfully produce a silly fish face. He duplicated the mouth so well that a little girl nearby pointed at him and gleefully exclaimed, "Look Mommy, it's a gold fish!"

After the aquarium they visited the Field Museum. For both of them it had been ages since they'd been to either tourist hotspot. Like youngsters, they were enthralled all over again, allowing an insatiable curiosity and interest to manifest itself. At one point, Heather extolled, "This is so cool! I feel like I'm ten years old again!"

It was nearly five o'clock by the time they got back to the parking lot, the skies pinkly foretelling that nightfall was soon to arrive. Heather directed Malcolm toward the area of Cabrini-Green. He'd forgotten how downcast and neglected the streets surrounding the region were. But it had grown even worse; a licentious embarrassment to city denizens.

"It's a shame your grandmother lives anywhere near here," Malcolm attested. "I've never even met her, but I'll tell you what, I would not let anyone in my family be subjected to such an ineffable mess. Not to mention the violence..."

Heather nudged Malcolm and said, "So that extra bedroom..."

"Yeah, well, let me meet her first. Make sure she doesn't mind my being black and all. We also need to make sure she's going to get along with Presley. But hey, if all of that goes well and things fall neatly into place, then yeah, she needs to come live with us."

After parking across the street from Silver Trails, Malcolm thoroughly checked his rearview and sides mirrors before he unlocked the car. "All clear," he reported.

"I don't think you have to worry that much," Heather said.

"When it comes to this part of town, doll face,...you do." Malcolm got out and opened Heather's door for her. Holding her arm in his, he escorted her across the street. After two long rings and one loud knock at the door, Myrtle, the starched pillar, answered.

"We're here to see Lily," Heather said politely.

"She's not in right now," the stodgy woman informed. "From what I understand she went out of town."

"Do you know when she'll be back?" Heather asked, thinking it very odd that her grandmother was gone at all.

"Not sure. May I ask who you are?"

"Her granddaughter."

Myrtle eyed Malcolm, wanting more.

"And this is my husband," Heather added, now annoyed. "May we come in, please?"

The pit bull employee retreated a step, allowing entry. "There are a few chairs down the hall. Don't know how long you plan to wait...might be a while." She trudged off, her white rubber soles squeaking along the recently mopped floor.

"They ought to think about getting somebody else to be their greeter," Heather whispered.

"You've got that right," Malcolm concurred. "So how long *are* we going to hang out here, waiting for your grandmother?"

Just then doors burst open down the hallway and up on the second floor. The elevator and stairways were suddenly flooded with a stream of seniors in murmurous chit chat, bustling toward the dining room for supper. One hunched-over granny spied Heather and Malcolm sitting in the front hall. In passing she craggily offered, "Want to join us, kids?"

Heather wasn't sure if the elder was in possession of all her faculties, so she simply smiled as the old woman hobbled on by. About five minutes later tall Thomas in his apron rounded the corner and accosted the waiting couple.

"One of our seniors came to the kitchen and told me you were sitting out here. We have plenty of food tonight. If you're waiting for one of the residents, you're more than welcome to join us," he said.

Heather looked to Malcolm and Malcolm looked to Heather and in unison they said, "Thank you!"

Thomas escorted them to the table where Lily usually sat. "There are two available seats here. Will this do?"

Both Malcolm and Heather nodded gratefully. As they took their seats they introduced themselves to the others at the table. Plates of pork roast with applesauce, green beans, and new potatoes were served. Thomas was standing in for Presley, playing busboy. As he filled the water glasses at the table, Heather smiled up at him and praised, "This is so good. My compliments to the chef."

"Thank you," Thomas said. "You're looking at him."

"You mean to tell me you cooked this meal?" Heather asked, incredulous.

"Most of it. Our head cook, Rosie, and our other chef, Tony, were busy earlier on today…so I took the lead."

"Well, then," Malcolm joined in, "Hats off, my man! I would've placed you on the free-throw line, not in a kitchen cooking a pork roast."

"Actually, I do both," Thomas replied with a grin. "Tonight I'm playing busboy, too." Acknowledging that water was needed at neighboring tables, he excused himself and sped off.

"We're lucky to have such an attentive kitchen staff here," relayed the perky, petite senior by the name of Primula.

"Yes, they're very adept," Heather responded making polite eye contact with the elderly woman who happened to have the tightest curls Heather had ever seen before. Tighter and smaller than a doll's. Heather had to assume that the senior got a perm every week rather than every other month or so.

"And what brings you to Silver Trails, dearie?" Primula queried.

"My grandmother, Lily, is a resident here..."

Primula slapped the table, "No wonder you're sitting in her place. Keeping it warm for her, are you?"

"Oh, well, actually my husband and I were instructed to sit at this table."

Primula didn't mean to, but she let go of a scowl. "That's your husband, dearie?"

Heather said curtly, "Last time I looked."

"Oh, silly me. I thought he was your driver."

Just then Heather felt soft hands fall upon her shoulders. When she turned to look it was her Grandma Lily. "Grandma! It's you!"

"Of course, it's me, darling. I live here. What are you doing here?"

"Waiting for you. They didn't expect you to be back until after dinner, so they gave me your seat."

Pointing at Malcolm, Primula announced, "And don't ask if he's the driver. I already made that mistake."

Turning all the way around in her seat, Heather said, "Oh, yes, Grandma, I'd like you to meet my husband...Malcolm."

Lily stole a deep breath as Malcolm confidently rose to his formidable height and reached for her hand. As he gently shook it, Lily gushed, "My, aren't you a handsome fellow." Looking back to her granddaughter she said, "Well, I can certainly see why you fell for him, sweetie...Mr. Debonair...mmm." At that instant she mocked fanning herself which caused even the prudish Primula to snigger.

Immediately taking a liking to his grandma-in-law, Malcolm offered Lily his seat. He pulled up another chair and positioned himself right next to his new friend.

"And why has it taken this long to be introduced to this charming gent?" Lily continued.

Heather swirled her head around. "Oh, Grandma. Let's not even go there. You remember how unsettled my past was. The good news is Malcolm was there to support me then and he's still here now. And we're back to claim the child we couldn't keep early on."

"Oh, my goodness. I guess that's where we'd left off, isn't it? You were in town on business and before leaving you squeezed a meeting in with someone from DCFS, right? I recall your phoning me after that meeting and you said you couldn't reclaim your child. So what's changed? How *are* you able to get your child back again?"

"Turns out our child is a boy, Grandma. We have a son!"

Lily clasped her hands together. "Oh, bravo, isn't that just the most wonderful thing in the whole wide world?" Elated to be sandwiched between the two, she placed one hand atop Heather's and one atop Malcolm's and declared, "I am so happy for you both!"

It was then that Presley, who'd darted from the limo to the kitchen, jazzed to be able to work one more night, wandered through the back of the dining room with two huge pitchers of water. He set one on the dessert table and proceeded to fill the residents' glasses with the other. Lily eyed the boy, trying to get his attention. When the child finally looked up and saw her wave, he hustled over with the frosty water jug in hand.

Before he could pour, Lily said, "No, no, dear. I'm fine on water. Thomas already got us some. I just hailed you over here so that you can meet my granddaughter, Heather."

Presley set the pitcher down, straightened and said in a cordial way, "So very nice to meet you, miss. Your grandmother has told me lots about you." Presley hesitated and then added, "Oh, and it's all been good."

"And this is her husband, Malcolm," Lily continued.

Again Malcolm rose like a rocket in gradual launching mode. He put forth his hand and shook Presley's in a strong but courteous fashion.

Presley couldn't hide his reaction. What he felt was intensely uncanny, as if he'd suddenly been born again.

"And what's your name, son?" Malcolm asked.

Still tongue-tied, Lily kindly responded for the boy. "Presley."

Like the tornado that had sent them flying years before, Malcolm was visibly blown away and Heather was leveled, tumbling right out of her chair.

Startled, Lily blurted out, "What's the matter? Heather, are you all right?" She gasped, clutching her stampeding heart.

Malcolm lunged in front of Presley, helping to gather Heather up. Presley jumped back, sensing that he'd done something terribly wrong. Lily teetered on the brink while Primula gawked, her mouth gaping like she had the word 'Oh!' plastered to her lips.

At nearby tables, seniors stirred in their seats, trying to take in the drama. It was Dickie who finally called forth to alert the kitchen staff. In a flurry, out charged Thomas and Tony, leaving Rosie rooted by the phone in the hallway, speedily dialing for help.

Gaining her wherewithal, on her knees Heather made her way over to the gradually retreating Presley. In the kneeling position she locked her son in a mighty embrace, Presley's face twisting into a contortion of horror and confusion.

"It's you! It's you!" Heather professed. "Presley, our son. Our dear, sweet son!"

Malcolm knelt down and diplomatically detached his overzealous, borderline maniacal wife. "Hon, don't scare the poor child. He's going to need a little time to get used to us."

Finally Lily let go of the breath she'd been holding. "You mean to tell me... You mean to tell me..."

Heather whirled around and crawled back to Lily's side. "Yes, Grandma! Presley is our son!"

"So that means...So that means..." she stammered, tears starting to well.

"That means Presley's your great grandson," Malcolm declared with aplomb.

At that instant, Lily's arms found heaven. Lifting them as high as they'd go, she sang out, "Presley is mine! He's family. He's my *great*grandson!"

The seniors in the room burst into applause. Some clinked their glasses like a memorable toast was soon to be proffered. Those that could get to their feet did. Others stomped their feet under the white table cloths. The thrill was vicarious and contagious. Those who knew the level of Lily's adoration for Presley were dizzied by it.

Malcolm stood by his son, pride overtaking every pore. Without so much as looking at Presley, he reached for his hand and it was there. He held that hand and immediately felt an impenetrable bond, one that was so distinct and familiar, yet new and auspicious. Then like he'd done with his own father, Malcolm squeezed his son's hand three quick times, meaning "I love you."

Without missing a beat, Presley returned the gesture.

Still on her knees, Heather returned to her son. She reached for his free hand and blissfully unloaded, "I love you. I always have. We always have. You know that, right?"

Presley nodded, his eyes searching deep within his mother's.

"We couldn't keep you when you were born. It wouldn't have been fair to you. Neither of us was prepared to be your parent. But that doesn't mean we didn't love you. We have *always* loved you."

Finally Presley whispered back, "And I've always loved you. Even though I didn't know you, I felt you inside of me."

"Really?" Heather asked. Then she put her hand to her son's heart. "Right here? 'Cause this is where you've lived inside of me."

"Yes," Presley replied. "And you know what else? I used to talk about you to my flowers. That's how I met Lily." The boy giggled. "I guess I'd better call her Great Grandma from now on."

"She'd like that, I'm sure." Heather returned to the subject, "So, you two met *how*?"

Suddenly feeling at home, Presley revealed, "Yes, I lived next door. And I planted daisies in big boxes between the buildings. And Lil...I mean Great Grandma noticed me and started talking to me while I was out there, taking care of the flowers. Then she got me a job here. Then she taught me how to play guitar. She introduced me to lots of her friends. Sal's the one I really miss. I just got back from singing at his funeral. He's giving me a daisy field of my own to take care of. And..."

Suddenly an urgent care team stormed in. Looking like the military on a mission, they infiltrated the orgy of frolic and excitement.

"Where's the heart attack victim?" the lead medic called out.

Heads turned and the unquenchable clamor gradually mellowed to a hushed buzz. Rosie finally appeared, throwing her weight side to side as she maneuvered through and around the residents and furniture. She was just about to explain why she'd called for help, but Presley recognized the head medic and beat her to the punch.

With combustible glee he called forth, "Hey, Black Jack, how's your crow?"

As the uplifting uproar returned, the dazed medic dropped his gear and lumbered over to Presley. "Hey, kid, how've you been?"

"Never better," Presley asserted.

"Ya know, I was thinking about you the other day. My wife and I are going on a vacation this summer and I need someone to watch my crow, Jasper. Ya want to be the man and help me out?"

Presley glanced at his parents and said, "I think I'm moving soon."

Black Jack stood tall and addressed Malcolm, "Oh, sorry. Didn't mean to be rude. My name is Jack. I do magic on the side, and I have a crow that accompanies me. That's how I know your son. We met here at one of my shows."

Malcolm extended his hand. "Nice to meet you. I'm Malcolm and this is my wife, Heather. We're Presley's real parents and we all met a few minutes ago."

"Ah, no wonder there's such a celebration going on here!"

Heather bounced into the discussion, asking, "So you have a trained crow? I hear they're very smart birds." Black Jack nodded as Heather continued, "Well, Presley doesn't even know this yet, but..." Facing her son, Heather foretold, "...we aren't moving him too far away. We've been living in California, but we made the decision to come back to this area."

With the sliver of a smile that turned from a crescent into a half-waxed moon, Presley said, "You mean I'm going to live near here?"

"Yes, we just bought a home in Morton Grove," Heather said. Then to Jack, she relayed, "And by this summer we should be settled into it. So, I have no problem with Presley bird-sitting." After the fact, Heather turned to Malcolm, a question mark in her eyes.

"That should be fine," he allowed. "I like birds so long as they aren't roosters that raise the roof at dawn."

Presley was almost jumping out of his skin. "Ya mean I can watch Jasper? And how about dog-sitting? Or actually how about adopting two dogs?!" Malcolm raised a conciliatory hand, but Presley blurted out, "Oh, man. We just have to!"

Heather stepped forward. "What's this? *Two* dogs? Weren't we just talking about one crow? How did we get on the subject of two dogs?"

Lily butt into the act, explaining, "Heather, dear, they're Sal's dogs, the gentleman who passed away. Presley is their dog walker. Right now they're with Dickie and Violet, but Dickie and Violet have their own dog, Boomer. If there's any chance of you adopting Squirt and Chimp..."

"A *monkey*?!" Heather exclaimed.

"No, *Mom*," Presley said for the first time and it took Heather's breath away, "Chimp isn't a monkey; he's a mutt."

Malcolm was now laughing. He took a deep breath and toasted, "To our extended family!" Gesturing to Lily, he added, "You're moving in with us, too, Great Grandma! We've longed for a full household and finally our wish has come true."

With a beatific grin to grace the child she deemed so deserving, Rosie approached Presley with enveloping arms, proclaiming, "Destiny has been fulfilled!"

"Amen to that!" Thomas underlined.

Tony added, "Seems more happenstance, very coincidental, but wonderf..."

"Hey," Presley interrupted, "that was one of our spelling bee words...coincidental. Let me think, its c-o-i-n-c-i-d..."

"Wait, you're a good speller, too?" Heather gushed with pride.

"Oh, that's not all," Tony exalted. "You should hear your son sing!"

Raising a finger of recall, "Now wait…it seems to me I may have heard him." Turning to Lily, Heather said, "When I called that day I was leaving town, there was singing in the background and you told me it was a child…"

"That was Presley," Lily guaranteed.

Looking at her son again, Heather extolled, "You have a memorable voice…absolutely mesmerizing."

Jumping through hoops, Tony said, "You should've heard him up on stage with Elvis!"

"My son sang with Elvis?!" After absorbing a roomful of nods, Malcolm said, "No way…how could a parent miss *that*? A quarterly recital or a school play, maybe; but a stint with Elvis?"

"Don't beat yourself up over it," Lily said. "His great grandma missed that one, too. But according to Tony and Rosie who were in the audience that night, there may be a repeat performance down the line. Elvis said he'd be following Presley's career…"

"And in the meantime," Rosie insisted, "we want you to bring him back here to perform for us at an occasional Happy Hour. Believe you me, we all just love his voice."

"It would be our pleasure," Heather said with conviction.

"So, Heather dear," Lily said, changing the subject, "will you be taking Presley back to California with you tomorrow or might you possibly entertain the notion of leaving him here until you sell your home and move back to Chicago?"

Unable to restrain himself, Presley put his two cents in. "Oh, please let me stay. I can live with Great Grandma and keep up with the things they need me for…like my busboy job and walking the dogs and pretty soon the daisies will be growing again. Oh, and there's a regional spelling bee coming up soon. My teacher probably wonders where the heck I've been. She counts on me, says I'm the school's star speller."

"But we just reunited," Heather said. "Aren't you going to miss us?"

Presley slowly nodded, torn.

"Aw, that was selfish of me," Heather continued, "I agree, I think you should stay put. We took years finding you. Wouldn't be fair to tear you up roots and all."

"My flowers hate that when it happens," Presley noted.

Everybody within earshot chuckled.

"Of course they do," Heather said consolingly. Addressing Malcolm she said, "We have two airline tickets back to California tomorrow morning. We'll let Presley and Grandma Lily hold down the fort here while we get our act together and move out."

Malcolm nodded. "Sounds like a plan."

"One thing, though..." Heather said, raising a brow, "we're going to call every day. So get used to hearing from your parents."

"I'd like that," Presley said.

"Deal!" Lily declared. She moseyed over to Heather and whispered, "Who would've thought after all these years... Wait until your folks hear about this one."

"Yeah, I should call them right now. And maybe we should send Black Jack and his medics over to their place because, when Mom gets wind of the fact that I married my high school teacher and the baby she wouldn't let me keep is now part of our family, she's going to have a big, fat heart attack!"

"Definitely a conversation for eavesdropping in on," Lily said with a wrinkly grin.

So, after the celebratory chaos died down and the residents returned to their rooms, Lily and Heather joined collusively to drop the bombshell news that they knew would be a penetrating blow to the ever-pretentious Ivy.

"Count on it, Grandma, my mom is going to dump gallstones over this...and I do mean *gall*stones."

Lily feigned a cinematic, award-winning scenario of how she envisioned Ivy's reaction. Contracting like she'd been stabbed, Lily dramatically wailed, "Yes, the gall of my daughter! How dare she!"

Heather took over, impishly acting out. "How dare she fall in love, marry, settle down and then decide to reclaim her birth child? 'Tis simply preposterous!" Heather contributed to the theatrics by waving her hands the way her mother often had when discord or some infringement challenged her immutable mindset.

"Oh, my," Lily said, applauding. "You have that down pat! But you know, above and beyond my daughter, Ivy, going berzerk over you having married and ten years later reclaimed the love child you conceived and bore...the heart-riveting explosion is going to occur when you mention the word black and mulatto." Suddenly Lily felt mortified for having broached the subject. "You know what I mean, right?"

"Grandma, it's okay. You don't have to explain yourself. I know how you feel."

Lily pulled Heather in for a hug. "Thank you, sweetheart."

"No, Grandma, thank you," Heather replied sincerely. "You've understood me all along." Reverting back to a whimsical mode, Heather rambled on, "And heck, go figure, you've been serving as a great grandma way before I showed up as Mom. I'm sure I owe you for at least a year's worth of babysitting."

"Go on," Lily scoffed. "I'm the one who lucked out! Lands! I have Presley as a great grandson and I'm part of a family again. What more could I possibly ask for?" Lily grabbed Heather's hand. "Come on, I can't wait to tell your folks!"

As anticipated, the phone call to Heather's parents was a tolerable sprinkle for Ted and a ferocious tsunami for Ivy. After chatting briefly, in his consolatory tone, Ted said, "Everything will be fine, Heather, dear. We can't wait for you to come visit us." At which point, Ivy grabbed the phone and declared to the daughter she hadn't seen in a decade, "You're making a big mistake bringing that child into your life. You don't know what you're getting yourself into!"

To which Heather resolutely replied, "The only mistake I made, Mom, is that I didn't *keep* him in my life to begin with. And for the record, I know what I'm getting myself into, and I can't wait. It's what I've wanted all along! Oh, and don't worry about your annual visit to see Grandma. She'll be well taken care of because she's moving in with us."

After her mother let loose a blood curdling shriek of "What?" Heather calmly underlined, "There's no need to worry about us anymore, Mom." Then with finality she said, "I assure you, we'll be fine."

Resolute in their plans to depart the next morning, Malcolm and Heather embraced Presley and gifted words of love that were so profound, so sacrosanct, that the bond they'd created seemed preordained. After giving additional hugs to Lily and reminding her that they'd indeed call daily, Presley's parents slipped out of Silver Trails into the welcome chill of a memorable Chicago night.

The next day after Presley left for school, a police patrol came looking for him. The officers were poised and ready to arrest Rosie, Tony and Lily for not delivering the boy to DCFS as promised. But after numerous phone calls were made back and forth to the agitated rep, Laurel, and a lengthy, convoluted explanation was proffered by the three presumed offenders, the intimidating warrants for arrest mellowed into one collective and tame reprimand.

And life went on in accordance of destiny's plan.

Chapter Twenty-Four

Perennial comforts for seasons to come

Whether you plant seeds or transpose a flat of flowers into cultivated soil, when you administer the proper care, you will get blooms. For the nurturing gardener the bounty to behold is generally as rendering as the initiative and effort it took to grow the plants and as gratifying to the soul and senses as the manifestation of beauty that prevails.

The daisies in planter boxes, in his urban gardens, continued to thrive because Presley was taken back to the Cabrini-Green area at least once a week during the growing season so he could tend to his flowers. The daisies in the field on the property in Door County didn't need as much attention because they were naturally doused with dew and quenching raindrops. And, too, they gobbled up the sunlight and generous nutrients the earth gifted.

In fact, early that summer when Presley and his flourishing family revisited the parcel of land Sal had willed to him, there was a field so full of daisies, so astonishingly resplendent, that Presley was fatefully driven to song. Going to the trunk of the car, he grabbed Blossom, hailed the family, including the dogs, to come partake of the blessed grandeur. He sang so every flower could hear, "*He was in the daisy field. Everything there seemed so real. He could laugh, talk, cry or sing. He could do most anything. In the daisy field...*"

About the Author

Amy Sutton is the author of a *Writer's Digest* award-winning short story, "Trench Warfare, Why Not to be a High School Sub," and "A Flight of Fancy," which secured a spot in the 2006 San Francisco Writers Conference Anthology. Her poem, "The Gift," can be found in Eber and Wein Publisher's anthology, *The Wishing Well.* Amy authored *The Healthy Executive,* a book on fitness and sensible lifestyle changes that promote one's physical wealth. Amy is a certified fitness instructor who sings professionally on the side. She volunteers her time as a puppeteer and docent. Amy taught AIDS awareness in Chicago area schools. After moving back to the Bay Area, she worked for the University of California's Lawrence Hall of Science in educational theater. Currently she is aligned with The Lindsay Wildlife Museum. Over the years, her copious volunteer efforts earned her Cal Berkeley's prestigious Rosalie Stern Award. Giving back has always been important to Amy. Thus, with this novel and all of the Zook's Books that are published, she plans to donate a percentage of her proceeds to deserving charities.

"We make a living from what we get. We make a life from what we give." —*Winston Churchill*